DUTCH ONLINE

LOVE IN THE LOWLANDS, BOOK #5

D.E. HAGGERTY

Also by D. E. Haggerty

Chapter 1

"Can I help you?" I ask when a man sits next to me at the restaurant where I'm waiting for my parents to arrive for Sunday brunch. This guy – whoever he is – is not invited, and he's certainly not welcome.

He winks at me. "I think it's me who can help you."

I groan. It's barely 11 a.m. It's way too early for some random dude to be sprouting stupid pick-up lines.

"I think you've got the wrong table, buddy," I tell him.

Before he can respond, I hear a ruckus at the entrance to the restaurant. Sounds like my parents have arrived. I check my watch. Ten minutes past eleven. Wow. They're barely late today.

I watch as Mama sends air kisses to everyone and anyone. She does like to make an entrance. If I'm being objective – a feat I find difficult to achieve with regard to Mama – she doesn't have to work hard at it considering she's six-foot-tall, has the legs of a ballet dancer, and the face of a model, which makes sense since she is a model.

I stand when she reaches the table. "Mama," I whisper in greeting as I kiss her cheeks.

"How are you, my little rabbit?"

Before I can answer, she notices the man sitting at the table and claps her hand. "I see you've met Tyson."

Awesome. I've been set up by my mother – again. I'm thirty-one years old. The last thing I need is for my mom to find me a man. Mama disagrees. She thinks a man is exactly what I need. It's not. Especially not the type of man she's always throwing at me.

I growl. "Mama."

"Now, now, don't be snippy with your mama." My father leans over and kisses my cheeks.

"Hello, *Pai*."

He pulls out a chair for my mother, and she sends him a wink over her shoulder. My parents are like yin and yang. *Pai* is Afro-Brazilian, whereas Mama is Russian with the palest of pale skins. I don't think she's ever enjoyed the sun on her face. I'm not exaggerating. As a model, Mama avoids the sun.

When I was young, I went through a phase during which I was convinced she was a vampire. All the facts lined up – she doesn't go out in the sun, she doesn't look a day over thirty, and she hardly ever eats human food. I might have been a bit obsessed with vampire romance in those days.

As soon as Mama's butt hits the chair, a waiter nearly trips over his own shoes in his rush to our table to take our order. Correction – Mama's order. While he bats his lashes at Mama, he doesn't bother to notice the rest of us. You get used to being invisible when your mother is a Russian supermodel.

My father was a model too, but he quit the business soon after I was born. While my mother continued her career, he raised me, and we followed her around the globe to wherever she was working. Being homeschooled while spending your days at various photoshoots throughout the world isn't as glamorous as it sounds.

"Let's get the introductions over with, shall we?" Mama says with a big smile on her face. I know this smile. It means she thinks she's won. Ha! As if. She can force me to have brunch with this man, but she can't force me to go out on an actual date with him.

"Tyson, this is my daughter, Fifi."

I cringe at her use of my childhood nickname. I extend my hand to him. "It's Sofia actually."

His hand is limp in mine. "Are you a model like

your mother?" He winks at my mom.

"Um, no. I'm a photographer."

His eyes widen like he's surprised. "You're Fifi Silva? The photographer?"

I stop myself before I roll my eyes. Mama loses her mind when I act 'childish' and rolling your eyes no matter your age is considered childish in her book. I nod instead.

Tyson places his hand on his chest and gasps. I hope this guy isn't trying to break into acting because I'm not buying his little act.

"Sasha didn't tell me her daughter is a famous photographer."

The snort is out before I can stop it. Mama clears her throat. If she were a normal mother – one who isn't worried facial expressions cause wrinkles – she'd be frowning at me big time.

"I'm not a famous photographer." My name is known in the fashion world, but it's not where my heart lies. Artistic photography doesn't pay the bills, though.

Tyson completely ignores my words. "What are you working on now? Do you have a shoot coming up? Do you know if they need any talent? Any male talent if you know what I mean."

How would I know if they need any talent? It's not like I'm in charge of selecting the models. My job is to show up when they tell me to, do my magic, and leave. I don't want to be involved with fashion photography any more than that. In fact, I'd give up fashion photography completely if I could. But I can't. It pays the bills. And there are always bills to be paid.

"But, Fifi, maybe you could see if Tyson could work on your next shoot," my mother pushes.

"I'm not working on any fashion shoots at the moment."

Pai leans forward. "What are you working on, baby girl?"

Pai and I share a special bond since we spent practically every waking moment together until I hit fourteen and was allowed to attend an actual high school. He knows my love of photography has nothing to do with taking pictures of beautiful people.

"I have a show coming up at a little gallery in Chelsea," I tell him.

"This is wonderful."

He raises a hand and snaps his fingers. A waitress appears within seconds. My *Pai* may be nearing sixty, but he remains gorgeous with his smooth dark skin, bright green eyes, high cheekbones, and strong jaw. Between mama and *Pai* we always receive good service at restaurants.

"A round of Caipirinhas," he orders.

Mama immediately corrects him. "You know I don't drink sugar. A bottle of vodka."

"Why don't you ask Tyson to tell you about himself?" Mama isn't asking. She never asks. She orders in question form. It's an art.

"Tyson, why don't you tell me about yourself?" I ask like the dutiful daughter I am.

His phone buzzes and he picks it up from where it's sitting next to his glass of water. He reads the message and types a reply before responding to me. "What did you say?"

Great. Another person who is as obsessed with his phone as he is with his appearance. Where does my mother find these men?

I force myself to repeat the question. "I asked if you could tell me about yourself."

He gives me what I call the model smile – all teeth and zero genuineness.

"I'm Tyson no last name, twenty-four, six-foot-two, one-hundred-sixty pounds, and I specialize in fashion modeling."

I don't bother responding to him. Instead, I cock an

eyebrow at my mother. Is she serious? She's setting me up with twenty-four-year-olds now? Did she forget how old I am?

I'm not allowed to say I'm thirty-one in her presence. If I'm thirty-one, then she can't pretend to be thirty-nine. I'll keep silent, but if she expects me to outright lie about my age, she's got another thing coming.

"He's in the prime of his life," is her response.

My dad clears his throat and puffs out his chest. "I'm in the prime of *my* life."

Mama pats his arm. "Of course, you are, dear. Of course, you are."

Tyson's phone buzzes again. He chuckles as he reads the message before typing in a response. I've had about enough of this.

"Excuse me," I say and stand. "I need the restroom."

He doesn't bother looking up from his phone as I step away from the table. Mama really picked a winner with this one.

I find the restroom and lock myself in. I wish I could claim a bad case of the stomach flu, but I can't. Mama is a complete germaphobe who would have an ambulance here before I can finish saying stomach flu.

I wash my hands and give myself a little pep talk instead. It's one Sunday a month. I can handle Mama and her scheming for a few hours once a month. Pep talk done I step out of the restroom to find my father waiting on me.

He doesn't say a word and hauls me into his arms. "I'm sorry, baby girl. Your mama doesn't mean to hurt you. She wants you to be happy."

"I am happy. I don't need a man to make me happy."

"I know, Sofia. I know. But she worries about you. You don't have a man. You don't date."

At his words, all common sense abandons me. "What if I had a man?"

He loosens his grip to gaze down at me. "You have a man? This is wonderful news."

"No, I meant—" I don't get a chance to explain I was speaking hypothetically before he's dragging me through the restaurant.

"Sasha, Sasha," he shouts as we approach the table. "Our baby girl has a man."

"I—" I open my mouth to explain the misunderstanding, but I don't get a chance before Mama is jumping from her chair and embracing me.

"This is wonderful news, my little rabbit. Such wonderful news." She releases me and I see she's smiling.

She's actually smiling and it's not for a camera. Shit. Shit. Shit. There's no way I can say I don't have a man now.

"Sit. Sit. Sit." She points at Tyson. "You go now."

At her words, he finally stops concentrating on his phone and looks up. "But you said—"

"Leave," I tell him. "Whatever she promised you isn't going to happen anyway."

"I should have known. There's a reason everyone in the industry calls you an uptight bitch," he snarls at me before spinning around and stomping out of the restaurant.

"Ignore him." Mama pours shots of vodka. "Now, we drink."

She hands me a glass and raises hers. "To my Sofia finding love."

Love? Who said anything about love? I've seen enough of the world to know the love my parents share is rare. I have a better chance of finding an Alpa Reflex Model I camera in perfect condition than love.

But my mama is a romantic. She's convinced I need to find love to be happy and now she thinks I've found it.

I slam my shot of vodka.

This isn't going to end well for me.

Chapter 2

M y phone buzzes with a message as soon as I enter my apartment after finally managing to extract myself from my parents and leave the restaurant. Mama cried – she actually cried – as she hugged me goodbye. She can't wait to meet my love. Me either.

Are you home yet? Call me!

I notice it's the fifth message my friend Zara has sent. Zara and I 'grew up' together. Until I was seventeen and escaped my parent's home for college, she lived in the apartment next to ours. Despite us hardly ever spending any time in the apartment, let alone the city, we became fast friends.

I better call her before she notifies the police I'm missing. You'd think the police wouldn't take her seriously. You'd be wrong. Zara's way of panicking is extremely contagious.

"Tell me everything," she demands as soon as she picks up the phone.

I rub my forehead where I feel a tension headache coming on. "Another blind date."

"Oh, goodie," she squeals. "What was wrong with this one? Was he legal? Did he try to pick up your mom? Did he leave without paying? Tell me. Tell me. I'm dying here."

I collapse on my sofa. The sad thing is she's not making up stories. Each and every one of those things has happened. Although, I don't think Mama actually brought Rodrigo, who was sixteen and a half at the time, to brunch as a date for me.

And I don't blame Mateo for leaving without paying. He's a starving model and my parents brought him to brunch at Gramercy Tavern. His eyes about popped out of his head when he saw a cookie costs twelve bucks.

But Alonso hitting on my mom? Yeah, I totally blame him for his actions. He asked my mom if she 'wanted to go somewhere more private' right in front of my dad. Of course, *Pai* thought it was hilarious. And Mama was living it up, being hit on by a man twenty years her junior. Fun times.

"It was another model who wants to use my connections as a photographer to get gigs."

"Your mom should come up with some sort of screening process."

"Better yet, she should stop setting me up with models. Or, you know, setting me up period."

"At least you get gorgeous men. My mom keeps setting me up with hippies. They all have long blonde hair, wear sandals, and have never heard of a bra before. I love boobs as much as the next lesbian, but letting it all hang out all the time? Some things are meant for the privacy of the bedroom. What about me spells hippie?"

"How about the tie-dye shirt you wore for like six months straight," I tease her.

"Ugh!" She growls. "I was ten years old. Two decades have passed. You'd think my mom would figure out I'm not into the hippie culture by now. I work at a bank for goodness' sake."

I giggle at the picture of my banker friend – who takes personal hygiene extremely seriously – going out with a sandal-wearing hippie. "Thanks. I needed a laugh."

"Uh oh. It sounds like today was worse than normal. What else happened?"

I sigh. "Way worse than normal. Mama thinks I'm in love and can't wait to meet my man."

She guffaws. "You're kidding me? You? In love?"

"Hey! I could be in love." I don't deny love exists, but it is extremely hard to find.

"Yeah. Yeah. And I'm going to burn my bras, too."

"Whatever. Mama is going to be very disappointed when she realizes there is no man."

"You could at least go out on some dates," Zara pushes.

"With who? The only people I meet are models. And I don't think I need to explain to you why I don't date models."

I'm not a complete model hater. There's nothing wrong with them, but when they hear I'm a fashion photographer, they forget all about Sofia the person, and I become Fifi the photographer. I'm more than my camera.

"What about online dating?"

"Online dating is the worst. People swipe left or right based on your appearance. Talk about superficial."

"Please." She scoffs. "You're gorgeous and you know it."

I'm not denying I'm attractive. I hit the lottery with my gene pool. I'm a perfect mix between my Afro-Brazilian father and my Russian mother – both of whom are beautiful. I'm two inches short of six-foot-tall, thin without having to diet, and have high cheekbones and plush lips. I also got *Pai*'s bright green eyes. Yeah, I'm not complaining.

"I want to be with someone because they like who I am on the inside, not because they think I'm pretty. Beauty will fade, personality is for life."

"What if I told you there's a dating service that isn't about appearances?"

"Sounds about as likely as me selling my Leica." Which will happen over my dead body – as in never.

"I'm serious. I sent you a link."

My phone beeps and I put her on speaker so I can read the text she sent. "Blind Love International." I chuckle. "Sounds like a dating service for Ukrainian women to find stupid American men."

"Don't be a hater."

I roll my eyes. "Fine." I click on the link. "Blind Love

International is the trusted online dating site for singles who are searching for more," I read the tagline out loud. "Wow. It sounds real special."

"Keep reading, Ms. Cynical."

I go back to reading the front page of the website. "They say love is blind. In a world where more than 90 million selfies are taken a day, appearances seem more important than ever. Here at Blind Love International, we believe there's more to life than appearance. We believe love begins with a conversation. Why not start your own conversation today?"

"And? Doesn't it sound perfect for you?"

Damnit. It does sound perfect for me. When I don't respond, Zara squeals. "Yes! I knew it! Let's get you signed up right away."

"Hold on. Give me a second to catch my breath." And think up an excuse for not signing up for a dating site. I suck at making up excuses, though. Guess I'm stuck with the idiotic truth. "I feel pathetic searching for love online."

"Please. Thirty-nine percent of couples met online."

"Really? Or are you quoting a fashion magazine quiz?"

"Says the woman who works for fashion magazines," Zara quips.

"Not by choice," I mumble.

"Sorry. Sorry. Sorry. And, trust me, I'll ask about your upcoming photography exhibit, but first, we need to find yourself a date before Mama Silva realizes you lied about being in love."

"I didn't lie. *Pai* misunderstood and then the whole thing kind of snowballed on me. You've met my mother. You know how difficult it is to change her mind once she's on a roll."

"Oh, I know. The woman continues to send me a bottle of rum for my birthday every single year. I don't know how many times I've tried to tell her I hate rum. I literally can't stand the smell of it without throwing up." She feigns gagging.

I laugh. "Maybe if you hadn't decided to drink an entire bottle of rum in one sitting when Brenda the bitch broke up with you, you'd still like the taste."

"I'm unsure which is worse. Knowing you had to help clean puke out of my hair or thinking I was in love with Brenda the bitch who was 'experimenting' with women but really loves the dick."

"Loves the dick?"

"Not my words. She told me those very words when she dumped me. It was fun, she said, but I love the dick."

"You're better off without her."

"Duh." She clears her throat. "Now, time to find you love."

"Do I have to?" I whine.

"Unless you want to explain to your *Pai* and mama why you don't have a boyfriend at next month's brunch."

"Maybe I'll be traveling next month and skip brunch."

"I'd like to see you try," she sings.

She has a point. No matter how much I travel for work, I always try to be home one Sunday a month for brunch with my parents. Mama doesn't hesitate to remind me of the few times I've had to miss a month. I had dysentery in India and couldn't board the plane in New Delhi for fear of not being within crawling distance of a toilet and still, Mama won't forgive me for missing brunch.

"Fine. How do we do this?"

"I already signed you up."

"You what?" I shout into the phone. "You crossed the line this time, Zara."

She snorts. She knows my threats are empty since she's the one person in the world who doesn't care about how pretty I am, what my parents can do to advance her career, or how I can get her a modeling gig.

"Ta da!" she shouts. "You're all set. I'm sending you your information now."

I groan when I read the profile.

Seeking a man to stop my mother from setting me up on blind dates with men who are trying to hit on my mom by dating me – her daughter! Must love Candy Crush, hate snakes, and be prepared to crush spiders. FYI – mom is happily married. Stop asking!

"How is this going to help me find love? Never mind. I don't want to find love."

"Cynic."

"Whatever." My phone beeps and I see I have a message from Mama.

Can't wait to meet your lyubov

Crap. She's breaking out the Russian.

"Fine," I tell Zara. "I'll do the online dating thing."

She claps. "You won't regret it."

I'm already regretting it.

Chapter 3

"I'm here!" Zara shouts as she strolls into my apartment.

I glance up from the photographs I'm editing. "I can see you're here. The question is why."

She rolls her eyes. "To review the responses to your dating profile, of course," she says and then proceeds to set herself up at my dining room table. She takes out her laptop, a bottle of wine, and a tray of sushi.

I see the sushi and my stomach grumbles. I can't remember when I ate last. I tend to get caught up in my work and forget all about food. I save my work before going to the kitchen to find some chopsticks and wine glasses.

"It's barely been a day," I say as I pour the wine and take a seat next to her.

"And you'll have tons of messages already."

I pop a tuna nigiri in my mouth while she switches on her laptop and navigates to the dating site.

"Okay. Here we go," she says and clicks on my inbox.

"Thirty messages! I didn't think I'd get any responses with my profile description."

Zara bumps my shoulder. "Oh, ye of little faith." The mouse hovers over the first message. "You ready?"

I take a sip of wine to fortify myself. "Let's do this."

Hello Sofia, My name is Luther and I'm a reserved man, happy in my career. I'd like to get to know you.

"Beep!" Zara shouts. "Reserved and happy is code for ugly and boring."

"I told you. Appearance doesn't matter."

"But you don't want to end up married to a troll either." She does an exaggerated shiver.

"Trolls don't exist. And stop being mean. I'm the cynic. Not you. Put him in the maybe pile."

She grunts before moving on.

Who's your mom?

Ugh! "Delete!"

Zara scrolls to the next message.

Does this mean your mom isn't available?

I groan. "Are all these messages going to be about my mom? Maybe we should re-write my profile."

She waves away my concerns. "This is good. We're weeding out the bad ones without you having to actually meet them. I have a feeling the next one will be good."

I promise I'll only make goo-goo eyes at your mom when you're not around.

"Maybe not," she mumbles as she quickly deletes the message.

"Who thought this was a good idea again?"

"Stop being Negative Nelly. We'll find a good guy in here."

Can you send a picture? I like to know what a person looks like when I'm talking to her.

"Ugh! The whole purpose of this dating app is to get to know someone based on the person and not their appearance, you jerk." I reach across Zara to delete the message.

The next message loads slowly. Once it opens, it's clear why. It's a dick pic. I tilt my head left and right as I review the picture.

Zara slaps me. "Are you seriously studying this dick?"

I wrinkle my nose. "No. Gross. But the shot is exceptional. Notice the angles and the lighting. It's almost professional." I lean in closer. "Hey! Wait a minute! I think this is a picture I took. Remember when I made the colossal mistake of doing the shoot for the adult magazine that shall not be named?"

I'm not proud of it, but adult magazines pay exceptionally well, and someone had her eye on a new Leica. Mama would have been happy to buy it for me, but she's helped me and my career enough. I want to know my work is worthy without the great Sasha the supermodel backing me.

Zara dissolves in giggles. "This is too good. Someone sent you a picture of a dick you took!"

"Unbelievable. This is copyrighted work. He can't use it without my permission. It's theft! Answer him and tell him I'm suing him for copyright infringement."

I reach across her to take the laptop, but she moves it further away from me. "Nope. We're not here to protect the copyright of some nude pictures you took. We're here to find you love."

"Blech. Love. As if it exists."

She sighs. "You're jaded. Love exists. Your parents are all the proof you need. They're in love and have been together for over three decades."

"They're also the poster children for co-dependency."

She waves away my concern. "Bah. Co-dependency is one of those terms people float around way too quickly. Not every loving couple who like to spend time together is co-dependent."

"Whatever."

The last thing I want to talk about is my parents and their love. Yuck! Trust me I've seen enough 'proof' of their 'love'. And by proof, I mean naked body parts no child should ever have to witness.

"Come on. Let's move on. I bet there isn't one normal guy in this entire inbox."

Zara rubs her hands together. "You're on."

Hi! We're wondering if you're interested in being our third in a threesome.

"Pass!"

Have you ever wondered what it's like to be a sister wife? Now is your chance to find out!

"Never wondered. Not interested."

Hi! How are you?

"Boring!" Zara shouts.

"Wait. I like boring, remember?"

"You don't like boring, but you've convinced yourself you like boring because you're afraid of love."

I glare at her. Afraid of love? I'm not some scaredy-cat. "I'm not afraid of love. How ridiculous! Love isn't scary."

"Yeah. Yeah. Whatever. Moving on."

Hi Sofia! How old are your children? I'm positive I'll make an excellent stepfather to them. I'm reliable, dependable, and not afraid to change diapers. Can't wait to hear from you!

"Um. Zara, did you write I have children in my profile?"

She shakes her head before moving onto the next response.

Are you into race play? I can be your slave master.

"What the actual fuck? How does he even know my ethnicity? Report him! Report him!"

Zara bites her lips. "I'm sorry. When I filled out your profile, there was a place for ethnic background. I indicated you're Afro-Brazilian."

I pat her arm. "I'm not blaming you, but we need to report this guy. This is not okay."

After she fills out a complaint about the guy, she returns to the inbox, but I stop her. "I don't know, Zara. I think I've had enough for today."

"Don't give up already. There's a gem in here somewhere." She bats her eyelashes at me, and I'm weak.

I can never resist her when she begs.

Hi Sofia! Your profile is totally cool. Moms, am I right? Anyway, I'm Cindi with an i. You indicated you're hetero but maybe you'd be willing to experiment? Wink. Wink. Give me a shout!

"Nice try Cindi with an i. If I were gay, I'd be all over my bestie and my life would be much simpler." True story. Unfortunately, I'm all about the dick even if they aren't pretty to photograph.

"Hey! Who said you're my type?" Zara crosses her arms over her chest and purses her lips at me.

"Whatever. You'd totally take this package for a ride if I'd let you." I waggle my eyebrows at her.

"In your dreams," she mumbles as we return to my inbox.

Hi Sofia! Great to meet you. My name is Dan and I'm a cancer survivor. Fuck the big C, am I right? Anyway, I've learned with facing death that there's no time for screwing around. Pardon my French. Can you send a nude picture of you? Like I said, I need to make certain I'm not wasting my time after I kicked the big C in the ass.

"Wow. Who thinks Dan is a big fat liar who didn't have cancer?" Zara asks and my hand shoots in the air.

I pick up my wine glass and notice it's empty. In fact, the bottle is empty. Before I can stand, Zara's removing another bottle from her bag.

"Geez. What do you have in there? An entire grocery store? Any chance of some chocolate?"

She snorts. "Of course, I have chocolate." She throws me a bag of M & Ms. I rip it open and shove a handful in my mouth before motioning to her to open the next message.

Afro-Brazilian, eh? I've never heard of it before, but it sounds like you're cool. Can't wait to get together with you and check out all your lady parts. Hint hint. Nudge nudge. I'll need to do a thorough inspection to see how they compare with other races.

"What a creep," Zara says before blocking the guy. "In what world is it okay to write those words?"

I shrug. Unfortunately, he's not the first man to make inappropriate racial comments to me and he most certainly won't be the last. "In this world apparently."

"Check this out. There's a bunch of messages from this one guy." She sounds excited, but I'm thinking a slew of messages from one person is not a good sign.

Hi, Sofia!

Are you there?

What's taking you this long to respond?

Stop being a bitch and answer me!

Who the fuck do you think you are ignoring me? You'll regret it!

I'm done with you. I'm blocking you!

"I guess he didn't block me," I point out when another message arrives.

The queen deems to talk to the lowly minions.

Why are you not answering?

"Does he think acting like a preschooler will get him a woman? Mama would have slayed him by now."

Zara feigns a shiver. "Lord help the man who crosses your mom." She slams her laptop shut. "Tonight may be a failure, but we'll find someone for you."

I drop my head onto the table. "Do we have to?"

"Yep. We can't disappoint Mama. Remember prom?"

She had to bring up prom, didn't she? Prom was not the wonderful experience those eighties films promised me.

My prom date, Dwayne, didn't deign to come into the house and pick me up. He honked his horn and shouted out of the window for me to 'hurry up'. Mama lost her ever-loving mind. She marched out to the car and yelled at him. I don't know what she said, but when the poor guy came into the house to pick me up, there was a distinctive stain on the front of his pants.

Pai had to lend him some trousers for the night. My father is over six-foot tall, and Dwayne hadn't hit his growth spurt yet. He spent the entire night pulling up his trousers. When he asked me to dance to a slow song, he – unfortunately – forgot about his pants situation.

When we stepped apart at the end of the dance, his pants were around his knees, and everyone noticed how happy he was to see me. At that point, I was done with the stupid prom. I marched right out of there and took a taxi home. Dwayne stayed, and I never talked to him again.

"Fine." I give in. "I'll keep searching."

"There's your spirit. Now, who wants more wine?"

Does she need to ask?

Chapter 4

A week later I'm waiting at the Mexican place for Zara to show up. I've managed to avoid another night of reviewing responses to my dating profile. In fact, I've kind of ignored the whole need to find a date altogether.

I'm going to have to disappoint Mama and tell her I broke up with my boyfriend. But what excuse to give? *Think, Sofia, think*!

I can't say my man died. Mama will expect me to go into mourning. And she takes mourning seriously – very seriously. She wore black for a month after our doorman passed. He was a good doorman and had been with the building since my birth, but a month?

Or maybe my man got deported? Nah. Mama will wonder why I didn't marry him to get him a green card. And then she'll refer to me as Andie MacDowell and him as Gérard Depardieu before forcing me to watch the movie *Green Card* for like the millionth time.

I've got it! I'll say he had a secret family he didn't tell me about and asked me to be a sister wife. Mama will want to gut him like a fish, but he'll be safe since *he* doesn't exist. I'll claim he lives with his real family in Utah somewhere on a ranch. Mama does not do countryside.

My phone buzzes and I pick it up to read a message from Zara.

I'm sorry.

Crazy bitch. What did she do now? Whatever it is, it can't be good. I stand, intent on getting the hell out of here, but a man drags the chair out across from me and sits down.

Damn. Too late. I sink back in my chair. It doesn't

take a genius to figure out my ex-bestie set me up on a blind date. Naturally, the man isn't plain or boring like I requested. Nope. He's gorgeous. Tall, broad shoulders, wavy brown hair, square jaw. Every woman in the place is checking him out and, judging by the smirk on his face, he knows it. Awesome.

"You must be Sofia," he says. I hold out my hand, and he lifts it to his mouth and winks as he kisses my fingers.

He probably thinks he's being charming. He's not. Creepy is what he is. I yank my hand back. My phone beeps again.

His name is Chad.

I switch my phone off and drop it in my bag. I'll deal with Zara tomorrow.

"And you're Chad?" I ask, like this whole setup wasn't dropped on me less than a minute ago.

Before he can respond, I hear a scuffle behind him and notice three waitresses pushing and shoving each other as they dash toward our table. One of them trips another one and she goes down, landing on her ass in the middle of the aisle. The distraction is enough for the waitress in front to pull ahead. She arrives at our table heaving for breath.

"Hello. My name is Darra and I'll be your waitress for the evening. Can I start you off with a drink? Today's signature drink is a raspberry limoncello prosecco."

"Yum. Sounds delicious. I'll have one of those."

Darra doesn't bother to look my way as she nods. "And for you, sir?" she asks all breathy.

See? This is why I have no interest in a man who's attractive. Attractive men are constantly surrounded by temptation. On top of which, other women won't hesitate to steal him away. I can do without the drama. Photographing beautiful people is enough drama for me, thank you very much.

Chad frowns at me. "Are you certain you want an

alcoholic drink? Alcohol ages the skin and, darling, you aren't getting any younger."

I'm thirty-one. I'm in the prime of my life. I give him the 'model' smile Mama taught me before I could crawl. "Oh, darling, I'm sure."

His frown deepens and he turns away from me to address Darra, "I'll have a mineral water with a twist of lime."

She sets two menus on the table before leaving to fill our drink orders. I don't need a menu. I've been eating here with Zara since we were teenagers, and we still eat here together whenever I'm in the city.

Quiet falls on our table and Chad stares at me expectantly. Great. Like I knew about this date for more than a minute. Ugh! Why didn't I tell him the truth about being blindsided by my friend? Zara has a lot to answer for.

I search my brain for a topic to discuss and say the first thing to pop in my head, "Do you have any vacation plans for Easter?"

Easter is a month away, but most people like to plan in advance, don't they?

"I'll probably head out to the Hamptons for a few days."

The Hamptons? Could this guy be any more not my type? How did Zara pick him anyway?

"No desire to go anywhere further? Somewhere with white sandy beaches and blue water?" Personally, I love a good beach vacation. Not in one of those all-inclusive resorts. Bah. No, give me a shack on the beach and a cold cocktail and I'm all set.

"I don't travel. I have everything I need here in New York City."

"But don't you want to see other cities? What about visiting Bangkok or Mumbai or Cape Town?"

He flicks a hand in dismissal. "Not interested."

"What a shame. The different cultures and

locations are fascinating as is flying in a jet watching the earth spin below you."

"Spin?" He scowls. "Everyone knows the earth is flat."

I feel my eyes nearly bug out of my head at his words. But I know better than to attack someone who believes in conspiracy theories. Trust me. It's a complete and utter waste of breath. Before I can figure out how to respond, our waitress, Darra, returns with our drinks.

"Your water," she says to Chad.

"Thanks, darling," he says and winks in response.

When Darra stares at him like she's starstruck, I clear my throat. "Ahem. Do you have my drink?"

"Yeah, of course." She places the drink in front of me but keeps her eyes glued to Chad. Another waitress arrives and accidentally on purpose slams into Darra. Darra glares at her before marching off after her. I guess we won't be ordering food then.

Chad checks his watch. "Okay, it's been fifteen minutes. How would you rate our date thus far?"

Is he serious? How the hell do I answer? "It's kind of early to rate, don't you think?"

He purses his lips. "No, not at all. Usually, I can tell within five minutes whether a date will be successful or not."

Do I dare ask? Why not. It's not like we're having some stellar conversation. "And how do you rate our date thus far?"

"To be honest, I'm pretty disappointed."

He's disappointed? How does he think I feel? I decide to play along. "Oh? Why are you disappointed?"

"I have the feeling you didn't bother to read my profile. I clearly indicate I'm a member of the flat earth society and yet here you are asking me about travel. You aren't prepared at all."

Profile? Damn Zara and her stupid internet dating idea. "You're right, Chad. I wasn't prepared because—"

My response is cut off when Chad farts – loudly.

My mouth drops open. "Are you okay? Are you ill?" Did you leave your manners at home I want to ask, but don't.

"Better out than in. Don't worry. You'll get used to it. I have irritable bowel syndrome. Having gas is a part of my life."

Awesome. This guy is getting better and better.

He glares at me. "I hope you're not one of those superficial pretty women like my ex-wife. She always complained about my farting in public. As if I can help it."

Can't he? I mean everyone farts. It's a natural biological action. But usually, people don't fart loudly in public. At least not if they can help it.

"And you can't help it? Is there no treatment for irritable bowel syndrome?"

"Now, you sound exactly like my ex-wife. She was always bothering me. Pushing me to go to the doctor as if doctors aren't all quacks."

Wow. Okay. The earth is flat, *and* all doctors are quacks. Could this guy get any worse?

"How long have you been divorced?" I ask instead of getting into a discussion about modern medicine.

"We're not like literally divorced."

I'm confused. "But you said ex-wife."

He shrugs. "Dates usually freak out when they realize I'm still married. But, hey, I need to see what else is out there before getting rid of the wife for good. You know what I'm saying?"

No, I do not know what he's saying. What I do know is I'm out of here. I down the rest of my drink. A waste of a delicious cocktail but I'm not sitting here any longer than necessary. The waitresses can have him.

I stand. "It was…" I pause. I'm not going to lie and say it was nice meeting him. I try again. "It was interesting meeting you."

I hook my camera over my shoulder and march my ass right out of there.

"Hey, wait!" I hear Chad shout after me, and I quicken my steps.

As soon as I'm out the door, I break into a run until I reach the subway entrance. I don't care what Mama says when she discovers I don't have a boyfriend. I'm done with this online dating bullshit.

Chapter 5

The next night I sit down at my computer to delete my profile from Blind Love International. After my wonderful date with Chad, I'm done with online dating. I don't care how many billion more times Zara tells me I have to give dating more of a chance. If online dating is such a great thing, why doesn't she do it?

Zara: Come on. It wasn't that bad.

Me: Need I remind you. Farting. Loudly. In Public.

Mama would give Chad the verbal dressing down of a lifetime if he farted in her presence. Hell, she'd probably drag him to the doctor for a check-up while explaining to him what an idiot he is for believing the earth is flat. Now I'm thinking about it, Chad could use a bit of Mama treatment. Lucky for him, I never want to see the guy's stupid face ever again.

My phone buzzes. Speaking of the devil.

Mama: It's been two weeks, little rabbit. When are you going to introduce us to your lyubov?

And where Mama is, *Pai* always follows.

Pai: Call your mother

I switch the sound off of my phone and lay it upside down on my desk. I'll deal with the parentals later. First, I'm deleting my online profile, because I am not going on another blind date again, thank you very much.

I flip open my laptop and navigate to the dating app. But when I try to log in, my password is no longer correct. Of course, it isn't. Zara knows exactly what my reaction to a bad date will be. Guess what? I know Zara pretty darn well, too. She has three passwords she always uses. One of which she doesn't think I know about. As if she can keep a secret from me.

I try her 'secret' password and voila – I'm in.

I sigh when I see the inbox has fifty messages. Too many crazy men with time on their hands. My finger hovers over the 'delete all' button. Damn it. I can't do it. It's rude.

I'll quickly scroll through the messages. Most of them probably don't require a response anyway.

Dick pic. Delete.

Request for naked picture. Delete.

Another dick pic. Delete.

I sigh before opening the next message.

Life is hard right now. I don't actually have time to date. Not to mention, I live across the ocean in Holland, but your profile made me laugh on a day I didn't think I'd ever laugh again. Thanks.

Who is this guy? I click on his profile. Name – Rafael van Dijk. It's a Dutch name, all right. Profession – Promotion and advertisement of famous fashion brand. He's discreet. I like it.

He hasn't filled in any of the other profile questions, and he says he doesn't have time to date. Why is he on a dating app then? I decide I need to find out.

Hi Rafael,

I'm glad I made you laugh during a difficult time in your life. But I'm curious. Why are you on a dating app if you don't have time to date? Inquiring minds want to know.

Sofia

I don't expect an answer. After all, it's nearly midnight in Amsterdam right now. But my laptop pings to let me know I have a new message.

Rafael: It's my sister's fault. She thinks I need a girlfriend. She snuck onto my computer and signed me up for this dating website.

Hmmm… sounds familiar.

Me: Ha! My best friend and your sister must be soulmates. My bestie signed me up, but after the date of doom yesterday, I'm done as in D O N E – done.

Rafael: Date of doom? Tell me more. I need to live vicariously through others right now.

Me: Let me see. Flat earther. Believes all doctors are quacks. But the icing on the cake was? Wait for it … He farted loudly and told me to get used to it. Oh, and he's married.

Rafael: What? I don't even know where to begin.

Me: And now you know why I'm deleting my profile and ending my adventure in online dating.

Rafael: I understand, but do you think we could maintain contact? I promise I'm not a creeper.

Me: Do you solemnly swear not to send dick pictures?

Rafael: Cross my heart and hope to die.

Me: Do you solemnly swear not to ask me for naked pictures?

Rafael: I swear.

Me: Do you solemnly swear you're not married?

Rafael: Like I have time for a wife.

Me: Not an answer.

Rafael: Sorry. I solemnly swear I'm not married.

Me: And, finally, do you solemnly swear you only fart in public quietly and as little as possible?

Rafael: Ha! Ha! I solemnly swear to try my best not to fart in public.

Me: Okay.

I give him my number before exiting the message board and deleting my profile. If Zara tries to set me up on another dating app, I'll have to resort to blackmail. As in I'll tell her mom what really happened that time in college when she came home for the weekend covered in blue paint.

My phone rattles on the table with a notification. I

grin when I see it's a message from Rafael. My curiosity gets the better of me and I enlarge his profile picture, but it's of a windmill.

Rafael: Good night, Sofia. I enjoyed chatting with you tonight.

I nearly respond before I realize my profile picture is of me smiling like a complete goof into the camera. I quickly change it to a picture of my beloved Leica before responding.

Me: Me too. Good night.

♥♥♥

I drum my fingers on the table at the bagel place the next morning while I wait for Zara to show. Naturally, she's late. My phone beeps and I expect it's her telling me she's running later than usual. I smile when I see the name Rafael pop up.

Rafael: Good morning. Or at least I assume it's morning where you are???

According to my profile on the dating website, I live in the US. It doesn't specify where in the US, though, and it is a big country.

Me: Trying to sniff out where I live. And here I thought you promised you aren't a creeper.

Rafael: You caught me! I'm a total creeper for wondering where you live.

Me: Since you confessed and all, I think it's safe to tell you I live in NYC.

Rafael: Cool. The big apple is awesome.

Me: And there go your cool points. No one who lives here calls it the big apple.

Rafael: No one who lives in Amsterdam calls it the city of sin either. Although there are plenty of opportunities to sin here.

"What are you smiling about?" Zara asks as she sits down across from me.

"I'm not smiling." I totally am.

Me: Gotta go. My bestie who thought I should try online dating is here.

Rafael: Go get her!

I switch off my phone before addressing Zara. "I don't care what you say. I'm not doing online dating ever again."

"Okay." She gives in without a fight before waving a hand at the waitress and motioning for a cup of coffee.

I narrow my eyes on her. "You're giving up awfully quick. What are you up to? You didn't sign me up for another site already, did you? I swear if you did, I'm going to tell your mother all about those dirty magazines you hid in your closet growing up."

"Please. Mom found those magazines when I moved out. We already had *that* discussion. Neither one of us wants to have it again."

Damn. Those magazines were prime bribing material.

"What I want to know is why you were smiling when I arrived and who you're texting."

I bat my eyelashes. "I have no idea what you're talking about."

"Ha!" She guffaws. "Sell it to someone who's buying."

"Fine." I sigh. "I met this guy."

She places her elbows on the table and leans forward. "And? Tell me more. Where does he live? What does he do for a living? Is he gorgeous?"

I don't bother trying to keep Rafael a secret. I never could keep a secret from Zara. "His name is Rafael. He lives in Amsterdam. And I don't know whether he's gorgeous or not."

"Yeah!" she screeches. "You met someone on Blind Love International. I told you the site was perfect for you."

"Did you miss the part where he lives in Amsterdam? It's not like we're ever going to meet."

"Come on. You travel to Europe all the time. I wouldn't be surprised if you have a shoot in Amsterdam coming up."

She's not wrong. I do travel to Europe often. In fact, I might have gotten an email from my agent about a possible shoot in Amsterdam. I hadn't considered it since I'm trying to finish preparations for the photography exhibit happening soon, but maybe I should. Hmm...

Chapter 6

Me: I'm nervous.

> **Rafael: No need to be nervous. Just remember – always double-tap and wear gloves.**

> **Me: Nope. Not a professional assassin. Keep trying.**

Although Rafael and I have been chatting quite a bit over the past weeks, I haven't opened up to him about my work yet. I don't want yet another person trying to use me for my connections.

I should be used to it. I grew up on the road following my supermodel mom. Even as a kid strangers would come up to me and ask me to introduce them to my mom. The worst was when people would use their children to get close to me and then ask for an introduction to Sasha the supermodel. There's a reason Zara is my one and only friend from childhood.

But I seriously like Rafael. I'd be supremely disappointed if he's another model hoping for a leg up in the business through me or my mom. And supremely disappointed is maybe putting it a bit mild. I'd be hurt. There, I said it. It'd hurt. But I do feel guilty for not opening up to him.

> **Me: I know. I know. I should tell you about my work.**

> **Rafael: Stop. I don't want to know. Don't ruin my fantasy.**

> **Me: Do I want to know?**

> **Rafael: Have I told you how sexy I find farmers? Those jean overalls and dusty boots. Please**

tell me you have straw stuck in your hair right now. Oh la la.

Me: And there are tons of farmers in New York City.

Rafael: I told you not to ruin my fantasy!

Me: Actually, I have a gap between my two front teeth.

Rafael: Oh, baby. And a big hairy mole on your pointy nose, I hope.

Me: I think you're confusing farmer with witch.

Rafael: I blame my sister. She's obsessed with Snow White.

Me: Blaming your sister for your obsession with Snow White? Low.

Rafael: Ew. You know Snow White was 14 when she went to live in the house with the dwarfs.

Me: WHAT??? You have ruined the fairy tale for me. Thanks for nothing.

Rafael: Sorry. Quick warning about Dutch people. We're direct and say whatever we're thinking.

Me: Now you tell me.

The door to the gallery opens and Zara dashes inside.

Me: Gotta go. This work thing begins soon.

Rafael: Don't forget to wash the cow shit off your boots when you get home.

"You're giggling!" Zara narrows her eyes at me. "Who are you and what have you done with my cynical grumpy best friend?"

"Hey! I'm not grumpy. Do I resemble a dwarf in any manner?"

Her nose wrinkles. "Um, why are you talking about dwarves? If you want to talk about mythical creatures you resemble, I'd stick to giants considering how tall you are and how big your feet are. Wait. It's hobbits who have huge feet."

I glance down at my feet currently encased in a pair of Michael Kors sandals. "My feet aren't big or hairy."

"Yeah, right," she chortles. "You keep telling yourself that."

I wrap my arm around her and give her a noogie. "Just because I'm not a midget like you, doesn't mean I'm a giant."

She ducks under my arm and tickles my ribs. I push her away.

I hear a loud over-the-top sigh before Mama says, "Children, perhaps we can behave this evening."

We immediately drop our hands and face my mother. "Yes, Mama," we say in unison before dissolving into giggles.

Mama sighs again before bending over to kiss my cheeks. "I'm proud of you, little rabbit."

Pai steps around Mama to draw me into his arms. "We're both proud of you, baby girl. This exhibition is wonderful."

Mama surveys the room and my pictures of trash and mimics *Pai*, "Yes, wonderful." Her voice makes it clear she's less than impressed.

Mama doesn't understand my art. She thinks I should stick with fashion photography. After all, I have the connections. She doesn't understand my desire to make it on my own. But I know better than to try and change her mind. After a childhood of listening to my mother's tales of woe about her difficult childhood before she was spotted by a talent scout, I've learned to keep my mouth shut.

When I study the photographs in the room, I don't see trash. I see art created from the things people throw away. The images themselves are in black and white, except for the so-called trash which I've highlighted in a variety of colors based on its composition. Plastics are in pink, biodegradable items are in green, and so forth and so on.

Zara threads her arm through mine. "Come on.

Let's get a glass of champagne. And I think your agent is trying to get your attention. We'll be right back," she says and leads me away.

Once we're halfway across the room, she whispers, "Are you okay?"

"Of course. She means well. Besides, I'm an artist. I'm meant to be misunderstood."

"A pain in my ass is what you are," she mumbles before taking two glasses of champagne from the bar.

I bite my lip and glance around the room. "Do you think anyone will show?"

The opening begins in fifteen minutes but there's no one here yet except for my parents, my agent, Zara, and the wait staff.

Zara bumps my hip and I nearly go flying. "Watch it. You know I can barely walk in these heels without breaking my neck."

She rolls her eyes. "I don't understand why not. Your mom had you practicing strutting a runway before you had boobs." She studies my chest and cringes. "Still waiting, huh?"

I slap her arm hard enough she nearly drops her champagne glass. "I may not need some complicated contraption to keep my boobs from drooping to my knees, but it doesn't mean I don't have any."

She arches her back and sticks out her chest. "You wish you had these babies."

Zara does not lack in the chest department. She's what the magazines like to call busty.

"I'd topple ass over teakettle on high heels for certain then. No thanks."

I'm full of baloney and she knows it. She had a front row seat to my angst filled teenage years waiting for my chest to fill out. The amount of Vaseline I rubbed on my chest hoping and praying for my boobs to grow is frankly embarrassing to think about. And then there was the protein diet guaranteed to give me boobs. Spoiler alert: It didn't.

"Is your boyfriend joining us tonight?" Mama asks from behind me.

I glare at Zara and mouth *you could have warned me.* She sniggers before meandering away. I'll get her back and remind her why payback's a bitch.

I whirl around to respond to Mama. I say the first thing to pop in my mouth, "He's not in town. He's in Amsterdam."

She claps. "How wonderful. Did you hear, Murilo? Our daughter's boyfriend is in Amsterdam. What's he doing there?"

Damn. Damn. Damn. Why have I let this whole boyfriend thing perpetuate this long?

"I'm happy you've found a man. It's exhausting trying to find a man for you who meets all your requirements," Mama says. Ah, yes. Now, I remember. I'm done with my mom setting me up with models who want to use my career to further theirs.

My agent, Dominique, approaches and cuts off my reply to Mama.

"Are you ready?" she asks.

"Ready for what? There's no one here."

She points to the door where I now see a line has formed. Holy cow. "Are all those people here for me?"

"Of course, they are. Grab a glass of champagne and follow me."

The rest of the night is a whirlwind. I don't know if Mama and *Pai* used their connections or what, but the place is packed. Dominique drags me from person to person, all of whom 'I absolutely must meet'. By the time my cab drops me at my place, it's after midnight and my feet are killing me.

I kick my heels off the minute I enter my apartment. My phone beeps with a message and I contemplate ignoring it. Oh, who am I kidding? I can no more ignore a notification on my phone than I can a smoke alarm blaring a warning.

> **Rafael: How did it go?**

> **Me: Shouldn't you be sound asleep in bed by now?**

> **Rafael: I couldn't sleep. I was too anxious to hear about how your work thing went. I knew how nervous you were.**

> **Me: It went okay. We got all the corn planted and I only stepped in cow dung once.**

> **Rafael: Did you slip and fall on your ass? There's nothing sexier than a woman who's all dirty.**

> **Me: Is that a sexual innuendo?**

> **Rafael: If you have to ask, then no. No, it's not.**

> **Me: I'll tell you all about my evening tomorrow. Right now, I'm exhausted.**

> **Rafael: Get some sleep. We'll chat tomorrow when you wake up.**

What a sweetie pie! He stayed up all night to hear how my showing went and didn't get mad when I put him off until tomorrow. I think Rafael might be the real deal. The nice, dependable man I've been searching for. I'll talk to him tomorrow and tell him all about my work I decide before falling asleep on my sofa.

Chapter 7

"Mama and *Pai* are going to flip," Zara sings as we enter the restaurant.

My parents think we're meeting for our monthly brunch. Nope. Unbeknownst to them, this is a farewell party because someone's moving to Holland. Mama will not be amused to hear I've sublet my apartment and shipped my stuff across the ocean.

I'm not in New York City a whole lot. I usually travel seven out of eight weeks, but the city has always been my home to return to when I need downtime or when I'm working on my art.

"You're supposed to be here for moral support. Teasing me about how my parents are going to lose their minds does not fall within the definition of moral support."

We take our seats and I remove my phone from my pocket to see if Rafael has messaged me. I'm worried about him. He's been stressed lately. I don't know about what, because despite my plans to do this big reveal about my life after my show, I chickened out.

Rafael: Can I exchange my sister for a new one? Tell me it's possible. I'm begging you.

Me: What did she do now?

Rafael: She made me watch her favorite Disney movies ALL NIGHT LONG. She's sixteen. Shouldn't she be watching romantic comedies by now?

Me: You'd prefer to watch rom coms with kissing and love in them with your sister?

Rafael: Ew. No. I take it back. I'll stick with the Disney princesses, although if she makes me braid her hair like Elsa from Frozen again, I may change my mind and force-feed her romantic comedies until she likes them.

Me: I bet you do the best braids. With ribbons and everything.

Rafael: Grunt.

Me: Gotta go. Lunch with the parentals. Chat later. XXOO

Eek! Why did I write XXOO? I've never done that before. I try to delete my message, but it's already marked as seen. Crap. I totally overstepped.

Rafael: XXOO

Phew. Okay. It's no big deal. I'm stressed about telling Mama and *Pai* I'm moving is all.

A cloud of Chanel No. 5 wafts toward me. Mama has arrived. Chanel No. 5 always reminds me of my mother. I can literally be standing in a Cambodian jungle and get a whiff of the scent from one of the models and I'll whip my head around expecting to find Mama standing behind me.

I greet Mama and *Pai* and everyone settles into their seats.

"And," Mama prompts, "what's this big news?"

"Big news? Why would you think I have big news?" I specifically didn't tell them why we're meeting today instead of in two weeks.

She scoffs. "You moved our monthly brunch up by two weeks. Of course, you have big news."

The speech I spent an hour perfecting in my mirror is completely forgotten as she raises her eyebrow and stares me down. I fiddle with my glass of water as I try to remember all the points of the speech I spent last night drafting.

Mama's head swivels back and forth between me and Zara. She studies us before finally giving us one of her rare dazzling smiles. "I knew it! You two have finally decided to make it official. You're a couple." She reaches across the table to squeeze Zara's hand. "I've always considered you my second daughter, but now it will be official."

I raise my hand in a stop motion. "Hold up, Mama. Zara and I are not a couple."

"Although there was the time you decided to experiment in college." Zara is such a shit stirrer.

I glare at her. "Everyone experiments in college. It's practically a requirement to graduate. Besides, my little experiment was a complete failure, remember?" Kissing Zara on the lips felt wrong and kind of icky.

She scrunches her nose up at me. "It was gross."

"And we know our baby girl already has a boyfriend, remember my darling?" *Pai* points out.

"I am thinking this boyfriend does not exist."

"He exists," Zara says. "She was chatting with him before you arrived."

Mama's eyes dart around the restaurant. "Then, he's here? Where?" She stands and surveys the room.

Several men notice her searching the room and get to their feet. Before they can approach, *Pai* stands and wraps an arm around Mama while giving the men the 'eye'. I roll my eyes. *Pai* is a puppy dog. He's completely harmless. The other men don't know it, though, and they sit back down.

"Mama." I wait until she focuses on me. "He's not here. He's in Amsterdam."

She collapses in her seat. And by collapse, I mean gracefully returns to her seat with a barely audible huff.

Pai takes her hand. "Maybe we can let our baby girl tell us what her news is instead of jumping to conclusions."

"Yeah." Zara needles. "What's this big news, Sofia?"

I narrow my eyes at her and mouth *moral support*. She bats her eyelashes at me like she's innocent. Not hardly. I should have known her definition of moral support is actually troublemaker.

"You remember the exhibit I had in Chelsea?"

"Yes, of course. It was a few weeks ago. I am not yet senile," Mama says.

"One of the attendees is a curator for the Photography Museum in The Hague. He contacted my agent Dominique because he wants to include my work in an upcoming exhibit."

Pai jumps to his feet and drags me out of my chair before hauling me into his arms for a hug. He lifts me off the ground and twirls me around like I'm a small child.

"I am proud of you, baby girl," he whispers when he sets me down.

Mama kisses my cheek. "This calls for champagne."

Before she can lift her hand to order a bottle of Moët, Zara says, "The exhibit isn't the big news." Why am I friends with this woman again?

Mama squeezes my hand. "What is it, little rabbit?"

"I think you're going to want to sit down for this." I wait until we're settled in our seats before continuing, "The exhibit in The Hague is going to take some time to set up, and then there will be this big grand opening."

I pause and Zara coughs. "Chicken."

I glare at her before returning to my long drawn out explanation. "I'll need to be there for several weeks to oversee things."

"Of course," Mama says. "It is right you are the one to place your art where it belongs."

I don't have any say in how the photographs are displayed, but there's no sense telling her anything of the sort.

"I also took a job doing a shoot in Amsterdam for a fashion magazine."

"Good." Mama nods her approval. "You can't neglect the fashion world. They will forget you and your phone number faster than I can say borscht."

"Oh my god! I can't take it anymore!" Zara shouts. "Sasha, Murilo, your daughter Sofia is moving to The Hague." She mimes dropping a microphone.

"Cancel the champagne!" Mama screams.

"You're what?" *Pai* shouts.

"But New York is your home. How can you abandon us like this? We hardly see you as it is. Soon, you'll forget all about us. You won't call. You won't come home for the holidays. You'll miss my birthday. We'll miss your birthday."

I take a deep breath and pray for patience. When none is forthcoming, I give up and respond. "I've been gone for months traveling before. This is no different."

"If it's no different, why did you invite us to brunch today?" Mama asks.

"She's got you there," Zara chimes in.

"Shut it," I order her. "At this point, I'm taking applications for a new best friend, because you're fired."

She snorts. "Yeah, right. You'll never get rid of me, and we both know it."

Damnit. She's right. I ignore her to concentrate on Mama.

"It's temporary. My lease is for six months."

"Six months! It's practically a year. And we're not getting any younger."

I cock an eyebrow. "Does this mean I can tell people my real age when I meet them?"

She clutches her chest. "You wouldn't dare!"

"There's more," I say instead of discussing Mama's age. It's a losing battle. Soon strangers will assume she's the daughter and I'm the mother.

"Oh, boy is there more," Zara mumbles.

"I also received a grant to live and work on my art for six months in Holland."

"Why didn't you say this to begin with, baby girl? This is wonderful. I am very proud of you." *Pai* places a hand on his heart.

"Congratulations, Fifi." Mama sounds sincere, so I bite my tongue to stop myself from complaining about her using my childhood nickname.

"Guess who else lives in Holland?" Zara asks, and I kick her under the table. Some moral support she is.

"The boyfriend!" *Pai* shouts. "She's moving for love."

"Ah, this is different. Why did you not say this at the start? You are such a troublesome child sometimes," Mama complains.

"You are officially off my Christmas card list," I tell Zara.

"Seriously? Was I on it? I've never gotten a card from you before."

"Not true. I send postcards all the time. I amend my statement. You are officially off my postcard list."

Zara slaps the back of her hand against her forehead. "How will I carry on?"

I roll my eyes at her. "Anyway, Rafael—"

"His name is Rafael? I love him already," Mama declares.

Pai frowns. "I need to have a chat with this young man. You are moving across the ocean to be with him, and I haven't met him. I don't like it."

"It's not… I'm not…"

My words explaining how I'm not moving across the ocean to be with Rafael get lost when Mama snaps her fingers for service. A waiter immediately scurries over.

"A bottle of Moët and some caviar."

Welp. I'm not explaining a dang thing now. Not when Mama is ordering champagne and caviar. Besides, it's not like I'm not moving for Rafael. I do want to be in The Hague in order to prepare my entries for the exhibit at the photography museum, and I did take a gig with a fashion magazine in Amsterdam. And the six-month grant is real. The stipend is barely enough to live off, but it's real.

But I can't deny one of the reasons I'm excited about staying in The Hague for six months is the chance to meet Rafael in the flesh. Who knows? He could be the nice and dependable guy I'm searching for.

Fingers crossed.

Chapter 8

I yawn as I step out of the taxi in Amsterdam barely two weeks later. What a two weeks it's been. Despite sub-letting my apartment furnished and renting a furnished place in The Hague, the amount of packing I've had to do is ridiculous.

I wanted to be absolutely certain all of my personal effects were either boxed and shipped overseas or stored before the tenant arrived. I kept imagining him finding a vibrator in a closet somewhere and I don't even own one. It's possible stress is causing my imagination to run rampant.

The idea of meeting Rafael soon hasn't alleviated my stress any. I should be excited to meet him. It's been over a month since we started chatting and thus far there are no red flags. Which is a red flag in and of itself.

Zara says I'm making problems where there are none. Easy for her to say. I've been here before. Thinking I found someone who doesn't care about my connections in the modeling world. Guess what? They always care about my connections.

I grab my camera equipment and trudge up the stairs to the magazine headquarters. Instead of heading straight to the photo shoot location, my presence here has been requested. Considering we're losing daylight, I'm less than happy about this plan.

I take the elevator to the fourth floor. When the doors open, I hitch my equipment higher on my shoulder and exit. The door to the magazine offices is shut, but I try the handle and it isn't locked. I knock before strolling inside.

As I enter, I hear a click above me. I glance up

right in time to see a bucketful of water come raining down on me.

"What in the world?"

I dash to the side before my equipment can be soaked and therefore ruined, but I don't move quick enough to avoid my hair and clothes being doused with water.

"Oh my god, this is classic!" someone says in between guffaws of laughter.

I lift my head to discover a man holding up a phone directed at me.

"Are you filming me? What the hell is going on? Was this some kind of prank?"

I lay my equipment on the sofa in the reception area before surveying the door. Yep, there's a contraption with string and pulleys all right.

"What in the world is wrong with you? You could have ruined my equipment."

"If you'd shut the hell up, I'd apologize."

"Apologize? As if there's an apology big enough for what you did."

"Calm down."

I feel my nostrils flare. I hate it when someone tells me to calm down. As if saying the words will magically make me calm. Not bloody likely.

"I'll calm down when I'm damn well ready to calm down."

"Real mature."

I grab the sides of my head to keep it from exploding. "Are you seriously saying I'm not mature right now? You, who barely five minutes ago, set up a prank in a professional office? I'm the one who's not mature?"

"You're the one having a hissy fit in this professional office."

I fist my hands on my hips to glare at him and realize he's been filming this entire time. You have got to be kidding me. Have I landed at the offices of Mad Magazine? I stomp over to him and snatch the phone from his hands.

"Hey! You can't take my phone. It's theft."

"Yeah," I mumble as I delete the video from his phone. "And you can't film me without my permission either."

I slap the phone on his chest. His incredibly hard chest. The t-shirt he's wearing is skintight and shows off all his delicious muscles. I continue my perusal and notice he has high cheekbones, a square jaw, and a slightly upturned nose. His smoky gray eyes are framed by long eyelashes, and his light-brown hair is perfectly styled, tempting me to run my hands through it and see if I can mess it up. Damn. Why are all the gorgeous ones crazy assholes?

"Ms. Silva," a woman calls as she enters the reception area. I drop my hand from where it's petting the crazy stranger's pecs – why am I petting a strange man's muscles? – and swivel to face her.

Her eyes widen when she notices I'm dripping water onto the floor. "I didn't realize it's raining. Oh no, this is an outdoor shoot. We're going to have to postpone and reschedule."

I point to the side of the room where there's a floor-length window. "The sun is shining. And the wind is minimal. It's a good day for an outside shoot. Apparently, it's also a good day to pull a prank on a perfect stranger."

I sound snippy, probably because I'm feeling mighty snippy right about now. Who pulls a prank on a perfect stranger in their workplace? An idiot is who!

"What a relief." The woman scrutinizes me and cringes. "I'm sorry. Ravi is somewhat of a troublemaker."

I think she means child.

"Let me get you a towel to dry off with and then we can go over our vision for the layout."

She's lucky I always braid my hair for a shoot to

ensure it stays out of the way. If my hair had gotten wet, there would be hell to pay.

She motions for me to follow her. I confirm my equipment is indeed dry before gathering it together and walking behind her.

By the time I leave the office two hours later, my t-shirt is dry. My irritation hasn't dried up any, though. I have no problem listening to an art director give me her vision for the shoot. I do have a problem with spending two hours on her vision, though, when we're losing daylight.

I hop into a car with the location coordinator, Geert, for the drive to where we're shooting. I had hoped to see some of the city of Amsterdam, but all I'm seeing thus far are highways and tall apartment buildings. I could be anywhere in the world.

Thirty minutes later, we arrive at the *Zaanse Schans*, and I now know I'm not anywhere in the world but Holland. In fact, I've been transported back in time to the Holland of the 18th and 19th Centuries. Green wooden houses with white trim and red shutters dot the area while canals flow around them. There are even old-fashioned wooden bridges to cross the water.

I want to spend the day exploring the area, but I haven't got the time. The light is nearly perfect. We need to get set up before we lose it. Although I've allotted a couple of days for this assignment, I'd like to finish as soon as possible.

I step out of the car and switch into work mode. "Come on. Help me lug this equipment so we can get started," I order Geert.

I march toward the entrance, but I slow when I realize I haven't got a clue where I'm going.

Geert passes me. "They want us to set up with the windmills as the background."

I follow him as we hurry through the outdoor museum. I slow down enough to get a glimpse of the various attractions. As we pass the bakery museum, I smell bread and cinnamon. It smells divine. I also spot a clog-making factory, a pewter foundry, and a cheese factory. I'm definitely coming back here one day when I'm not lugging camera equipment around.

We continue to the furthest end of the museum where there are four windmills situated on a dyke. I survey the area. On one side is a river. The other side is a small canal beyond which is pastureland. It's going to take some work to use all of the windmills as a backdrop for the shoot as they're spaced a bit too far away from each other.

There's already a location tent set up by the time we arrive. Geert leads me there. The art director, Fleur, charges toward me the minute I step foot under the tent.

"Good. You finally made it."

My eyebrows raise of their own accord. Finally? I wasn't the one who needed to give a PowerPoint presentation on my 'artistic vision'.

Fleur motions me to follow her. "This is your team. They'll get you set up in the pasture."

"The pasture?"

She points outside of the tent to where someone is placing my stabilizing tripod in the middle of a muddy field. A cow lifts its head and moos in her direction.

I peer down at my feet. My Tire Bottega Veneta boots are going to be covered in mud by the time the day is finished. Mama would kill me if she knew I went into a pasture with the boots she gave me for my birthday. I keep telling her to stop buying me expensive clothes and shoes, but she doesn't listen. It's not like she ever listens to what I want.

With a sigh, I hitch my bag on my shoulder and march toward the pasture. Someone bumps into me, and I spin around to discover the prankster is here.

"What are you doing here?" I hiss.

He smirks. "I'm your star model."

Great. Just great. Could this day get any worse? First, I get doused in water by some stupid prank. And now I'm going to have to trudge through mud and cow dung for this shoot. My first week living in Holland is not shaping up in the way I expected it to.

Chapter 9

I groan when I hear my phone beep. I squint my eyes to see the time. 7 a.m. Who the hell is sending me a message at this gawd-awful hour? I unlock my screen and see it's Rafael. Yeah! I sit up in bed before opening the message.

> **Rafael: Good morning, Sunshine!**

> **Me: It's 7 a.m. Normal people are sleeping.**

> **Rafael: Someone isn't feeling very sunshiny today.**

I gaze out my bedroom window and notice it's gray and rainy. It's May. Doesn't Mother Nature know it's supposed to be springtime in Holland?

> **Me: Have you seen outside? The sun isn't feeling very sunshiny today.**

> **Rafael: Welcome to Holland! Where we have two seasons – cold and rainy and slightly less cold and rainy.**

Now he tells me.

> **Me: Why did I move here again?**

> **Rafael: For an awesome job of course! Dutch farmers are state of the art. Your little farmer's heart must be going pitter-patter with all the new technology.**

Yeah, yeah. I still haven't told Rafael what my real job is. There's nothing wrong with being cautious. I don't care what Zara says. Being cautious doesn't make me a cynic. It makes me smart. Besides, when I told him about being in Holland for work, he suggested waiting until we meet in person before telling each other private details about our lives. I jumped to agree.

Me: Ha! I did end up in a pasture this week. Mud up to my eyeballs.

Rafael: There's my dirty girl.

Me: Insert eye roll here.

Rafael: Crap. I need to go. My sister is calling me. Can't wait to meet up with you!

I set the phone down and roll out of bed. I'm awake now. There's no time like the present to get some unpacking done. There's a knock on my apartment door a few hours later. Who could it possibly be? It's not like I know anyone in The Hague.

I open the door to find a short woman with reddish-blonde hair, blue eyes, and pale skin standing in front of me. She takes a deep breath before speaking, "*Hallo. Ik ben Charlotte. Ik—*"

I hold up my hand to stop her right there. I have no idea what she's saying since I don't speak Dutch. Being able to speak rudimentary Russian and Portuguese is no help with the Germanic Dutch language.

"I don't speak Dutch."

The tension in her shoulders releases. "Thank goodness. You're American."

"I'm actually Brazilian and Russian," I explain. "But I grew up in the US." For the most part. She doesn't need to know how I was carted around from country to country as a child.

"Oh, okay. Cool." She clears her throat. "Anyway, I'm wondering if you're a photographer."

"What was your first clue?" I ask and point to my t-shirt. It says *eat, sleep, shoot.*

"Great. Do you do private gatherings? Or are you one of those fancy photographers who takes pictures of food for magazines? I saw a documentary about it. The food isn't edible half the time. Totally ironic since it always looks super yummy. But you can't eat it. They use paint and all kinds of stuff on the food that will make you sick, maybe even poison you."

I bite my tongue to stop from laughing at her. At first, I thought she was yet another model angling for an in with the business. But, based on her rambling, she has no clue what kind of photography I specialize in.

"Maybe you can tell me your name."

She bobs her head. "Of course. I'm Charlotte. You can call me Char or Charlotte, but never Charlie because it's a boy's name and I am most definitely not a boy."

Alrighty then. I grin and extend my hand. "I'm Sofia. You can call me Sofia. Do you want to come in and discuss this?" I glance over my shoulder and grimace. There are boxes everywhere. And I thought I packed light. Guess not. "Maybe not. I'm not done unpacking and it's a mess in there."

"No problem. There's a little coffee shop across the street. I mean café. Coffee shop means something entirely different here in Holland. Trust me. I won't make that mistake again. But now I know. Marijuana is not for me."

She wrinkles her nose, and I bite my tongue to stop from laughing at her. She's at least half a foot shorter than me but what she lacks in height, she makes up for in talking capabilities.

"Let me grab my bag." I remember my bare feet. And some shoes, too. I hook my camera bag around my neck and slip into some shoes.

"I'm ready," I announce as I exit my apartment into the hallway.

"I didn't mean you have to take pictures like right now."

What a weird thing to say. Of course, I'm not going to take any pictures right away. I feel the weight of my camera against my chest. Ah. She obviously doesn't know any other photographers.

"I always carry a camera with me. You never know."

She shrugs. "The café's this way."

We exit the building and cross the street before walking a block to the café. I'm expecting a little coffee shop but the place we enter is stylish and chic. The barista counter is marble and the wall behind it has sleek black metal shelving. The seating area has dark blue velvet couches and a polished concrete floor.

Once we're seated at a table with coffee, Char caresses the cup and moans after she takes a sip.

"Long night?"

"You have no idea. I didn't know almost five-year-olds were this much work. I thought they were little independent beings by now. Wrong."

I wouldn't know. I've never spent any time around children. The door to the café bangs open and Char whips her head around to watch as two women hurry inside. One is tall, although not as tall as me, and skinny with purple streaks in her hair. The other woman has a mess of blonde curls on her head and ivory skin Mama would be proud of.

The blonde is trying to hold the other one back. She doesn't stand a chance. The tall, skinny woman easily gives her the slip before marching to our table. What the hell kind of drama did I land in the middle of?

"I'm sorry about this," Char mumbles.

I don't get a chance to ask her what she's sorry about before the skinny woman slams her hands down on the table. She glares at Char. "How dare you?"

"Um, what? Hire a photographer without your permission?" Uh oh. I hope she's not bringing me into the middle of their drama. I don't do drama. Correction – I don't do drama unless it's Mama or some other model I can't avoid.

The blonde tugs on the tall woman's shirt. "Maybe we can leave Char alone to talk to her friend. Let's get a coffee. No. An herbal tea to calm you down. Stress is not good for the baby."

But they don't go anywhere. Instead, Char sighs before introducing me, "Sofia, these are my friends. The crazy one is Abby. And the blonde trying to hold her back is Mia. They're both pregnant and shouldn't be chasing me around."

I look back and forth between them. "Are you two a couple? How adorable you're both pregnant at the same time."

Mia's eyes widen. "No. We're not. I mean. I have a Dutch husband." She shoves her hand in my face to show off her ring. It's a nice ring. Not a diamond but a ruby surrounded by little diamonds.

Abby giggles. "Once you go Dutch, you never want another man's touch."

Another woman bounds into the café and rushes over to us. "What's going on? Why did I have to get my ass over here?" She bends over and places her hands on her knees as she gasps for breath.

"Duh." Abby rolls her eyes. "We can't induct a new member into our girl gang without unanimous approval."

My eyes widen as I stare at the women now surrounding our table. "Girl gang?"

I don't know what kind of induction ceremony they have but considering the drama about nothing going on right now, I'm concerned. I survey the room and make note of the exits in case I need to make a run for it.

"I'm using the definition of gang as in a group of persons having informal and close social relations, not the definition as in a group of persons working to unlawful or antisocial ends. Although, I'm not against unlawful ends. But these two." Abby thumbs her finger toward Avery and Mia, "are law-abiding citizens to the end." She feigns gagging.

Her definition is not reassuring. I slowly rise from my chair.

"Please." Char grasps my hand. "Ignore the crazy lady. She's actually a nice person once you get to know her."

I'm not convinced. "Define nice."

Abby opens her mouth to respond, but I cut her

off. "It was a rhetorical question, encyclopedia lady."

Abby grins as she raises her hand. "I vote she's in. What say you?"

"I say I need the largest coffee this place has. Can I get anyone else a drink?" Avery asks. Abby opens her mouth to respond, but Avery wags her finger at her. "No coffee for the pregnant lady."

Avery goes off to order drinks and we move to another table to accommodate our growing group. *Our* group? These aren't my people. I like to limit my life to one crazy woman and the role is already fulfilled by Zara.

Avery returns with herbal teas for Abby and Mia and a large coffee for herself. Before Avery has a chance to take a sip of her coffee, Abby grabs the mug and sticks her nose in it. "I need to smell it. I promise I won't drink any."

Avery snatches the mug from her. "I don't need your cooties in my drink."

Abby frowns before picking up her herbal tea. She sniffs it, makes a face, and sets it back down. "All right, Sofia. What's your story, morning glory?"

Char rolls her eyes and tells me, "Ignore her. She thinks she's in charge of the world. Spoiler alert. She's not."

My lips tip up before I can stop them. These ladies may be full of drama, but they're also way fun to watch interact. "It's fine. My name is Sofia. I'm a photographer."

"And what are you doing in The Hague?" Abby rubs her hands together. "Tell me it's for a man. We're all with Dutch men."

Char slaps Abby's arm. "Stop prying."

"Actually." I clear my throat. "There is a man." Kind of.

Abby rests her elbows on the table and places her chin in her hands. "I'm all ears. Where did you meet him? Is he gorgeous? Is he Dutch? Does he live in The Hague?"

"All ears, my ass," Mia mumbles.

"We haven't met yet," I admit.

Not for lack of trying, but since I arrived a few days ago it's been go, go, go for me. I thought Rafael and I might meet up tomorrow, but he's got a work thing. I have no idea what. I didn't ask since we agreed to keep the details of our lives private until we meet in person.

"Oof. Like you haven't met in person yet because you're a scaredy-cat?" Abby fixes her gaze on Char and raises her eyebrows. Char sticks her tongue out at her. There's a story there. "I'm having a mighty powerful case of déjà vu right now." Yep. Definitely a story.

Avery sighs. "Maybe we can let Sofia speak without interrupting her every two seconds."

Abby rolls her eyes. "Ms. Uptight is in the house."

Four women focus on me, and my mouth opens before I realize I'm going to speak, "I met Rafael online."

"I like the name Rafael. Sexy," Mia says.

"And I do plan on meeting him in person, but work is busy right now. As soon as things calm down, I'll arrange to meet him."

"And you're a photographer?" Avery points to my camera case.

"Yep. A fashion photographer to be specific. I'm here doing a shoot for a Dutch fashion magazine." I don't mention my artistic work. Most people don't understand my art.

Char cringes. "I'm sorry I asked you to take pictures of a five-year-old. I didn't realize."

I roll my eyes. "Trust me. A five-year-old is mature compared to models. They think the world revolves around them because they're pretty. As if. I can make anyone seem pretty with the right light and the proper lens."

It's true. I can. Hell, my whole photography exhibit revolves around making trash into art.

Abby leans in closer. "Have you photographed anyone famous? Please tell me supermodels are all bulimics. How else do they stay skinny?"

Mia snorts. "Like you're one to talk."

"It's the lingerie models I don't get." Avery motions to her oversized breasts. "How are they skinny and still have boobs and ass for days?"

I snicker. "Because their boobs and ass are all fake." Not to mention the women themselves are as fake as can be.

Avery's eyes widen. "Even their asses?"

"Even their asses."

"Let's get back on topic," Abby says like she wasn't the one who got us off topic and onto the whole supermodel thing, to begin with. "When are you going to meet this Rafael? What do you know about him? Is he sexy?"

I make a face. "I hope not. I get enough sexy at work. I want a nice, dependable man who isn't superficial."

"Awesome!" Abby claps. "You're in the right place then. Dutch men are the best." She winks. "I may be a bit biased."

"Can you recommend a photographer for a kid's birthday party?" Char asks before we can get into a discussion comparing the virtues of men from different cultures.

"I'll do it. When is the party?"

"You will?" She squeals. "It's next Saturday."

"No problem. I should be done with the current shoot then." I won't be able to meet Rafael for another week, but I'm in Holland for several months. There's no hurry. It's not because I'm a chicken.

"Wonderful. You can meet our men and we can meet yours," Abby says.

Char leans over and whispers in my ear, "I'll cover you if you want to make a run for the border."

Chapter 10

Rafael

My feet are dragging as I exit the van at the *Zaanse Schans* for another day of shooting. We had one day of shooting last week but then, as it tends to do in Holland in the spring, it rained the next day. Today is the first day the sun has deigned to grace us with its presence.

I yawn as I follow the group of models to the shoot location by the windmills. I was up most of the night helping my sister who spent the night throwing up over and over again. I wanted to take her to the hospital, but she refused. She's in the hospital enough, she told me.

I notice the photographer who got accidentally caught in my prank last week. I've tried to apologize to her since then, but she has been nothing but a bitch to me. It's always the gorgeous ones who are complete and total bitches.

And make no doubt about it. Fifi Silva is gorgeous. She's tall and thin and moves with a dancer's grace. She has mocha colored skin and thick black hair with blonde streaks in it. Her cheekbones are high, and her nose is delicate. And then there's her dark red, plush lips. Every time she opens her mouth to berate me, I want to kiss the snark right out of her.

I avoid Fifi and trudge to the other side of the tent to change my clothes. These jeans make me feel like my junk is being strangled, but I wear what they tell me to wear. I'm not into fashion. It's not like I have the money for brand name clothes now anyway.

I'm drowning in medical costs for my sister, Mieke. Everyone thinks medical care in Holland is free. I'm here to tell you it's not. Although most of the costs are covered, there are all kinds of extras you have to pay out of pocket. Like a caregiver to come and be with Mieke when she's having a bad day and I can't stay home.

And then there are all the non-health care costs no one talks about. Such as me losing my job for missing too many days of work. Dutch employment law says I can't be fired for taking unpaid leave to handle a medical emergency of immediate family, but it doesn't stop companies from refusing to extend my contract.

I'm piecing together enough money for us to live on with several part-time jobs. The modeling gigs pay the best, but they're hard to come by and the days are long. I also design websites on a freelance basis and bartend on the weekends.

Between working three jobs and caring for my sister, I'm exhausted.

Fee, who happens to be my favorite make-up artist, grunts when I sit down in her chair. "The bags under your eyes need their own chair."

I yawn. "I'm sorry."

She squeezes my shoulder. "No worries. How is Mieke anyway?"

Fifi stomps our way. "Are you seriously sitting here gossiping right now? We're losing light."

Fee frowns. "I can talk and do my work at the same time."

Fifi sighs. "Sorry. Fleur is on my ass. We were supposed to finish the shoot last week and she's blaming me for the rain. As if. If I could control the weather, I sure as hell wouldn't be traipsing around here taking fashion pictures."

She peers down and notices me in the chair. She purses her lips. "Great. The prankster is in the house." She doesn't give me a chance to apologize before whirling around and stomping off.

"What did you do to her?" Fee asks.

"Nothing."

She snorts. "Yeah, right."

I try to speak without moving my lips while she works on my make-up. "She got caught in the crosshairs of a little prank is all."

"Little prank? Why do I not believe you?"

"Women are weird when they get their hair wet. Doesn't your hair get wet in the shower? What's the big deal?" Mieke would kill to have luxurious hair instead of the limp strands she now has while Fifi is being a precious princess about hers getting wet.

Fee pats my shoulder. "Honey, you have a lot to learn about women."

She spins me around so I can see myself in the mirror. "You've done it again," I tell her before standing and kissing her cheek.

"I am a miracle worker," she shouts after me as I walk away.

The stylist stops me. She motions with her finger for me to twirl around. I do as she says. You get used to being treated like a piece of meat when you model.

She frowns and reaches forward to unbutton my shirt. Her hands are cold as they brush against my skin. "There. Much better."

I peer down. Great. My entire chest is practically exposed despite wearing a shirt. I resemble some sleazy man on the prowl. I don't know what style they're going for, but I wouldn't buy these clothes if I had all the money in the world.

"She wants you over there in front of the dyke."

I peep down at the leather shoes I'm wearing. If I walk to the location the stylist indicated with these shoes on, they'll be ruined. I take them off and roll up my pant legs before tiptoeing toward the spot she indicated.

"Oh my god. Can you stop being a diva? Hurry up. I don't want to have to come back here tomorrow," Ms. Perfect Photographer yells at me.

"I don't want to get mud on the clothes," I shout back because I'm done listening to her bitch at me.

She doesn't respond and instead places her camera back in front of her face. Whatever. When I arrive at the indicated spot, I put my shoes back on. I don't bother asking for a towel to clean my feet first. Ms. Perfect Photographer's head is going to explode if I take any more time than necessary.

And while I might want to see her head explode, I can't afford to lose this gig. Not only is the money more than I can make in a week of bartending, the modeling world in Holland is tiny. If I get a reputation as a diva, I can kiss my next gig goodbye.

"Good. You're finally ready," she snipes when I finish wiping the mud spots off of my pants.

I give her my best model smile.

"No," she grunts. "I don't want you smiling. Peer off into the distance like you're dreaming of your lover. As if anyone could possibly put up with you."

I take a deep breath and let her words flow over me. She's not important. No, the only women in my life who are important are Mieke and Sofia. Although I've yet to meet Sofia, I know she's genuine and down-to-earth. Exactly what I need.

"Good. Good. Now focus on the sky like you're missing her."

This pose isn't difficult. I am missing Sofia despite never having met her. Since she arrived in Holland, she's been busy with work and Mieke had a flare-up. I haven't been able to get away to meet her in person.

Before I know what's happening, my eyes close of their own accord.

"Are you seriously falling asleep out there? Am I boring you?"

I jerk awake but don't say a word. Telling a famous fashion photographer the whole modeling thing is a bore isn't going to land me any new gigs anytime soon.

She has me twisting into different poses for what feels like an eternity, although in real life only a few minutes pass before another model, Jasmine, joins me.

"How did you piss her off?" she asks without moving her lips.

Not moving your lips while talking is a skill most models have acquired. Staring off into the distance unable to move while waiting for the perfect shot takes time.

"Prank gone wrong," I admit when we're moving for a different pose.

"You and your pranks. How is Mieke by the way?"

I smile before I can stop myself. Thinking about my sister always puts a smile on my face.

"Did I tell you to smile?" Ms. Fashion Photographer of the World screeches at me.

No worries. There's nothing to smile about now.

Jasmine pats my back where the photographer can't see. "Sorry. I didn't mean to get you in trouble."

We pose for another thirty minutes before Fifi finally shouts at us that we're finished. Somehow when she says finished, I don't think she means for the day.

Damn. I hope she isn't going to try and ruin my career. Losing modeling money is the last thing I need right now.

Chapter 11

Me: Sorry I can't meet up today like we planned. I have this work thing.

Rafael: I understand. When it's time to milk the cows, it's time to milk the cows.

Jokes on him. The closest I've been to a cow is this week when one decided to wander near to where I was set up for the fashion shoot. I tried to shoo it away, but let me tell you, cows are not the docile beings everyone claims. The thing mooed long and hard in my face.

No one – and I do mean no one – can ever make me feel guilty for eating beef again. Cows are mean and scary. They are not big dogs like my vegan friends claim.

Me: Next weekend.

Rafael: You found a babysitter for the cows then? Or is it a cow-sitter?

Me: Enough with the cow shit.

Rafael: I think it's called dung.

Me: I need to get to work. Chat later. XXOO

Rafael: XXOO

I grab my camera equipment and head to Char's apartment. The door opens and a Greek god stands there. Wowzah! Dark brown, curly hair, olive skin, chocolate brown eyes all put together in a package I'm guessing is around six-foot tall.

"I'm Nico," he says and extends his hand.

"Sofia, the photographer."

"Noooooo!" A little boy shouts before I hear pitter-patter and he appears wearing a white oxford shirt and no pants. Not even underwear. Nope, his little wee-wee is hanging out for all the world to see.

"Do you need me to come back?"

Nico chuckles and waves me inside. "Nah. We only have a small window of opportunity to get his picture taken."

"And by small window of opportunity, you mean when he's not streaking through the apartment?"

Char races past. She's carrying a pair of pants and underwear while chasing after the little boy. "Tobias, you can't run around naked."

The little boy, Tobias I presume, stops and spins around. "What naked?"

"It means having your penis out," Nico informs him.

"You know not to say the p-word in front of him," Char hisses at Nico.

"Penis!" Tobias shouts at the top of his lungs before grabbing his. "I's got one!"

Char shoves the clothes into Nico's hands. "Tag. You're it." She motions to me. "Come on. I could use a coffee and a shot of vodka."

I follow her into the open living kitchen dining area. Despite her threat to do a shot of vodka, she pours us two cups of coffee.

"I'm sorry. I should have planned better. But in my defense, Tobias was completely dressed five minutes ago. Unfortunately, his good behavior lasted exactly for those five minutes."

Nico strolls in holding a squirming Tobias in his arms. "*De mooie vrouw gaat foto's van jouw maken.*"

I have no clue what Nico said, but his son is not impressed. No worries. I came prepared. I remove a bag of candy from my pocket and wave it in the kid's direction. Since I've never photographed children before, I called a friend for advice. She suggested I be prepared to 'bribe' the kid into behaving.

"*Snoep! Ik wil een snoepje!*"

"*Snoep* is candy," Char informs me.

I tease Tobias by extending my arm until the candy is dangling in his face. "No *snoep* until I get a picture." I lift up my camera and say, "click."

The candy works like a charm. Within thirty minutes, I've taken hundreds of pictures of Tobias and his parents.

"This is a great shot of Tobias with his mom and dad," I say to Char as I show her the picture of them standing in front of the window. Nico is dangling Tobias by one arm with his other arm thrown around Char. While Char is smiling down at her boy, Nico is gazing at Char like she hangs the moon.

"Actually." She clears her throat. "I'm not his mom. And Nico isn't his dad. At least not his biological dad. It's a long story."

I cock an eyebrow. "I can't wait to hear all about it with a glass of wine sometime."

"You're on. But for now, we need to get to someone's birthday party."

"Me!" shouts Tobias. "*Ik ben jarig!*"

I have no idea what he said, but I ruffle his hair and tell him, "Congratulations, young man." I wave to Char. "I'll see you out there."

An hour later I'm shaking my head as I glance around the outdoor common area of our apartment complex. Char went totally overboard for Tobias' fifth birthday. In addition to a bouncy castle, there's a face painter, and somehow I got roped into taking pictures of all the kids with their faces painted.

Abby strolls over with a baby girl in her arms. "Hi Sofia, this is my daughter, Sylvia."

"Me lion!" Sylvia shouts.

"You sure are," I tell her before asking Abby, "Do you want me to take her picture?" I have a white backdrop set up. Tomorrow, I'll photoshop a jungle into the pictures. The kids are going to love them.

"Picture!"

"Sorry." Abby sighs. "She's a bit excited today."

"I can't blame her. Birthdays are awesome."

"Speaking of birthdays," she says. "When does Rafael have his?"

I snort. "Nice try. I'm not giving out any more details about him." It's not like I know any personal details anyway.

"Abby," a tall man with curly dark hair and nerd glasses rebukes as he joins us. "Don't pry."

Abby rolls her eyes. "This is my husband, father of my children, and fellow nerdy engineer, Jasper."

I wave at him. "Nice to meet you, Abby-wrangler."

"Ha!" Abby shouts. "As if anyone can wrangle me." She wiggles her eyebrows. "Unless I want him to. In fact, I'm thinking we should play cowboy and lawman."

I hold up my hand. "Too much information."

"Your loss," she sings as she gathers Sylvia before sauntering off with Jasper.

I take pictures for a while until Abby organizes the kids into a game of hide and seek and gives me a break. I stand and stretch my legs to get the blood flowing again. I could use a breather and a refreshment. I find my way to the tables laden with food and drink and grab a bottle of water.

"You doing okay? The kids aren't bothering you too much, are they?" Char asks. I'm learning the woman can be a bit of a worrywart.

"Please. This is a walk in the park compared to my normal photo shoots."

A woman I don't know wrinkles her nose before speaking. "Except for the peeing."

I chuckle. "You'd be surprised at the amount of bodily fluids I see. I'd be okay if it were only pee." I wish I were kidding. I'm not.

Char's eyes widen. "Do you mean...? I thought

you were a fashion photographer."

Ugh. I hate when people refer to me as a fashion photographer. I mean, I am. But there's more to me than fashion photos. Of course, I would need to tell my new friends about my exhibition for them to realize it. I haven't told anyone except my parents and Zara about the show, though. I still can't believe it's actually happening.

"I am. But an erotic magazine, whose name I won't mention but everyone knows, pays really well. Like, obnoxiously well. I learned my lesson, though. Money is not worth what I saw. I can make anyone attractive, but penises are their own special challenge."

Although, considering men are stealing my photos for their dick pics, I think I did an okay job making *that* particular body part into a work of art.

Tobias jumps in front of me and screams, "Penis!"

I cringe. Oops. Lesson learned. No saying penis around the little boy who likes to show his off.

Mia bursts out laughing. Char glares at her. "I hope you have a boy."

Mia's laughter dies off and her face gets all dreamy. "I'd love a little boy who resembles Matthijs."

I watch as Char picks up Tobias and gets a dreamy expression on her face, too. I slowly step back. I hope this pregnancy thing isn't contagious.

"I'm with you," Avery says before threading her arm through mine. "I don't want children. At least, I don't think I do."

"I don't understand why. Between your brain and this handsome body, we'd create the perfect child. Scientists would want to clone him. And beauty companies would fight amongst themselves to use him as their model," a man says as he throws an arm around Avery.

Avery slaps his chest. "Sofia, this is my boyfriend, Niels."

Niels bows his head. "You can call me Niels or if you're like Avery, Norse god."

Avery slaps his chest again, but he's not wrong. With his blond curly hair and blue eyes, he does remind me of a Norse god.

An extremely tall man joins our group and wraps an arm around Mia. "You doing okay, honey?" She stares up at him, the love clear to see on her face.

Char clears her throat. "This is Matthijs, Mia's baby daddy."

Mia waves her hand with her wedding ring plain to see. "And my hubby." Her voice sounds all breathy. Like the very idea of being married to this mountain of a man is all her dreams come true.

Maybe he is. What do I know? In my experience, men are users. They use you for your connections and then throw you away.

Not Rafael, a little voice reminds me. He's a good guy. Nice and dependable.

I hope the little voice is right.

Chapter 12

"**A**re you off to see Rafael?" Abby shouts her question at me as I walk to the waiting taxi on Monday morning.

"Shouldn't you be at work?" I shout back instead of answering her question. The woman is a pest. Every time I turn around, she's popping up out of nowhere to ask me a question about Rafael or my life in New York City. I get the feeling she's creating a dossier on me.

"I'm the boss, baby. I can be late." She wiggles her eyebrows at me.

"Shouldn't the boss be early to set a good example?"

She checks her watch. "One thing to know about Dutch office workers. They are not early risers. As long as I make it to the office before nine, I'll be the first one there."

I don't know why she's sharing this information with me. I don't work in an office. Blech. I can't imagine a worse work scenario than getting dressed in a suit to sit in a tiny cubicle working on a computer all day every day. Although Abby isn't in a suit. She's wearing a pair of ripped up jeans and a t-shirt with the words *I'm an engineer so while it's possible I'm wrong it's highly unlikely* printed on it.

"I'm off to work," I tell her before waving and opening the door to the taxi. She shouts at me, but I pretend I can't hear her and close the door.

The taxi from The Hague to the magazine office in Amsterdam takes more than an hour today. We stand completely motionless in traffic several times. I'm wondering why I didn't brave the train when the taxi finally arrives at the office.

I spent all day yesterday editing the photos from the shoot at the *Zaanse Schans*. I'm satisfied with the final product. Even the pictures with the jerk Ravi are good. Of course, the man is gorgeous. You could put him in a prison uniform, and he'd still be gorgeous. Too bad he's more than well aware of how handsome he is. The jerk.

The elevator dings open, and I stroll into the reception area of the magazine. Unlike the first time I entered, there's no bucket of water hanging over the door. Thank goodness. I spent an hour styling my hair this morning. I'd have to cut a person if it got wet.

The receptionist grins when she notices me. "You must be Ms. Silva. They're almost ready for you." She indicates a sofa. "Please have a seat."

Once I sit down, she says. "Oh, and don't look up."

What do you do when someone says, 'don't look up'? You look up, of course!

I look up at the ceiling and see one of the ceiling tiles is missing and a woman is trying to crawl out of the ceiling. Holy cow! I jump to my feet and scream. It takes at least five seconds – okay, maybe a minute – of me screaming to realize the woman isn't a woman at all. It's a papier-mâché doll.

I'm clutching my chest, trying to get my heart rate to return to normal when Ravi strolls in. Of freaking course, it's Ravi.

"What is wrong with you?" I shout at him. "You scared me half to death."

He grins. "The footage is awesome. Mieke is going to love it."

I growl at him. "Did you videotape me getting scared out of my mind?"

He suddenly finds the ground fascinating. "Noooo."

I stomp to him. Despite being five-foot-ten, Ravi is several inches taller than me. I glare up at him. "Give me your phone."

"Sorry. No can do. I don't have my phone with

me."

"Bullshit. Everyone has a phone with them." I hold out my hand and wiggle my fingers. When he doesn't move, I poke him in the chest. "Give." Poke. "Me." Poke. "Your." Poke. "Camera." Poke. Poke.

No matter how much I try, I can't seem to force my hand to move away from his chest. It's almost as if a magnet is keeping my hand right where it is. Little zaps of electricity travel from his chest to my hand. I stare down at it. What the hell is happening here?

I wrench my hand away from him and force myself to take a step back. "I want the video footage." My voice comes out all breathy. I take another step back.

"I'm not going to put it on the internet," Ravi says, and my eyes snap to his.

His forehead is creased in confusion as he studies me. He's not the only one who's confused. I'm around sexy men all the time with my job. Why is this sexy asshole causing my body to wake up and imagine him naked?

Oh no. Now I'm imagining Ravi with no clothes on. I felt his chest. It was hard as a rock. I'm certain his t-shirt is hiding defined muscles. He's not one of those super skinny models who make me want to feed them heaping mounds of spaghetti. I glance down and notice his jeans are stretched over his thighs. There's a distinct lump clear to see in the crotch area.

Oh god. Now I'm imagining Ravi's manhood in all its naked glory. My belly warms and tingles spread down to my lady bits. Shit. Shit. Shit. This is not good. I don't want a superficial model. I want a nice, dependable man. One who isn't involved in the fashion world and won't use me for my connections.

At the idea of being used for my connections, an ice bucket splashes over my libido. I clear my throat.

"If I discover the video online anywhere, I will make you regret it."

He opens his mouth to speak but before he can

answer a woman arrives in the reception area and motions me to follow her. To my surprise, Ravi trails behind us.

"What are you doing?" I hiss at him.

He whistles and ignores my question. Fine. It's his funeral.

To my surprise, when we enter the conference room, Ravi is right on our heels. I whirl around. "What are you doing? You're a model. This doesn't involve you."

The art director, Fleur, clears her throat. "Actually, Ravi also does some freelance work for our website."

"Whatever," I mutter and find a seat.

Ravi takes the seat directly across from me and smirks. I narrow my eyes on him for a second before concentrating on Fleur.

The next hour is spent going through the pictures from the shoot and discussing whether and how they fit with Fleur's vision. This is the part – besides getting scared by cows – I hate about working in fashion.

I don't like being in the same room as people discuss my photographs. I want to send my work out into the world and let everyone make their own interpretation of my art. Although, fashion photography isn't exactly an art.

I feel a nudge on my foot. I peer across the table to find Ravi tilting his head toward the floor. I know better now. I will not fall into his trap. I don't care what he's up to now. But then there's another nudge on my foot and I can't help myself. I glance down to discover there's a snake.

I stand and scream, "Snake! Help! Snake!"

I climb onto the chair. But the chair isn't high enough. I scurry onto the table.

"Get it! Get it out of here!"

Ravi chuckles and gets down on his hands and knees to crawl around under the table. "Be careful. Does someone have a snake bite kit?"

I used to always keep a snake bite kit in my bag. There was a time when all the big fashion magazines and brands wanted to shoot exclusively in the desert. I wasn't taking any chances and made sure I had a kit in my bag with all the antivenom I could find on the market whether legal or not.

Ravi pops out from under the table with the snake in his bare hands. "What are you doing? Are you an idiot? You're going to get bit."

He rattles the snake in his hand and my heart races. I may not like the guy, but I don't want him to die either.

"It's a rubber snake. See?" He throws the thing across the table toward me.

I jump back, lose my footing, and end up sprawled on the table. I stare at the snake, waiting for it to attack me when I realize everyone in the room is laughing. I peer closer at the reptile and realize it is indeed a fake. Great. Just great.

I take a deep breath before rolling myself off of the table and getting to my feet. I pick my bag up from the floor and hitch it on my shoulder.

"I'm done here." I nod to Fleur. "If you have any questions, feel free to contact me."

I glare at Ravi. "You need to grow the eff up."

With those final words, I stomp out of the room and out of the office. I don't look back. There's no need to watch the bridge burning behind me.

Chapter 13

Rafael

What a shit day. I nearly lost my best paying client in my web designer business due to Fifi the Great having a snit when I pranked her with a rubber snake. I don't see what the big deal is. It's not like she got hurt. In fact, she couldn't have gotten hurt because the snake was fake.

I take a deep breath and force all the stress and worry about money and keeping my three jobs afloat out of my body. My sister doesn't need to know how stressed I am. She has enough stress in her life considering she's reaching end-stage kidney disease while we wait on a kidney for her.

"Mieke!" I shout as I open the door to the apartment.

"What are you shouting for? My kidneys may not function, but my ears work fine."

I hate it when she jokes about her kidneys not working. There's nothing funny about waiting for someone to donate a kidney. But I force a smile on my face. Mieke doesn't need to see me upset. She needs me to be her rock.

"How was your day?"

"Well, you know, the same old, same old. I took a ride on a magic carpet, fought with a den of vampires, and to top it off, I got bit by a werewolf when he realized I'm his true mate." She sighs and places her hands on her heart and pretends to swoon.

Mieke has a vivid imagination which is fueled by her obsession with reading. She loves reading all kinds of paranormal romances. I tried to get her to read books on the list from her school to no avail. At this point, I can barely manage to force her to do any schoolwork at all. And, let's face it, schoolwork is the least of our worries.

"A boring day then?"

She huffs. "I'll have you know my new mate, Connor, is not boring."

I feign gagging. "I don't want to know."

"You don't want to know how we made sweet love under the moonlight before he bit me in the shoulder to make me his?"

"Does this mean you're a werewolf now? Should I add kibble to the shopping list?"

"Kibble! I am outraged. The werewolves of the Crimson Shadow Pack are of noble descent. They are not dogs to be fed kibble."

"Yeah, right." I survey the coffee table where the oatmeal I made her for breakfast still sits. "Did you eat anything today?"

She shrugs and tilts her head down to avoid my stare.

"Mieke, you need to eat to keep your strength up. When they find a kidney for you, you have to be strong enough for the surgery."

"When?" She scoffs. "I think you mean if."

I hate how my sixteen-year-old sister has become a pessimist. I won't allow it. "Hey now. Connor will be devastated if you don't get better. In fact, won't he die without you?"

I've read enough werewolf romances to know the details. Hey! Don't judge. When your teenaged sister is sick, you'll do all kinds of weird stuff to take her mind off how she's feeling. Including reading werewolf romances. Although, I draw the line at the graphic sex scenes. I quickly learned to skip them. Mieke insists I mark the pages so she can go back and read them when I'm not around.

"It is true Connor would fade into the nothing were I to be no more."

"What do you want to eat? How about some soup and crackers?"

"Yeah!" She claps. "I haven't had soup and crackers in ages."

"Stop being a little shit, or I'll make you drink one of those nutrition shakes." She rolls her eyes. "The banana flavored one."

Someone hates bananas. I'd probably hate bananas too if it was the only fruit I could stomach for years on end.

I heat up bowls of soup for both of us and sit next to Mieke on the sofa to eat.

"How was your day?" she asks. "Please tell me the prank with the scary papier-mâché doll was a hit."

This is why I do all the silly pranks. The videos entertain Mieke to no end and I will do pretty much anything to make my sister happy. Even if I do end up losing my best paying customer.

I slide my phone out of my pocket. "It was classic."

She snatches the phone from my hands and clicks play on the video of Fifi getting scared to death by a doll.

Mieke giggles. "This woman is pretty. Did you ask her out?"

Ask Fifi the Great out? Never. My body doesn't agree with my head. When she put her finger on me today, I nearly lost my mind and wrapped my arms around her to draw her near. I must be desperate for a woman's touch if the cranky photographer is causing my body to heat.

"Keep watching," I tell my sister.

Her eyes widen when she gets to the part where Fifi pokes me. "She's more than a little bit mad."

"Yep."

Mieke groans. "Uh oh. What did you do to her?"

"Me? Hurt Fifi the Great?"

She raises an eyebrow at me. "Fifi the Great?"

"Her name is Fifi. I added the great."

"Okay. What did you do to Fifi?"

"What makes you think I did something?"

"Please. As if I can't read you like one of my books."

I shrug. "I may have thrown a rubber snake at her feet."

She dissolves into giggles making all the yelling from Fleur worthwhile. I switch on the television, and we watch a movie while we eat. By the time the movie is finished, Mieke is fast asleep. I carry her into her bedroom and get her settled.

When I lay down on my bed, I take out my phone and message Sofia. I've become addicted to our little chats. I can't wait to meet her in person, but every time we schedule a date, something comes up.

Me: Hey Sofia! How was your day?

Sofia: Horrid. Absolutely horrid.

Me: Uh oh. Don't tell me the cows ran away from you.

Sofia: I wish. Cows I can deal with. People on the other hand...

Me: What happened?

Sofia: I don't want to talk about it. Suffice it to say, some people shouldn't be allowed out of their houses to mingle in society.

Me: I hear you. I met one of those people today, too.

Sofia: Tell me all about it. Make me forget my horrible day.

Me: I think the word cranky was invented for her.

Sofia: Rubs hands together. Tell me more.

Me: She lost her mind when I joked around. She has no sense of humor.

Sofia: Sounds like a hag.

Me: I don't want to talk about her. I want to talk about how we're going to meet this weekend.

Sofia: Ugh. Sorry. I got another gig for this Saturday.

Damn. I can't hardly tell her to refuse a gig for me. I have no idea what she does for work, but I know how difficult some work is to come by.

Sofia: Are you there? I really am sorry. I promise I'm not avoiding you.

Me: Are you absolutely certain you aren't avoiding me? It's okay. I understand. Some women can't stand the awesomeness I am.

Sofia: Feeling less guilty about cancelling on you already.

Good. That was my intent.

Me: We'll reschedule for next weekend.

Sofia: It's too bad you work on Sundays. I'm free then.

Sunday is my day to rest and catch up on sleep. Between taking care of Mieke and trying to keep three jobs, I need a day of rest. Besides, I bartend on Saturday nights and usually don't roll home until six in the morning.

I consider making an exception for Sofia. I could probably sleep until noon and be semi-conscious enough to meet her.

Nah, I can't. Mieke and I spend our Sunday afternoons watching movies together. My sister is alone enough. I can't abandon her for an entire afternoon because I want to get together with some woman I met online.

Me: Sorry. No can do.

Sofia: No worries. I understand.

I yawn. I need to get some sleep, or I'll be worthless in the morning. Some twenty-nine-year-old I am.

Me: Off to bed. Chat tomorrow.

Sofia: Don't let the bed bugs bite!

Chapter 14

I didn't lie to Rafael. I do have a gig this weekend. It's not exactly a paying gig. More like a favor for a friend, but I couldn't say no. Who can say no to Abby? Not me.

When I step out of the elevator onto Char's floor in the apartment building, I find the hallway is crowded. Abby, Mia, Avery, and a woman I don't know are gathered outside of Char's apartment. Abby actually has her ear to the door.

Jasper stands on the opposite side of the hallway with Niels, Matthias, and some man I haven't met yet.

"Why are we standing outside? What are we waiting for?" I ask the group of women.

The woman I don't know answers, "Abby's up to her old tricks. I'm Jenny by the way. My husband is Bram." She points to the guy I haven't met.

"Sofia. What do you mean up to her old tricks?"

"She promised Nico she'd give him thirty minutes to propose," Avery explains. "But then she dragged us all here before five minutes expired."

I hold up a hand. "Wait a minute. Char and Nico aren't engaged yet? But I'm here to do their engagement pictures."

"Which you will," Abby says before using a key to unlock Char's apartment and strolling right on in like she owns the place. "Stop whatever you're doing!"

I hear scrambling and a thunk in the bedroom before Char hisses at Abby, "What are you doing in here?"

Abby stands at the entrance to the bedroom. "Celebrating you and Nico moving to the next level, of course."

Avery, Mia, Jenny, and I stand in the hallway behind her out of view while the men head to the living room. I contemplate following the men instead of standing in the hallway with the nosey women, but I can't help myself – I'm as nosey as the rest of them.

I hear Char and Nico talking inside the bedroom, but I can't make out the words. Abby steps closer to talk to them. The woman knows no boundaries.

"She's half naked," she shouts over her shoulder.

No need to contemplate any longer, I have no interest in seeing Char naked. I scurry to follow the men to the living room with Avery and Mia on my heels.

"Come on," Abby says when she stomps into the room, not a minute later. "We've got fifteen minutes to get this party set up."

She drags two bags from under the kitchen table and dumps the contents onto the table. Party decorations of all kinds spill out. Within a few minutes, the place is transformed into party central.

I hear a door open and whirl around to see Char, Nico, and Tobias exit their bedroom. I hurry to the mouth of the hallway, drop to my knees, and lift my camera. Char sees me and throws me a dazzling smile.

I manage a few pictures of the entire family before Tobias squirms to be let down. Once he rushes off, Nico kisses Char's cheek and wanders off.

"Group hug!" Abby shouts before throwing her arms around Char. Mia, Avery, Jenny, and I join her.

"Congrats, Char," Mia says. "I'm excited my little girl will have a big brother to watch out for him."

Char squeals. "You know you're having a girl?"

"Matthijs is freaking out and making all these obnoxious rules about her not dating until she's thirty. He's a police officer. He should know better than to think he can control our daughter, especially once she hits her teenage years."

The doorbell rings. "I'll get it," I offer. Trying to keep up with all the names of the partners of my new friends is giving me a headache. I could use a break.

I open the door. My mouth drops to the floor when I see who's standing there. My surprise doesn't last long before irritation overwhelms me. "What the hell are you doing here?"

Ravi stares at me like I'm the one who isn't where she belongs. As if. These are my friends. Mine. His mouth gapes open and closed but he doesn't speak.

"Get out of here! You're not welcome here!"

He finally finds his voice. "I was invited."

"Invited? By whom?" I whirl around to confront my friends, but they've suddenly disappeared. I'm all alone with Ravi in the hallway.

He shrugs. "Abby something or other."

My nostrils flare. I knew Abby was a troublemaker the second I met her. I knew it! I should have escaped out of the café when Char offered to cover for me.

I twirl around and stomp off to find the troublemaker. I don't have to search very far. She's standing right around the corner where she can spy on us.

"Who do you think you are? And why would you invite Ravi here?"

Abby pats my hand. "My dear Sofia, I didn't invite Ravi. I invited Rafael."

"Rafael?"

I glance over my shoulder to find Ravi – or is it Rafael? – staring at me with his mouth hanging open. "Sofia?

Abby herds us out of the living room into a bedroom. Judging by the bunk beds and mounds of toys, this must be Tobias' room.

"I'll leave you here alone," she says as she shuts the door behind us. I follow after her. I don't want to spend any more time in this man's presence than I have to.

"You're the bitch." Rafael's words have me spinning around to face him. How dare he!

"Me? I'm the bitch? Maybe if you weren't such an unprofessional ass, I wouldn't need to be a bitch."

"Unprofessional? You're the one who lost her mind about a little prank."

I step closer and poke his chest. When the heat of his muscles hit me, I yank my hand back before my body decides climbing Rafael like a tree would be a great way to burn off some anger. My belly dips in excitement at the idea. *Nuh-uh, body. Not happening.* I take a step back.

"Little prank? You threw a snake at my feet."

He grunts. "It wasn't a real snake."

"But I didn't know it was fake, did I? I thought there was a real, live snake slithering on the floor in the conference room." Even talking about the incident now and knowing the 'snake' was rubber makes my heart speed up and beads of sweat form on my brow. I truly hate snakes.

"You were bored. I was helping you out."

"Enough." I slash a hand through the air. This conversation is getting us nowhere.

"You lied to me. You told me you were in marketing."

He shakes his head. "I didn't lie. I told you I promote and advertise famous fashion brands, which is exactly what I do."

"It was misleading, and you knew it."

"Like you told me the truth about your job," he sneers.

"I didn't tell you about my job, because we agreed to keep the details of our lives private until we met in person. If I told you what I do for work, you would have figured out who I am."

He crosses his arms over his chest, and I hate the way my eyes follow the movement. I hate how my hands want to touch his biceps and feel how strong they are. I tear my eyes away from his arms when he speaks.

"Because you're the famous photographer Fifi Silva. Think a lot of yourself, don't you?"

"It's not like you think." I consider explaining how people have used me in the past. How no one cares about Sofia. How all they care about is Fifi the photographer and her famous supermodel mother, Sasha. But I don't.

What does it matter? It's obvious Rafael and I are not compatible in any way. He's not the nice, dependable man I thought he was.

I indicate the door. "I think you should go."

"My pleasure," he says as he opens the door and marches out without a backward glance.

My eyes itch, but I refuse to cry. It's not like Rafael and I were a couple. I'm not heartbroken. I'm just disappointed. I've been excited about meeting Rafael since I arrived in Holland is all. *Liar.* Okay, fine. Maybe I'm a little hurt, too.

The Rafael I've been chatting to for the past few months is nothing like the man Ravi. Ravi is a completely different person. And not one I want to spend any time with.

I take a deep breath and straighten my back while forcing thoughts of pretty boy men and their stupid pranks out of my head. I have a party to attend.

Chapter 15

*B*ang! Bang! Bang!

I jump in my chair when I hear the loud knock on my door. I've been hunched over my computer reviewing pictures for the exhibition at the photography museum for hours. I stretch my back until I hear a crack and stand to answer the door.

Apparently, I'm not moving fast enough as someone shouts, "We know you're in there! Come out, come out, wherever you are!"

Sounds like my new best friend, Abby. What is it about me that attracts crazy friends? Is there an invisible sign on my forehead? *Looking for crazy friends. Apply inside.*

"What's up?" I ask when I open the door and find Abby, Mia, and Char in the hallway.

Abby lifts up a bag. "It's cheer up your girlfriend time. I brought my official 'cheer up a girlfriend'-kit. Patent pending."

I scrunch my nose. "Why are you cheering me up? I don't need cheering up."

Abby rolls her eyes before pushing her way past me into my apartment. "Yeah, right."

I bug my eyes out at Mia and Char.

"I find it's best to let her get on with it," Mia says.

Whatever. I wave them in. Before I can shut the door, Avery comes racing down the hall.

"I'm here! I'm here!"

"You're late!" Abby shouts in her direction.

"If you'd give me more than a fifteen-minute heads

up, I could be on time."

"It takes exactly nine minutes and fifteen seconds to bike from your house to this apartment building giving you a five-minute and forty-five-second buffer."

"I was in the middle of something. I can't drop everything the minute you call."

Abby stops emptying her bag onto my kitchen counter and lifts her head to study Avery. "Whatever it was, it obviously wasn't a booty call. Thus, it's not important."

Avery huffs. "I'll have you know my job is important. I'm responsible for all legal aspects of Petroix Oil in Europe and the Middle East."

Abby rolls her eyes. "Yeah, yeah, Ms. Uptight. We all know how 'important' you are."

I cringe. Using air quotes around important is asking for trouble, but Avery gives Abby her back. Phew.

"Wow!" Char says from behind me. "These pictures are sublime."

I whirl around and rush to my laptop. I reach out to slam it shut, but Abby's hand stops me.

"What are these?" Avery asks as everyone crowds around my computer.

"I'd say someone is more than a fashion photographer," Abby answers. "In fact, I wouldn't be surprised if someone has an exhibit coming up soon."

I glare at her. "Who do you think you are? The CIA?"

She scoffs. "I'm way better than the CIA. Would the CIA have figured out Rafael and Ravi are the same person?"

Mia raises her hand. "Since Ravi is an artist name and Rafael is his real name, I think the CIA wouldn't find it too difficult."

Abby sticks her tongue out at Mia, but whatever she responds is lost on me. My head is too busy reeling to pay attention to their sniping at each other.

I spent hours tossing and turning in my bed this week racking my brain to figure out how the hell Abby found Rafael and invited him to the party. She claimed she invited Rafael, but now it seems she knew Rafael and Ravi are the same person? How? I don't know.

"How did you know?"

"I have my ways. Although if you like, you can call it divine intervention." She winks. "I'm the divine in this scenario in case you were wondering."

"Divine? I think you're confusing the word divine with interfering busybody."

She shrugs. "You say potato, I say po-tah-to."

I growl. An honest to goodness growl. She acts like what she did was no big deal. Like betraying a friend is some everyday occurrence. With friends like her, I don't need enemies.

Avery sighs before stepping forward and taking my hands. "I'm not going to lie and tell you Abby's harmless. She most certainly isn't. But her heart is in the right place."

I frown. "How can you defend her after what she did?"

"Consider it this way – is Rafael the man you thought he was?" No need to think about my answer. I shake my head. "Here's the thing about Abby – she has no family. We are her family, and she will do literally anything to protect us."

I get wanting to protect your family but, "I barely know the woman."

"Doesn't matter. You've been inducted into the girl gang and there's no escaping."

I do an exaggerated shiver. "I'm thinking I need to reconsider this whole girl gang thing. How do I get out?"

Avery cackles. "Not happening."

Great. What kind of drama den have I landed in? My eyes find Abby who to my surprise actually appears contrite. "I'm sorry. I'm sorry if I hurt your feelings, but I was—"

Mia slaps a hand over Abby's mouth. "No. No buts. No excuses. Leave it at I'm sorry." Abby nods and Mia removes her hand.

Everyone waits for me to respond to Abby's apology. I consider letting them sweat. But I want to move on. I want to forget all about Rafael slash Ravi. I never want to see the immature childish man again. *Liar.* I shove the little voice into the back of my mind where I can properly ignore it.

"Fine," I grunt. "I accept your apology."

"Can we talk about the pictures now?" Abby asks.

I don't like to talk about my art. Not when most people don't understand it. Least of all Mama.

"I thought you were here to cheer me up. Prying into my life isn't cheering me up any."

Abby waves a hand in dismissal. "Trust me. We'll get to the cheering you up portion of the evening. I have wine and snacks and all the best chick-lit movies."

"Did you finally remove the vibrator from your 'cheer up a girlfriend'-kit?" Mia asks as her cheeks darken.

Abby clutches at her non-existent pearls. "What kind of girlfriend would I be if I didn't include a vibrator in my 'cheer up a girlfriend'-kit?" She addresses me. "Don't worry. I replaced the one Char got from the last 'cheer up a girlfriend'-evening."

I raise my hands, palms up. "I'm good."

"Your choice." She points to my laptop. "Now, can we talk about your art?"

"Isn't it time for wine and snacks?"

"I hate to admit it, but I'm with Abby on this one," Char says. "These are fabulous. Why do you claim to be a fashion photographer when you can do these? And how can I apologize for making you take pictures of Tobias?"

I wink at her. "And miss you chasing after a naked boy showing off his penis? Never."

She shivers. "We don't say the p-word out loud anymore."

"Here it is." Abby shows her phone to Avery, Mia, and Char.

I peer over Mia's shoulder to see Abby's screen. She's showing them the poster for the photo exhibition I'm taking part in.

"Oh my gosh. This is exciting. I know a real artist," Mia says.

Abby rolls her eyes. "The woman is a billionaire. She's probably bought and sold artists."

"Like you're one to talk, Ms. Millionaire."

My brow wrinkles. Mia's a billionaire and Abby's a millionaire? "I thought you taught history at the American School? And I thought you were an engineer at Petroix Oil?"

"I do teach history at the American School. I gave up the billions for love." Mia rubs her pregnant belly and gets a faraway look in her eyes.

"And I am an engineer at Petroix Oil. I also have a few patents. They bring in a decent second income," Abby says with a shrug like it's no big deal.

"A decent second income?" Char snorts. "Her little doohickeys make her millions. Trust me, I know. I'm a financial advisor at Petroix Oil and we pay to license one of those doohickeys. Why do you think she lives in the penthouse?"

"Our little Sofia didn't bat an eye at my penthouse. She's used to living in the lap of luxury," Abby responds.

I cock my eyebrow. "Did you do a background check on me?"

"I like to thoroughly vet the women who are inducted into the girl gang."

I cross my arms over my chest. "Translation – you did a background check on me."

"If it's online, it's in the public domain and considered common knowledge. I didn't go digging around in your financials or private emails."

"And you found out about my photo exhibition

online?"

"No. I saw there's an upcoming exhibition about turning trash into art and was interested."

Avery bumps her hip. "Abby is what you like to call a crusader for the earth."

"Someone has to be. It isn't like the governments are doing enough to stop the earth from being destroyed."

Avery mouths, *Told you.*

"If I tell you about the exhibit, can I have a glass of wine? And maybe some snacks? I forgot to eat lunch today."

Everyone gathers around my computer, and I show them some of my photographs. They ooh and aah, but unlike Mama, they sound sincere. They ask questions about when and where the pictures were taken.

"Welp," Abby says as I close my computer. "I'm impressed."

I blush as everyone murmurs their agreement. "Do you want to come to the opening? It's an invite-only thing and I can invite people."

I invited Mama and *Pai*, but Mama has some work engagement. I'm used to it. She always has a work engagement. I thought *Pai* would come alone, but he said he needs to stay with Mama.

"Oh, my goodness. I thought you'd never ask. Oh wait. Can I bring Matthijs? He's a little overprotective at the moment. In fact, I'm surprised he hasn't shown up here yet to check I'm resting with my feet up." Mia rolls her eyes but it's obvious she isn't bothered by it.

Right on cue, the doorbell rings.

Lucky girl. I wish I had a man who worried about me. Wait. I don't need a man. Mia and Abby must be emitting pregnancy hormones into the air and it's affecting my common sense is all.

Chapter 16

"I can't thank you enough for this," a woman says as she ushers me into the building. "This campaign is our biggest yet and to have a world class photographer volunteer her time…" She places her hand on her heart. "It's more than I could have hoped for."

"Maybe we should introduce ourselves? I'm Sofia Silva. Please, call me Sofia."

"Sorry. I got a bit overexcited there, didn't I? I'm Daphne."

She pumps my hand up and down as we shake. Overexcited is an understatement. I manage to extract my hand before she crushes the bones.

"Come this way. We also have a videographer who will be videotaping the different patients as they tell their stories."

I follow her into a room the size of a classroom. There are between ten and fifteen children here varied in age from around five to seventeen.

"These are our young heroes." Daphne motions to the children.

As we watch, one of the boys reaches into his backpack. He jerks his hand out and screams. The adults run to help him while he points at his backpack and shouts in Dutch. I have no idea what he's saying. I haven't bothered trying to learn the language.

All the children gather around the boy and his backpack as one of the teachers peeks inside. He sighs before reaching inside and removing a snake. A rubber snake.

A girl pushes her way to the front of the crowd and

glares at the boy before hissing at him in Dutch. I'm regretting not taking those Dutch classes now.

When the girl stomps off after giving the boy a piece of her mind, I follow her. She sits down, and I take the seat next to her.

"What's your name?" When she doesn't answer, I realize I'm an idiot. "Do you speak English?"

"Of course, I speak English. My kidneys may not work, but my brain is perfectly fine."

"Ah, okay. I don't speak Dutch, and I didn't want to presume."

She wrinkles her nose at me. "Who are you?"

I lift my camera. "I'm Sofia. I'm the photographer."

"I'm Mieke. Can I see your camera?"

I unwind the strap from around my head and hand it to her.

"Do you like to take pictures?"

"Nah, I don't have much to take pictures of since I spend most of my time at home."

"Can you take pictures out of your window?" I suggest.

She returns my camera. "I prefer to read."

"Really? What kind of books do you like to read?"

"I like paranormal romance." When I don't respond, she explains. "Werewolf and shifter romances. Oh, and vampire romances."

"I used to love those kinds of books, too. Although," I glance around as if making certain no one's listening, "they kind of went to my head and I convinced myself my Mama was a vampire."

Mieke leans closer. "Maybe she is a vampire. Does she drink blood?"

I feign gagging. "I don't know, but she hardly eats, she's very pale, and she doesn't age."

"She's totally a vampire," she says before dissolving into giggles.

I wait until she calms down before speaking again. "One time when I was around your age a boy called me a monkey."

Her eyes widen. "What did you do?"

I smirk. "I filled his locker with banana pudding."

She raises her fist and I bump it. I tilt my head toward the boy. "What did he do?"

She glares across the room at the boy. "Boudewijn is a dick."

I roll my eyes. "Obviously. What did he do?" She doesn't respond and I bump her shoulder. "Come on. He must have done something. Otherwise, you wouldn't have put a snake in his bag."

"He called me a scarecrow." Her lower lip wavers for a second before she takes a breath and juts out her chin. "I'm skinny because I'm sick. He was rude and I took care of him. If my brother were here, he would have punched him."

"Sounds like a good brother to have."

She huffs. "He's overprotective."

"Aren't the best brothers? At least, I assume so. I don't have a brother. I'm an only child, but I always wanted a sibling."

"You can have mine. I had to practically beg him before he 'allowed' me to come here alone today. I'm at the Kidney Foundation. What does he think is going to happen?"

"You could get bit by a snake," I tease.

"Or meet some strange woman who thinks her mom is a vampire."

"Touché." I tilt my imaginary hat to her. "What about your parents? Are they as protective as your brother?"

Pain flashes in her eyes and I'm quick to retract my question. "Sorry. Forget I asked."

"It's okay. My dad took off when I got sick, and my

mom died about six years ago. It's just me and my brother now."

I squeeze her thigh. "That sucks."

Daphne wanders over to us while chewing on her fingernail. "I'm sorry, Ms. Silva. The kids can get rambunctious."

"I told you to call me Sofia. And sometimes kids need to be taught a lesson." I wink at Mieke before standing. "Shall we get started?"

Today's photoshoot is to update the Kidney Foundation's website. There's a page dedicated to the 'young heroes' aka kids who have kidney disease and are waiting for kidney transplants. My job is to take pictures of all the heroes while they tell their stories to a videographer.

A friend of a friend of a friend called me yesterday in a panic. Apparently, the original photographer for the project has a cold and didn't want to come today as a cold can be dangerous to these children. Of course, I agreed to step in. Who wouldn't?

After an hour of shooting, Daphne finds me. "I can't thank you enough."

It's nice to be thanked for donating your time, but what's a few hours of taking pictures compared to what these kids are enduring? I can miss a day of work.

"Please help yourself to some refreshments before you leave." She motions to a table laden with all kinds of goodies. Wow. "We have very generous donors," she explains.

"Hey, Mieke. How's it going?" I ask as I sit down next to her with a plate of cookies and a soft drink.

"My brother has texted me twenty times in the last hour," she grumbles.

"He worries about you," I say. I don't know her brother but anyone who's willing to take in a sibling and raise them is a good egg in my book.

"Whatever." She rolls her eyes, and they catch on my plate. "Did you try the chocolate chip cookies? They are divine."

I rub my hands together. "I love chocolate chip cookies." I take a small bite but instead of the heavenly taste of chocolate on my lips, it's oatmeal and raisins. I spit the cookie out into my napkin.

Mieke waits until I take a sip of my drink before speaking, "That's what you get for taking my brother's side."

"You're a menace. Everyone knows you never lie to a woman about chocolate. Ever. I'll get you back."

She reminds me of another Dutch person who's a menace. But while Mieke is an annoying teenager, Rafael is a pest. And pests should be exterminated. Too bad I can't stop thinking about the man.

"What if I were allergic to raisins? Huh?"

She motions to the room where in addition to the young kidney patients, there are a few doctors being interviewed for the Kidney Foundation website.

"I think you would have been fine."

"All right, troublemaker." I find my phone in my bag. "I'm sending you a friend request. Someone needs to keep her eye on you."

She sighs. "Because I don't have enough people being overprotective."

"I don't care about your kidneys. I need to warn the world about your pranks."

She takes out her phone and accepts my friend request before frowning.

"What's wrong? You too cool to be friends with a thirty-one-year-old? Remember. I have vampire connections."

"My brother's here to pick me up."

I survey the room, but I don't notice any new faces. "He is? Where is he?"

"He's illegally parked. I'll meet him outside." She stands.

"Do you need me to walk you out?"

She points to her legs. "These things work fine. My kidneys not so much."

I cringe at her flippant referral to her illness for the second time today. I know it's her way of dealing with a serious disease, but it's hard to listen to.

"I guess you better get those legs to working then before your brother sends you another message."

She wiggles her phone at me. "Too late." She salutes. "Nice meeting you Sofia Silva."

"I'll see you around, kid."

I watch as she leaves the room before relaxing back in my chair. I pick up my cookie and take a bite before realizing it's still oatmeal raisin. I spit it out before standing. I'm done shooting for the day. Since Mieke is gone, there's no reason for me to stay. I see Daphne heading in my direction. Sigh.

"Ms. Silva. I wanted to thank you again."

I know she means well, but a lifetime of watching people kiss Mama's ass has made me somewhat adverse to an overabundance of thank yous.

"You're welcome. Can you show me where the restroom is?"

"Down the hall to the right."

"Thanks," I say and then hightail it out of there.

Chapter 17

Rafael

"Remember, call me if you need anything," I tell Mieke.

She rolls her eyes at me. "Gee, good thing you reminded me. It's not like you've told me like a gazillion times already."

"The teenager is strong with this one."

"Dork," she mutters before stepping out of the car.

"Text me," I shout as she slams the door. She's not going to text me.

I drive to the bar where I usually work Friday and Saturday nights. With my sister off doing a photo shoot, I figured I could pick up some extra hours.

Remembering Mieke is at a photo shoot reminds me of a photographer I'm doing my best to forget. And failing, if I'm being perfectly honest. I can't believe Sofia and Fifi the photographer are the same person. Sofia is sweet, funny, and down-to-earth. Or at least I thought she was. Fifi is a cranky cow who can't take a joke.

I admit the bucket of water was ill-timed. The receptionist was supposed to be the next person to open the door, and if ever there was a person who deserved to be drenched it's Juul. The bitch had the nerve to call Mieke a sick orphan.

If Sofia or Fifi or whoever the hell she is would have given me the chance, I would have apologized and explained. But, no, Ms. Butter Doesn't Melt in My Mouth Photographer didn't give me the chance to speak let alone to apologize.

What are the chances she would end up in the

middle of one of my pranks again? I would have said none, but then she shows up at the office for our meeting and Juul tells her to look up. At least I scared the pee out of Juul before Sofia saw the creepy doll.

I will admit the snake was all prank all directed at Fifi. In my defense, she was obviously bored out of her mind. I was trying to help her loosen up. How could I know she would take such a long time to realize the snake was rubber? It was hilarious watching Ms. Perfect climb onto the table, though.

And then I get this message inviting me to a party where Sofia is going to be. It was weird. I have no idea who this Abby person is or how she knew who I am, but I couldn't resist the opportunity to meet Sofia.

I wish I had resisted. A little voice in the back of my head shouts liar. It says I need to give Sofia another chance. Why? *Because you need to explain about the pranks.* Whatever. I shove the voice back and enter the bar to get to work.

The bar is on the *Leidseplein* in Amsterdam, which is tourist central, and we're right in the middle of tourist season. I thought dealing with foreign customers would give me a chance to practice my English before I met Sofia. Now? Who cares?

I spend the first hour of my shift restocking the bar and cleaning glasses. And texting Mieke to check on her. I have to resort to threatening to come back there before she finally texts back.

Mieke: I'm fine. I'm alive and having a good time. Thanks for ruining it by being Mr. Overprotective.

Ugh. Mieke can switch from grumpy teenager to guilt-tripping sister in a blink of an eye.

Me: Have a good time.

I put down my phone, but I can't resist picking it up and adding to my text.

Me: Be safe.

Mieke: You crossed the line *GIF of donkey

blowing up the line*

I'm smiling as I return my phone to my pocket. If she's sending GIFs and making jokes, she's okay.

I watch as two guys stroll into the bar. Their gazes dart around the room as if they're nervous. Did I mention how much I hate tourist season?

"What can I get you guys?" I ask in English, not bothering with Dutch.

While one of them hangs back, the other motions me to the end of the bar. I grunt before I follow him.

"Is there a problem?"

He leans in close before he whispers, "I want to buy some drugs."

Why do tourists think every Dutch person is a drug dealer? Yes, drug use is legal in Holland. Yes, selling drugs is tolerated in Holland. But, hell no, to all Dutch people being stoned out of their minds all the time.

"What kind of drugs?" I whisper back to fuck with him.

"You know, like hash."

I snort before stepping back. "Dude. Hash isn't a drug. And this isn't a coffee shop." I point to the place across the street. "Try over there. You know, the place with the big hash leaf on the sign."

They scamper out of the bar and practically sprint across the street. Good riddance.

The lunch crowd arrives, and I'm swamped for the next hour. I'm wiping down the bar when two kids sit down across from me. One clears his throat before saying, "Um, can I have a beer?"

"Tap?"

He slides a card across the bar. "Here's my ID."

I glance down at it while I pour his beer and chuckle. "Dude, your ID is the worst fake ID I've ever seen." The card isn't even plastic.

The kid snatches the ID back and jumps to his

feet. "Where are you going? Don't you want your beer?"

"But you said my ID was fake."

"Show me your actual passport and you'll be fine," I tell him.

He leans forward and whispers, "But we're not twenty-one."

"Yes, and?"

"We're American."

I nearly roll my eyes. As if I didn't spot they were Americans the minute they walked into the bar. "I'm not understanding what the problem is."

His friend finally speaks up, "Our parents told us we can't drink in Amsterdam because we're not legal to drink back home."

I chuckle as I pour another beer. "Show me your passports and these beers are yours."

They scramble to dig their passports out of their fanny packs and show them to me.

"No getting crazy drunk and puking all over my bar," I tell them as I slide the beers their way.

Their eyes widen before they bob their heads in unison. "Yes, sir."

They wander away to find a booth to sit in and I check my phone. No message from Mieke.

Me: Is there a bratty teenager available?

Mieke: No bratty teens here. A magnificent teen with a new career as a model is available, though.

Me: Be good.

Mieke: *GIF of a camel sticking its tongue out*

I return my phone to my pocket and get back to work.

When another group of male tourists clamors to the bar fifteen minutes later, I have to force myself to not growl at them. What now?

"Hey! Hey! Hey!" One of them whisper-shouts at

me.

"Can I get you a drink?" I ask them like the good bartender I am.

"I want something to drink all right." He waggles his eyebrows.

I gotta admit. I have no idea what he's trying to insinuate. "What can I get you?"

"How about a tall glass of water?"

"Tap water okay?"

He knocks on the bar and shakes his head. "No, not water *water*. A tall glass of water." He tilts his head and motions to a woman sitting at a table by herself.

"Do you want to offer her a drink?"

He rolls his eyes. "No." He's obviously frustrated with me, but in my defense, he's not being very clear.

"I'm sorry, but you're going to have to explain. I don't know what you want."

"You're not some undercover cop, are you?" another guy asks.

Undercover cop? The confusion continues. "Why would you think I'm an undercover cop?"

Another man in the group pushes his way to the front. "We would like to acquire her services for the day," he says.

The guy next to him slaps his arm. "Are you crazy? We haven't established he's not a cop."

They forget all about me and start arguing amongst themselves. "Ahem." No one pays me any attention. "Guys!" I shout and wait for them to quiet down.

"One, prostitution in the Netherlands is legal. No undercover cop is going to give the first shit about you hiring a hooker. Two, the woman over there is not a prostitute. She's dressed in a suit and is on her lunch break. Three, we're not in the red light district. Now, do you need directions?"

I don't wait for them to answer and go ahead and

give them directions to *De Wallen*. The medieval city center with its narrow alleys and canals is where the red light district can be found.

The next hour passes slowly before it's time for me to clock out and leave to pick up Mieke who hasn't answered any of my texts for the past hour.

Me: I'm outside.

Mieke: On my way, sir. Right away, sir.

Such a smartass. When she slides into the car five minutes later, the happiness plain to see on her face is worth all the stress I suffered today worrying about her.

"How did it go?"

"It was awesome. I finally got Boudewijn back. You were right. The fake snake worked like a charm. Oh, and I met this cool photographer."

She chatters on as I drive us home. I nod at the appropriate moments, but my mind is once again wandering to a certain photographer.

Sofia aka Fifi may make me want to yank my hair out, but at the same time, I can't deny the way my skin sizzles whenever she's in my immediate vicinity. My body doesn't care how cranky the photographer is. It wants to haul her near and taste every inch of her mocha-colored skin.

Good thing I'm never going to see the woman again because my willpower with regard to her is non-existent.

Chapter 18

Mia is bouncing on her toes as she rings the doorbell to Abby's penthouse apartment. Her husband Matthijs stands next to her with his arms crossed over his chest.

"You are not doing any lifting," he orders her.

She rolls her eyes at him before winking at me.

"What's got you all excited?" I ask before I have to listen to another lecture about what pregnant Mia can and cannot do according to her protective husband.

Mia rubs her hands together and her eyes sparkle with mirth. "I finally get to snoop in Abby's stuff. Like she did to me when I moved."

Abby opens the door with a flourish. "No need to snoop. I hereby grant you permission to go through my undergarments." She does a bow before motioning to her bedroom. "All the drawers are open for your perusal."

Mia frowns. "But it's not snooping if you grant permission."

"I know," Abby says before winking at me.

Avery pushes her way past Mia. "She's not stopping me," she declares before marching off to the bedroom.

"The muscles have arrived," Niels announces and flexes his bicep.

Matthijs glances at Niels before snorting. I can't blame him. Matthijs is only a couple inches taller than Niels but he's miles wider. According to Mia, he was a semi-professional rugby player before he quit the team when she got pregnant.

"What did we miss?" Char asks as she strolls in

carrying a squirming Tobias.

"*Ik wil spelen,*" the boy pouts.

Char sets him down. "Sylvia is here."

He promptly announces, "She's my girlfriend." And darts off to find Abby's daughter.

Char groans, but Nico chuckles as he throws an arm around her shoulders. "He's five. He doesn't know what a girlfriend is. It's fine."

She widens her eyes before pointing to the living room where Tobias is giving Sylvia a sloppy kiss. Sylvia pushes him away and shouts, "Cooties!"

Abby's gaze is full of pride for her daughter, but Jasper sighs. "You had to teach our daughter to shout cooties whenever a boy touches her?"

"It's a scary world out there. I'm preparing her for it, not coddling her." She rubs her bulging belly. "Of course, when her little brother arrives, he'll help to protect her."

Jasper frowns. "What if the baby is a girl?"

Abby rolls her eyes. "Then, the house will be overrun by women."

Matthijs opens his mouth, but Mia slaps his stomach. "No, don't you dare say a word about girls and all the rules necessary for keeping them safe."

He grunts at her but wisely keeps his mouth shut.

Avery stomps out of the bedroom. "All your clothes are already packed in boxes." She crosses her arms over her chest. "And the boxes are sealed shut with some kind of wonder tape."

Niels takes her hand and pulls her close before kissing her forehead. "Sorry, sweetheart. You'll have to snoop when we unpack at the new house."

"Actually," Abby says and then pauses for dramatic effect. "There will be no unpacking."

Huh. What is she talking about?

"Are you not moving?" Mia asks before bouncing

on her toes. "Yes!"

Matthijs growls. "No jumping. It's not good for the baby."

She glares at him. "Says who? The doctor said I can do normal activity. In fact, she said I can jog if I want to."

"You are not jogging!"

She fists her hands on her hips. "I'll jog if I damn well want to."

Tobias sprints into the hallway. "Damn!"

Mia's mouth drops open when she realizes the little boy heard her. "Shit, Char. I'm sorry."

Tobias doesn't waste a second before shouting, "Shit!"

Mia's face is now bright red. "And now I said shit."

"Shit!" he shouts again.

I'm starting to think the little boy is way smarter than everyone gives him credit for.

"And now I did it again. Shutting up now." Mia clamps a hand over her mouth.

Char picks Tobias up. "It's fine. What did I tell you about repeating the words of grown-ups?" she asks as she carries him away.

"Ahem." Abby clears her throat. "Can we get back to my announcement now?"

Avery rolls her eyes. "Yes, Wonder Woman, please tell us your announcement."

Abby dips her chin. "Thank you."

Avery huffs. "I was being sarcastic."

"Really? Good thing you told me. Otherwise, I would have never noticed."

Jasper arrives holding Sylvia in his arms. He places an arm around his wife before announcing, "We are moving. The movers are coming tomorrow."

This is confusing. "Why are we here then?" I ask.

"Duh. This is our going away party." She tilts her head to my camera. "Thanks for being our photographer."

"Will you stop taking advantage of Sofia?" Char asks when she returns without Tobias.

"I didn't ask her to bring her camera, so I'm not taking advantage. Those are the rules."

"Whose rules?"

Abby whips out her phone. "It's right here. How to know if you're taking advantage of your friend."

Avery peers over Abby's shoulder at her phone. "You're referring to a quiz in a women's magazine? Since when do you read women's magazines?"

"Since my obstetrician put up a big 'No Phones' sign in her waiting room."

Jasper nudges her. "Tell them what the rest of the sign says."

She grunts. "This means you Abby." When everyone laughs at her, she snarls. "It's not my fault someone called with an emergency while I was waiting for the doctor."

"But it was your fault you told the doctor to wait while you finished your call," Jasper points out.

"I don't see what the big deal is. I have to wait for her all the time." Abby seems genuinely confused.

I don't bother trying to explain the rules of etiquette in a medical setting to her. The woman lives by her own rules. Instead, I ask, "This party is all of us standing around in your hallway talking? Should I take pictures already?"

"Why is everyone standing in the hallway? Come in. Come in." Abby motions to everyone to follow her as she waddles to the living room.

Mia gasps when she sees the table. "Did you do this? How is it you're further along in your pregnancy and you have the energy to prepare a brunch for nine people? I feel like I'm a gazillion years pregnant and I will never get enough sleep again. Ever."

The table decoration is pretty impressive. The tablecloth is a deep blue while the runner is gold with lace trimming. In the middle of the table are several bouquets of flowers and bunches of candles. Each place setting has a different colored charger plate on top of which is a white plate with gold trimming. There are several different glasses per setting, too.

"I'll sleep when I'm dead," Abby quips. At Jasper's frown, she admits, "I was super tired during my first pregnancy. This second pregnancy is much easier."

Mia groans as Matthijs helps her into a chair. "I don't think I can handle another pregnancy." When her husband grunts at her, she throws up a hand. "No, I'm not talking about how our child needs a sibling right now."

I take several pictures of the table, flowers, and place settings before motioning for everyone to take their place.

"Nuh uh," Abby says and waves her hand in front of my camera. "I know you have a timer on that thing. Don't try to deny it. I reviewed the instruction manual."

I move the camera away from my face to ask the room, "I get having energy, but does this woman ever sleep?"

I do as Abby says and set up the timer to take a picture of the entire group, including me. You'd think as the daughter of a model, I'd be used to getting my picture taken. You'd be wrong. Why do you think I took up photography to begin with?

Once we take our seats, I notice there's an extra place setting across from me. Did Abby think I would bring a date to 'moving day' turned into 'going away party day'?

I'm saying no to dating. I don't care how much Zara bugs me and Mama pushes me to introduce them to my supposed boyfriend. I don't need a man.

An image of Rafael pops into my head. My body likes the idea of getting to know Ravi slash Rafael better way too much. It doesn't matter how often I remind it of what an immature child he is. My body doesn't care. It's convinced Rafael knows exactly how to use his sexy body.

It doesn't matter what my body thinks. I am in control, not my hormones that have decided to act like a lovesick teenager. I survey the room and notice all the love passing between the couples.

Love is all well and good for them. But it's not for me. Not when every man I meet wants to use me. And Rafael would be no different.

Yes, he would.

I ignore the little voice and reach for my glass of wine.

Chapter 19

I sigh when I see Zara is calling. I'm not avoiding my best friend. Not exactly. But I haven't told her about the whole Rafael Ravi debacle yet. After how I talked him up, I'm kind of embarrassed what a jerk he turned out to be.

You don't ignore a call from Zara, though. The woman doesn't speak Dutch and has never been to Holland, but you can bet she'd figure out how to order the police to check on me to make sure I'm not dead in my bath. I don't even have a bathtub, but try to tell that to Ms. Over The Top.

I accept the video call and infuse my voice with happiness I'm not feeling, "Hey banker lady! How's life?"

She purses her lips. "I told you. I work in a bank. I'm not a banker."

"What's the big deal? Is there something wrong with being a banker? I didn't know you were this prejudiced."

She rolls her eyes. "Nice try but you won't distract me this time. I want to hear all about Rafael. Is he dreamy?"

"No one says dreamy anymore." See? I can distract her.

"Stop stalling or I'll tell Mama Silva about the time you switched out her pricey anti-aging cream with a drugstore brand."

"You helped. You'd be implicating yourself, too," I point out.

"Maybe, but she won't threaten to come to Holland to meet my young man."

I snort. "Because you don't like the dick."

She makes a face. "You have to admit it's not the most attractive anatomical feature."

I waggle my eyebrows. "It's not about how it looks. It's about what it can do."

She feigns gagging. "Stop."

"When it's hard—"

"Enough! Stop stalling and tell me what happened with Rafael when you met him. Or have you not met him yet? Are you a chicken? Bwak! Bwak!"

"Ugh. Fine. Here goes nothing." I explain how Rafael is Ravi. She knows who Ravi is since I told her all about the childish unprofessional annoying as hell model.

"You. Are. Shitting. Me."

"I wish I were. Once again, a man isn't the person I thought he was." I sigh.

"Oh no, you don't. You are not going to use the whole Rafael Ravi incident as an excuse to stop dating."

I totally am. Dating is for suckers. No thanks. I don't bother telling Zara my decision, though. She'll argue with me. But I'm going to do what I want.

"I can practically see the wheels churning in your head from here. The word stubborn was invented for you."

"Not hardly. You have met Mama, haven't you?"

She does an exaggerated shiver. "Remember when she was convinced air-conditioning would give you a lung infection and refused to use it all summer long? Despite your dad having a doctor come to the house and discuss air-conditioning's benefits to her?"

"It was one long, hot, sweaty summer."

"But, seriously, about you and dating—"

I hold up my hand. "I have another call. You'll have to give me the 'I have to date to find love and love really does exist and is wonderful'-lecture later."

"I'll pencil it into my schedule."

She's not joking. She'll make a note of it in her

phone, the crazy woman.

We say our goodbyes and I answer my other call.

"Hey, Mieke. What's going on?"

She sighs. "My brother is driving me crazy. He doesn't even have to be home to drive me up the wall."

"What did he do now?"

"The usual crap. Texting me every thirty seconds to check I'm not too hot or too cold and to ask if I've eaten and what I've eaten. It goes on and on and on."

"He worries about you. It's sweet."

She blows a raspberry. "I think you mean annoying."

"Why don't you send him a message every once in a while telling him you're okay?" I suggest.

She huffs. "Now, you sound like him. If you'd message me, I wouldn't have to message you all the time," she mimics.

"I hate to tell you this, but he's not wrong."

"On top of everything, he's been a total grump lately."

"He has? What happened?"

She shrugs. "I don't know. He won't tell me. I have to tell him every single detail of my life, but does he tell me anything about his? No. He does not."

"Hmmm… maybe it's girl problems."

She snorts. "Girls throw themselves at my brother. It's disgusting."

"He must be as handsome as you are beautiful."

"Actually, we aren't similar in appearance. We have the same mom but different fathers. I take after our mom, but he must take after his dad."

"You've never met his dad?"

"He died before I was born. And then my mom remarried the jerk and had me."

"What was your mother like?"

"She wasn't a vampire like your mom."

"I never should have told you about that. I'm never going to hear the end of it."

Thankfully, she moves the conversation on. "Mom was awesome. She had to work a lot since we always needed extra money because having non-functioning kidneys is really expensive. My brother had to babysit all the time."

"Is your brother a lot older than you?"

"He's twenty-nine. Hey, how old are you?"

"Thirty-one. Why?"

"Awesome. You're the perfect age for my brother."

Uh oh. I don't like where this is going. "What are you talking about?"

"I've decided you should date my brother."

"The same brother who is overprotective and drives you crazy?"

"I think he only drives little sisters whose kidneys don't function crazy."

At the mention of her kidneys, I ask, "How are you feeling?"

"*Et tu, Brute?*"

"*Nemo, ne me.*"

"You speak Latin?"

"Not really. My dad tried to teach me, but I didn't get very far. I do speak a bit of Portuguese and Russian, though."

"Wow. Impressive."

"Not really. My dad is Brazilian, and my mom is Russian."

"Cool. Where did you grow up? Moscow? Rio?"

I chuckle. "New York City. When I wasn't traveling with my parents."

"You have such an exotic life and I'm stuck here in my apartment most days." She sticks out her bottom lip and does a proper pout.

"Why don't you come to the opening of my exhibit at the Photography Museum?" I suggest.

Her eyes widen. "You have an exhibit at the Photography Museum? No wonder Daphne kept kissing your ass at the photo shoot for the Kidney Foundation."

"Don't say ass. Although, you're not wrong. She did kiss it. A lot. So, will you come to the opening?"

She frowns. "I don't know if my brother will let me come alone."

"Bring him with. Then, he can't complain. And he can't text you all the time if he's with you, right?"

"I'll ask him. *Nee heb je, ja kun je krijgen.*"

"What did you say?"

"It's a Dutch saying. It means 'you have no, you can get yes'."

"I hope he says yes. I'll send you all the details."

"Speaking of the brother, he's calling now." She shows me her phone which indicates *The Jailor is calling.*

"Answer him. We'll talk later. And don't forget to ask him about the exhibit!"

It takes me five minutes to realize Mieke played me. She totally maneuvered me into inviting her brother to the opening. The brother she wants to set me up with. I'm such an idiot.

Never mind. Mieke does need to get out and about more and if I have to meet her brother in order to give her a nice time out, then I'll meet her brother. Fingers crossed he's not a total asshole.

Chapter 20

Rafael

I ruffle Mieke's hair before plopping down on the couch next to her. "What do you want to do today?"

It's Sunday. The one day of the week I don't work. Unless you count working until 5 a.m. at the bar, which I don't. Mieke and I always spend the day together having some fun. Unfortunately, fun for her often involves Disney movies. Although, if I'm being honest, they're not too bad.

"Movie marathon?"

Mieke sighs. "I don't want to sit on the sofa all day long."

Fuck. I hate this. I hate how my baby sister is stuck at home most of the time. And when she's not at home, she's at the hospital getting dialysis. It's a crap situation, and it's not fair. Why wasn't I the one born with kidney disease? Not her.

"You know what you need? A prank day!"

She pumps her fist. "Yes!"

I rub my hands together. "Where shall we begin? Finn in apartment 203 gave me the stink eye when I came home this morning."

He was grumpy because it was five in the morning but no one in the apartment building is safe when it comes to Mieke and her pranks.

"I have the perfect idea."

Ten minutes later I'm standing in front of Finn's apartment door with a box of laxatives and a note saying *We heard you were having trouble pooping.* Mieke is at the end of the hallway with a camera.

"You ready?" I ask her.

She gives me a thumbs-up, and I knock on the door.

"Hey, Finn," I say when he answers. "Got a delivery for you."

I angle myself to prevent Mieke from seeing my face and wink at him. His chin dips slightly indicating he understands. Finn is a good sport. He knows he's being pranked, but he takes the box with a smile on his face.

"What's this? A surprise for me?"

I roll my eyes. I hope he's not into acting because he sucks at it. I place the box in his outstretched hands. He opens it, and his eyes widen to the size of saucers when he sees it's full of laxatives.

"There's a note, too."

He finds the note and reads it. "Trouble pooping? How the hell would you hear I'm having trouble pooping. I mean, I am. But I don't go around telling everyone I'm constipated. How would the conversation go? Hey, Finn. How are you? Not too good. I can't seem to poop."

"You must have told someone because the whole apartment building has been gossiping about it."

"This place is a bed of rumors. It's worse than when I was in the military. And, let me tell you, soldiers are gossipmongers of the highest order. There's not much else to do when you're stuck in the desert on watch for hours at a time."

I hear Mieke giggle, and I glance over my shoulder to see she's bent over laughing with her hand over her mouth to prevent any sound from escaping. The camera is abandoned on the floor.

"Um, I hope your pooping works out," I tell Finn and leave.

I take Mieke's elbow and pick up her camera before leading her to the elevator. "Did you get it on camera?"

"I...I..."

She bursts out laughing and warmth spreads throughout my chest. Seeing her happy fills my heart and makes the endless hours of work worth it. I would do pretty much anything to make her happy, including nearly lose a good paying gig because of a prank gone wrong.

"What's next?" I ask once we're settled on the sofa at home once again.

"Counterfeit money," she says as she draws her laptop near.

I watch as she opens Photoshop and starts a new project to design a fifty euro note. Unlike American dollars, euro notes don't portray people. Instead, each banknote depicts bridges and arches in different historical European styles. They aren't existing monuments. I don't want to imagine what the political fighting amongst the member states would have been like if they were real.

"What am I supposed to do?" I ask Mieke as we stand in the hallway with her fake fifty euro banknotes and a bottle of glue.

She grabs the items from me. "Here. Let me show you."

She glues the fake money to our next door neighbor's welcome mat, rings the bell, and then runs away giggling. I bite my tongue to stop myself from yelling at her for running. Running down one hallway is not going to kill her, I remind myself.

We hide around the corner, and I position my phone to record our neighbor, Laura, while we watch.

Laura opens the door. When she notices there's no one standing at her doorstep, she surveys the hallway. She doesn't spot my hand with the camera. She huffs and is about to return to her apartment when her eyes land on the supposed fifty euro bill.

She grins as she reaches down for it. Her brow wrinkles when she can't pick it up. She paws at it, but the bill doesn't move. She grunts before kneeling to study it closer. She shakes her head when she notices the tiny picture of Mieke waving from inside the Renaissance era archway.

"Good one, Mieke," she shouts.

"Don't tell anyone," Mieke shouts back.

"I won't," Laura says before closing her door behind her.

I'd bet money – real money – she's on the phone messaging the entire apartment building about the prank before we return to our place. Finn didn't lie about our apartment building being a hotbed of gossip.

"You done?" I ask Mieke when we're on the sofa once again.

"One more," she says and opens her laptop again.

"Esmay has a new Wi-Fi printer, but it's not password protected. She should know better."

I watch as she types out a message: *Hello! I am a demon taking over your printer. If you don't send an apple pie to your next door neighbor, I will take over your dishwasher.*

She selects Esmay's printer and hits print. "Now we wait."

I stand. "Ready for lunch?"

"Meh. I guess."

I turn away so she doesn't see my frown. She hates it when I get upset about how little she eats. She thinks I'm a worrywart. My sister needs a kidney transplant before dialysis no longer works for her. Of course, I worry.

I can't resist telling her, "You need to eat."

"Yes, Mom."

"Soup and sandwich?" I ask, but I don't wait for an answer. I'm already walking to the kitchen to prepare the food. I warm up a can of tomato soup while I make us sandwiches.

"Do you think Esmay will send over a pie?" I ask when we sit down to eat.

"She will if she doesn't want me to send all kinds of nasty messages to her printer."

If it were up to Esmay, she'd bake Mieke a pie every day. I had to take her aside and tell her to stop with all the baking since my sister hardly eats. I gained five kilograms within a month of Esmay moving into the place next door.

I can't get any modeling gigs if I have a pudgy belly. I wish I could give up on the modeling. I hated it before I had the misfortune of being photographed by the great Fifi Silva. And now? Now, I don't want to see a fashion shoot ever again. Unfortunately, my bank account doesn't care about my wants.

"Are you dating anyone right now?" Mieke asks, and I nearly choke on my sandwich.

"I thought we agreed not to discuss my dating life."

It's not as if I have much of a dating life to discuss. I don't have the time. If I need sexual release, I pick up a woman at the bar around closing time. I let her take me to her place, I give her a good time, and then I return to my bed all by myself.

"When did we agree to this?"

"When you picked up my phone and the caller didn't realize it wasn't me and she said—"

She holds up her hand. "Stop! It's bad enough I had to hear about the size of your male anatomy once. I don't need to hear it again." She feigns gagging.

"Why are you asking anyway?"

She plays with the crust of her sandwich. "Just wondering."

Wondering my ass. "What are you up to?"

"I thought I could set you up with my new friend. Remember I told you about the woman I met at the Kidney Foundation photoshoot?"

I'm shaking my head before she finishes speaking. "No. I don't have time to date."

"But you shouldn't be alone. You're nearly thirty. You're practically an old man."

I mock glare at her. "I'll show you an old man."

"If you won't let me set you up on a date, at least let me go to this photo exhibition. I was invited to the opening."

I don't want to tell her no, but her health is too important for her to be traipsing around at a museum.

"I'll only go if I'm feeling well. And I promise to tell you if I'm feeling even the teensiest, tiniest bit sick." She flutters her eyelashes at me, and I cave.

"Fine. You can go, but I will be going with you. I will check your temperature before we leave. And you can stay a maximum of one hour. Not a minute more."

"Thank you!" she shouts and jumps up to kiss my cheeks. "Thank you. Thank you. Thank you."

"Sit down and eat your lunch. And don't make me regret it."

The doorbell rings. "Pie's here!" she yells as she skips to the door.

Seeing how happy she is now I truly hope I can take her to the museum exhibition. I couldn't care less she's obviously trying to set me up. Let her have her fun at my expense. I can take it.

Chapter 21

"**I**'m nervous."

Dang it. Saying the words out loud reminds me of the last time I was super nervous and messaged those very same words to Rafael who I thought might be the nice, dependable man I want.

Obviously, I shouldn't be trusted to find a man myself. But then again, Zara didn't do a much better job when she set me up with Mr. Married Stink Bomb.

"Why?" Abby asks as she surveys the exhibition. It's opening night at the Photography Museum and my new friends are here to support me. "Your photos are da bomb."

"I don't think anyone says da bomb anymore. The nineties called. They want their slang back," Char says.

"Actually, 'the bomb' can be traced back to the jazz scene of the forties and fifties," Mia aka the history nerd says.

"Whatever. I love how you changed items everyone ignores into art. But here comes the question. Did you pick the trash up after you took the pictures? And, even more important, did you recycle it properly?"

Avery slaps Abby's arm. "Leave her alone. You don't have to crusade for the planet twenty-four seven."

"Of course, I do. Do you realize what's happening to the planet? Have you read the news about the fire tornado? Have you seen how many wildfires there have been this year?"

"Slow your roll, Crusader. We're here to celebrate the opening of the exhibition and Sofia's participation in it, not discuss the planet."

"I'm here for the free champagne," Char says. I widen my eyes at her, but she waves away my concern.

"Don't get me wrong, I will wander around the exhibit and ooh and aah as necessary. But I already know you're brilliant and I've seen all the photographs at your house. But since Abby and Mia are pregnant, I don't have anyone to drink wine with anymore. Thus, champagne."

"I'll drink wine with you," I tell her.

"And what am I? Chopped liver?" Avery asks.

"You're a workaholic who doesn't finish work until after happy hour every night," Char says.

"You forgot uptight," Abby points out.

"Sometimes I wonder why I'm friends with you," Avery says to her.

"Because I'm awesome. Duh."

"I think I need some champagne now," I say. "Do you want an orange juice?" I ask Mia.

"Mia needs to sit down," Matthijs says as he joins the group. "She's been standing for ten minutes now." And then, proving he isn't the most intelligent man in the room, he points to his watch where the stopwatch is ticking off the time.

"I'm going to get an orange juice with the artist. And you're going to go back to the horde of men and think about what you've done wrong." Mia doesn't bother waiting for his response. She hooks her arm through my elbow and marches off.

"Is he watching?" she whispers to me when we're halfway to the bar.

I glance over my shoulder. "Yep. Staring at you like he has no clue what he did wrong."

She snorts. "Such an idiot. Using an actual stopwatch to time how long I'm allowed to stand."

"Do you want to get a drink and sit over there?" I point to a table in the corner.

"God, yes. My feet and back are killing me. Why

did I think wearing heels was a good idea?"

"Because you wanted to look pretty," I say as I escort her to a table and make sure she's comfortable before going to find her a drink.

As I'm returning to Mia with our drinks, I glance across the room to the entrance. My eyes narrow when I see someone with perfectly styled light-brown hair. Oh no, he didn't. I slam the drinks down on the table and march over to the entrance.

Abby appears at my side. "This is going to be good." She motions to Avery and Char. "Hurry up or you'll miss it."

"What is it now, Wonder Woman?"

I ignore their chatter and continue my march to Rafael. "What are you doing here?" I hiss at him.

At my question, he swivels around, and I notice Mieke has arrived. I push past Rafael the Immature to hug her.

"I'm glad you could make it. Did your big brother not come? Did he actually let you leave the house without him?"

"No. He did not," says a voice sounding suspiciously like Rafael's.

"Ha ha! I can't believe I didn't know this. This is even better than I could have planned." Abby is bouncing on her toes in excitement.

I point at her. "Stop bouncing. You already look ready to have the baby any minute now. I'd prefer you didn't give birth in the foyer at my exhibit."

"Not again." Mia glares at Abby. "Have you been in secret labor all day again?"

"Geez. You act like I go into secret labor all the time. It was the one time. And we made it to the hospital before I gave birth to Sylvia."

"Because I forced you into a taxi. You were too busy trying to find Jasper to realize you needed to get to the hospital pronto."

"Who are these people? And can I be friends with them?" At Mieke's questions, the chatter dies down, and everyone focuses on her. She smiles and waves.

"Are you going to introduce your friend?" Char asks. "Not the male one. We know who he is. Everyone in our apartment building knows who he is because man can Sofia shout when she needs to. But we don't know who the girl is. Unless Abby knows. She's quite the spy. I wouldn't put it past her. Sorry. Switching off my motormouth right now."

Nico comes up behind her and wraps an arm around her. "Did someone call you motormouth again? Who do I need to beat up this time?"

She beams up at him. "You've never hit anyone in your life. You're a lover, not a fighter."

Abby claps. "Now, we're getting somewhere. Let's hear how Nico is a lover."

"Ahem. There's a child present," Rafael says and Mieke scowls.

"I'm not a child. I'm sixteen years old, you know." Mieke pokes him in the side. "Be nice or I'll tell everyone how you pee when I tickle you."

"I don't pee when you tickle me."

Mieke smirks. "Yeah, but they don't know I'm lying."

"I like her. Let's adopt her into the girl gang. All in favor raise your hand," Abby says with her hand already in the air.

Char, Mia, and Avery lift their hands in the air while I stand there staring at them. "I'm sorry, Mieke. I'd say I should have never let them initiate me into their girl gang, but then I wouldn't have met Tobias."

She surveys the group. "Which one is Tobias?"

"He's not here," Char explains. "He's my son. Well, not my son as in my biological son, but the son of my fiancé." She sticks out her hand to show Mieke her engagement ring. "Although, he's not the biological son of my fiancé either. It's a long story."

"Family's complicated," Mieke says like she's some wise woman and not a teenager. "This guy here is my brother, but he's actually my half-brother who's raised me since I was ten."

My eyes practically bug out of my head. "Ravi the immature, unprofessional asshole is your brother?"

"Fifi the cranky bitch fashion photographer is your artist friend?" Rafael sneers.

Mieke's head whips back and forth between us. "You know each other?" She bounces on her toes. "I knew it! I knew Fifi the Great was Sophia. I guess this isn't a blind date anymore, then."

"Blind date? You set your brother up with Sofia, the woman who hates him? I'm in love. I seriously want to adopt you right now." Abby throws her arms around Mieke but considering the size of her pregnant belly her arms can't circle Mieke. She drops one arm and settles for an awkward one armed hug.

Mieke doesn't seem to mind. In fact, she's beaming.

"Why don't we leave these two lovebirds alone while we go check out the exhibition," Abby suggests, and I want to punch her. Unfortunately, Matthijs is a cop and he'd probably have me in handcuffs before my fist reached her face. Also, I don't know how to punch someone.

"Why don't you mind your own business?" I hiss at her.

She laughs. "You really don't understand the rules of the girl gang."

"What rules?"

"I'll send them to you," Abby says.

"Are you serious? You wrote down rules?"

Abby rolls her eyes. "Of course, I did. Don't all gangs have rules?"

I don't respond. There's no response to her madness.

"These are your pictures?" Rafael asks as he points to one of my photographs on the flyer for the exhibit.

"Yeah. What did you think? I actually like doing fashion photography? Why do you think I was such a grump at a photoshoot?" He opens his mouth to respond but I raise my hand to stop him. "Don't answer. It was a rhetorical question."

"Sounds like you two have some misconceptions you need to clear up," Abby says in a sing-song voice.

"I think she's right," Rafael says.

"I hate it when she's right. She lords it over you for days." But I can't deny my curiosity is officially piqued. Have I been wrong about Ravi all along and right about Rafael? He's not two different people, I remind myself.

"Sounds like someone I know." He winks at his sister.

"Shall we get a drink?" I motion to the bar.

"Why don't we have a coffee sometime this week? I don't want Mieke out and about for too long."

"Why can't Mieke be out and about?" Abby asks because she couldn't mind her own business if her life depended on it.

"Because my kidneys don't work. Big bro thinks since my kidneys are kaput, the rest of me is fragile." Mieke rolls her eyes.

"Our agreement was you can stay for one hour."

Rafael crosses his arms over his chest, and I can't help but notice how the material stretches tight across his muscles. Damnit. Was I all wrong about the guy? Or right and then wrong? I grasp my head before it can explode. I'm confusing myself. The sight of his chest is not helping any. I drag my gaze away from his body.

"Fine. Come on, Sofia. Show me how awesome you are." Mieke wiggles her fingers as if she's daring me.

"I'll send you a message about meeting up later this week," I tell Rafael before taking Mieke's hand and strolling to the start of the exhibit.

Don't look back. Don't look back.

I look back. Of course, I do. Rafael is standing in the foyer his smoky gray eyes following our every move. His legs are planted shoulder width apart and his biceps bulge as he crosses his arms over his chest. He has the appearance of a modern day knight ready to come to his lady's protection.

I wish I were his lady. Whoa. Slow down. *No, you don't, Sofia. No, you don't.*

Liar.

Chapter 22

"Thanks for meeting me in Amsterdam. I don't like to be too far away from Mieke if I can help it." Rafael rubs a hand across his jaw, his perfectly square jaw. A jaw I want to lick and bite. *Stop it, Sofia.* You don't know who this man is.

"Who are you and what have you done with the immature childish Ravi?"

He grunts before motioning to the waiter and ordering a coffee. I order a cappuccino.

"Sorry. I desperately need caffeine. Mieke had a bad night."

"Oh no." I reach across the table to squeeze his hand without thinking about it. When I realize what I've done I try to pull my hand away, but he holds tight. "What happened? Is she okay?"

"The dialysis makes her feel nauseous. It makes for a long night."

I study his face and notice the dark circles under his eyes and brackets of strain around his mouth.

"Can I ask what her prognosis is?"

Whenever I bring up her illness to Mieke, she shuts me down. I get it. She doesn't want to talk about it, but I have a need to know. She's my friend. I want to know how to help her.

The waiter returns with our coffees, and I wrap my hands around my drink. I'm feeling cold all of a sudden.

Rafael clears his throat. "It's not good. Without a kidney transplant, she…" His words trail off and he stares at his cup of coffee.

I feel my eyes itch with unshed tears, but this

moment isn't about me. I squeeze them tight for a few seconds until the tears retreat.

"What are her chances of receiving a kidney transplant?" I ask once I'm sure I won't start bawling.

"She's pretty high up on the donor list, but the idea of someone having to die for my sister to live? It fucking kills me. Kills me." A look of anguish crosses his face.

"What about a live donor?"

"I'm not a match."

"What about her father?" I know her father abandoned her, but surely he'd be willing to give up a kidney to save his daughter's life.

"The rat bastard wouldn't buy her a coffee, let alone donate a kidney to her," he snarls.

"This sucks. I'm sorry." I take a deep breath and force myself to continue with an apology. "And I'm sorry I judged you about the pranks. But you're lucky my hair was braided when I got doused with water or you'd be missing a limb right now."

"And I'm sorry you got caught in the middle of my revenge prank. The receptionist Juul called Mieke a sick orphan and I couldn't let it go."

My nostrils flare. "Are you serious? She called Mieke a sick orphan? What a fucking bitch!"

"Don't worry. I got her good already."

I lean forward. This I've got to hear. "How?"

"You know the creepy doll?"

I shiver. "How could I forget?"

He smirks. "Juul saw it and peed her pants."

My eyes widen. "No?"

"Yep. And everyone saw it, too. Last I heard, she was searching for a new job."

"Awesome." I raise my hand to give him a high-five.

"I hope this means you'll forgive me for the pranks."

How could I not forgive him? "Of course. But if you ever place the rubber snake near me again, it will be a different story."

He cringes. "Sorry. I forgot about the whole snake thing from your profile. I promise to get rid of the thing."

"Good." I take a deep breath before continuing, "I hope you'll forgive me for being such a bitch."

"You weren't so bad." He winks.

Yes, I was. "I hope all the stuff I said at the shoot won't affect your career as a model." I cringe. If he develops a reputation of being difficult to deal with, other fashion magazines will refuse to work with him. I never meant to get him blacklisted.

"It's fine. Modeling isn't my career. It's merely a way to earn some extra money. As is the bartending."

My eyes widen. "Exactly how many jobs do you have?"

"Three. I take modeling gigs whenever I can. I bartend on the weekends. And I'm a freelance website designer."

It's possible I was a bit hasty in my judgment of Ravi aka Rafael.

"Is website design where your passion lies?"

"Yes." He takes a sip of coffee and sighs before continuing. "I went to college for design."

"And you went freelance straight out of college?"

"No. I worked for a website platform, helping to design website templates, but when Mieke's illness got worse and she began dialysis, they let me go. Don't get me wrong. The company was understanding at the onset. But it got to be too much. Racing around to take Mieke to her appointments several times a week and trying to meet the demands of the job was an impossible combination."

"I'm impressed. And, trust me, I'm not often impressed. My best friend, Zara, calls me the world's biggest cynic." I roll my eyes. I'm a tiny bit cynical, but my best friend likes to blow things out of proportion.

He shrugs. "I do what I have to do to take care of my sister. I'd do anything for her."

"You're amazing with her. How old were you when her mother died?" I slap my hand over my mouth when I realize what I said. "Shit. I'm sorry. I forgot she was your mother, too. Talk about insensitive."

He pats my hand in reassurance. "It's fine. Mom died six years ago when Mieke was ten. I've raised her as my own since then."

"You were what? Mid-twenties then? Most men in their mid-twenties wouldn't have taken on the burden of raising a sister."

"What else was I going to do? Her parents were gone. None of her father's relatives were willing to step up to take care of her, and my mom didn't have much of a family. I wasn't going to let her grow up in foster care."

Wow. I was totally and completely wrong about Ravi. He isn't an immature jerk. In fact, he's the furthest thing from immature there is. Taking on raising a sister when he was barely an adult himself. *Now can we jump him?* my heart, the stupid organ, asks.

"Can we stop talking about me now?" Rafael asks, and I cock an eyebrow. "What?"

"Most men can't stop talking about themselves."

"I think I've proven I'm not most men."

He certainly has.

"What do you want to talk about?"

"Sofia Silva. Who is she? Where did she grow up? And why is she doing fashion photography when she can make art?"

I feel my cheeks warm at his last question. "Art?" I squeak.

He snorts. "If those pictures you're exhibiting at the photography museum aren't art, I don't know what is."

My belly warms at his praise. "Thanks."

"Why the fashion stuff when you can take those

pictures?"

I sigh. "Unfortunately, the art stuff doesn't pay the bills." I pause before admitting, "And I have connections in the fashion world."

He cocks his head and studies me. "Is this the infamous mother all the other men hit upon?"

"Yep," I say but refuse to elaborate.

I don't usually volunteer information about my mother to men I'm interested in. And I can't deny it any longer. I'm definitely interested in Rafael. But can I trust he's not using me for my connections? My heart reminds me all the other men knew who my mother was before they met me. But here Rafael is completely clueless as to who she is.

"You don't have to tell me who she is," he says when the silence drags on. "It doesn't matter anyway."

"I think I do have to tell you. I think I have to start trusting you if we're going to be friends or whatever this is." I bite my lip. I want more than friendship, but I don't know what he wants. I probably should ask.

Rafael reaches across the table and takes my hand. His thumb rubs circles on my wrist and goosebumps break out on my skin. He stares at my skin for a long moment before raising his head to gaze into my eyes.

"I want more. I don't have much time to date, but I'd like to see where this can go."

The warmth in my belly spreads to the rest of my body. "I do, too."

I take a deep breath and make a leap of faith. "My mother is Sasha Silva," I blurt out. He stares at me with confusion clear to see in his eyes. "You know, the supermodel." He continues to stare at me. "The Russian supermodel."

He shrugs. "I haven't exactly had much time to follow the fashion world over the past years."

"I believe you. But please don't tell Mama you don't know who she is. Her ego will be crushed. And no one, not even *Pai*, wants to be near Mama if her ego is hurt."

He chuckles. "I'll keep it in mind. Your mother being a supermodel does explain why you're gorgeous, though."

I'm not comfortable with compliments about my appearance. I got lucky with good genes. It's not like I worked hard to be pretty.

"My *Pai* was a model, too."

His eyes widen. "You weren't kidding about having connections in the fashion world."

"Nope. Let's change the topic." I know I sound abrupt, but I don't like talking about my parents. I'm trying to trust Rafael here. To believe he isn't interested in me for my connections but I'm still being cautious. And cautious doesn't mean cynical no matter what Zara says.

"Okay. Let's talk about when we can go out on a date."

I like this topic of discussion. Because despite being cautious – not cynical – I do want to date this man. A man who dropped everything in his life to raise his little sister? That's what I call dependable.

Chapter 23

"**P**ut the phone down. I want to see what you're wearing," Zara insists.

I huff but do as she says. "Wowzah. Rafael is going to lose his mind when he sees you in your dress."

I may have gone a bit overboard with my outfit for my first date with Rafael. But come on. The man is sexy wearing a t-shirt and jeans. I want to look my best for him. And this dress gives me curves I usually don't have.

"Is it too much?" I ask Zara.

"If you're going for him wanting to ravish you, two thumbs-up."

I roll my eyes. "It's our first date. There will be no ravishing."

She wiggles her eyebrows. "You sure? Ravi is one hot dude."

"You don't like dudes."

"Just because I don't want to have sex with men doesn't mean I can't appreciate when a man's sexy."

The doorbell rings. "Shit. He's here. You're sure this outfit is okay?"

She snorts. "You're sexy and you know it. Now, go get 'em tiger."

I blow her an air kiss before disconnecting.

I open the door and Rafael's eyes widen before they heat as he takes in my outfit. He clears his throat before his gaze returns to my face. "You look beautiful, gorgeous."

I beam up at him. "You don't look so bad yourself."

He's wearing dress slacks with a button-down

shirt. The shirt stretches across his wide shoulders drawing my attention to his narrow hips. His pants don't do much to hide the bulge below his waistband. Maybe ravishing is on the table for tonight after all.

He winks before leaning down to kiss my cheeks. I went with flats as I'm used to towering over my dates at five-foot-ten, but I needn't have. Rafael is at least four inches taller than me.

"These are for you," he says and hands me a bouquet of red roses.

"Wow. They're gorgeous."

After I put the flowers in some water, Rafael leads me out of the apartment building and down the street.

"We're walking?"

"The restaurant is only a few blocks away, and the weather is mild. I thought a walk would be nice."

I slip my hand into his, and he laces his fingers through mine. "I agree. I do feel bad about you coming to The Hague, though. I could have gone to Amsterdam. Then, we'd be close to Mieke in case she needs us."

"Mieke pretty much ordered me out of the house. She even made the restaurant reservation."

"The girl is going to rule the world someday."

My phone beeps as we take our seats in the French bistro. "Sorry. I'll switch it off." I remove my phone from my purse to power it down and read the message. I gasp at what it says.

"What's wrong?" Rafael is immediately by my side wrapping his arm around me.

"It's good. Abby's in labor." I feel my lips tip up. "Another Van de Berg is entering the world whether we're ready or not."

"Do you want to go to the hospital?"

"Nah, it's okay. It'll be hours before mini-Abby is born. Although, Sylvia arrived pretty quick."

He squeezes my shoulder. "Okay. Let's go."

"But, it's our first date."

"Gorgeous, we can have a date anytime. You can't see your friend having a baby every day."

I take a breath before giving in. "Okay, let's go."

When we arrive at the hospital twenty minutes later, chaos reigns. Mia and Matthijs, Char and Nico, Avery and Niels, and Jenny and Bram are all gathered in the waiting room, and the staff doesn't appear happy with the situation.

"What's wrong?" I ask Niels.

"They claim you can only have one person per patient in the waiting room," he says.

"Which is completely untrue. I checked the hospital regulations. There's nothing about limiting the number of persons in the waiting room in there." Of course, Avery checked the hospital regulations. The lawyer thinks the world can be reduced to rules and regulations. Not hardly.

"At least sit down," I hear Matthijs growl at Mia who has Sylvia perched on her hip. She's bouncing the baby girl up and down as she paces the room.

"I'll sit down when I'm good and ready to sit down, Mr. De Vries."

"She's using the last name. Someone's in trouble," Niels sings.

Avery bats his arm. "Stop making problems."

He chuckles as he throws an arm over her shoulder. "Don't ask for the impossible, sweetheart."

"Where's Tobias?" I ask Char to interrupt the lawyers' verbal sparring.

"He's with the neighbor," she says. She bites her lip before asking Nico. "Do you think he's okay?"

"You mean has something horrible happened in the two minutes since you last chatted with the neighbor?"

She slaps his stomach. "We left in such a hurry. I'm concerned he felt our stress and is worried."

Nico chuckles. "Did you miss how he shouted

about having a new brother?"

She bites her lip. "We need to talk about giving him a brother."

My eyes widen. "Are you trying to get pregnant?"

Char frowns. "I wish. I can't have children. But I'd like to adopt another kid. Not another kid. I haven't actually adopted a kid already. I can't adopt Tobias for a while because of stupid Dutch laws." Avery coughs. "Sorry, Avery, but it's true. It's stupid and cruel to make me wait. Anyway, what do you think?"

Nico cocks an eyebrow at her. "Of the Dutch adoption laws?"

She sticks her tongue out at him. "You know what I mean."

He kisses her forehead. "I think we're on the same page. And I also think the waiting room in the hospital while we're waiting for Abby to have her baby is not the time or place for this discussion."

She sags against him. "I guess you're right."

"This is why I love the girl gang," Jenny announces. "There's always something happening with you guys. My life would be beyond boring without you."

Her husband Bram grunts. "Thanks, babe."

She shrugs. "You know what I mean."

Before anyone else can make any other life-altering announcements, a baby's cry erupts from Abby's room. I search the area until my eyes connect with Rafael's. He smiles at me, and it takes my breath away. This man could be my everything. He motions to me, and I sit next to him, our hands entwined, as we wait for news.

A short time later, a haggard looking Jasper enters the waiting room. He's holding up his phone to show us Abby and the tiny bundle in her arms. Everyone stands to crowd him.

"It's a boy," he tells us.

"I told you the baby was a boy," Abby shouts into the phone.

"How are you?" Mia asks. "How is the pain?"

"Indescribable," Abby answers and Mia cringes as she rubs her hand over her pregnant belly. "Jasper's lucky he's got the snip, or I wouldn't let his sexy ass come near me again."

"How many drugs did they give you, *mijn schat*? I haven't gotten the snip."

Abby's brow wrinkles for a second before she snaps her fingers. "Oh, that's right. You have an appointment for next week."

Jasper groans but he doesn't fight her. Whether it's because he knows it's a losing battle or because he doesn't mind getting a vasectomy seeing how he already has two children, I don't know. And I'm not asking. I don't want Abby to direct her wrath my way on a good day. On the day she's given birth? I'll keep my mouth shut and give her a wide berth.

Jasper takes Sylvia from Mia's arms. "Are you ready to meet your brother?"

"Ollfy," she shouts.

"Olivier. Can you say Olivier?" Jasper prods her.

"Ollfy," she shouts again.

Jasper sighs before walking back to Abby's room with Sylvia in his arms.

"I guess we should get back to Tobias," Char says once they're gone.

"I'm not leaving until I meet little Ollie," Mia announces, and Matthijs groans. "Don't you dare tell me I need to go home and rest. I'm pregnant, not a brainless invalid." Her husband wisely keeps his mouth shut.

Rafael tugs on my hand. "Do you want to stay, gorgeous?"

"Do you mind?"

He bops me on the nose. "Of course not. But you need to eat." My stomach rumbles in agreement. He frowns at me. "Do you eat at all today?"

Telling Rafael I sometimes get too caught up in my work to remember to eat was obviously a mistake. I keep my mouth shut.

"I'll go see what food I can scrounge up for you." He kisses me on the forehead before leaving the room.

I can't help but watch him walk away. Dress slacks were made for him. I could watch him and his ass walking away from me all day.

Avery, Mia, and Jenny surround me.

"Are we forgiving him for being an ass?" Avery asks.

"Based on his ass alone, she should forgive him," Jenny says.

"Appearances are superficial. Sofia needs a man who isn't superficial. Is Rafael that man?" Mia asks.

I bite my lip. I don't know yet. I'm leaning toward saying yes, though.

Chapter 24

Rafael

I stroll down the hallway in search of a quiet space to call my neighbor, Esmay, and ask her to watch Mieke. Mieke will be pissed at me, but I can handle her being mad. What I can't handle is her laying in her own vomit when she's too weak to make it to the bathroom.

"Can I make a pie?" Is Esmay's response to my query if she can stay with Mieke until I can make it home.

I don't know how long it takes to make a pie, but I don't want my sister alone for any longer than necessary. I've already been gone several hours more than I planned as it is.

"Maybe you can make it at my place? Have Mieke help you?"

"I'll pretend I'm out of flour but having a massive sweet tooth attack."

Mieke won't be fooled, but she's too nice to slam the door in anyone's face.

"Sounds perfect. Thanks, Esmay. I owe you one."

She scoffs. "You don't owe me a thing, Rafael. Mieke's a good girl. I didn't have any plans tonight anyway."

I check my watch. It's after nine on a Saturday. "Sorry about calling this late."

"Stop apologizing and go spend time with your girl."

"She's not my girl – yet."

We hang up and I turn around to find Niels,

Jasper, Matthijs, Nico, and Bram waiting on me. I guess it's time for the big brother inquisition, but I won't make it easy for them.

"Shouldn't you be with your wife? You know, the one who gave you a son like fifteen minutes ago?" I ask Jasper.

Niels chuckles. "Abby's high on whatever painkiller they gave her and is describing how Olivier was conceived to anyone who will listen."

Bram grunts. "You're one of my oldest friends, Jasper, but I don't need to hear how you had sex against the wall in the hallway. You know Jenny is going to make me recreate the whole thing when we get home and I have a bad back."

I find my next target. "Shouldn't you be making sure your pregnant wife isn't standing too long or bending over or breathing too heavy?"

Matthijs lifts his phone to show me the timer ticking down. "She gets ten minutes of baby time and then we're going home even if I have to drag her by her hair."

Niels' chuckle becomes an all out laugh now. "I can't believe I tried to convince Avery to stay home tonight. This is too much fun."

Nico grunts. "Can we get this over with? I need to get home to Tobias."

Jasper taps his chin. "I don't know. Is this strictly necessary? He was just on the phone with his neighbor to make certain someone is with his sister. His sick sister he's taking care of. Maybe we should give him a pass."

Nico frowns. "He's not getting a pass. Not after what he did."

I don't want a pass. I want Sofia's friends to think I'm good enough for her. Since Sofia is indeed the sweet, kind woman I chatted with every single day for weeks, I've decided I'm not letting her go anytime soon.

I open my arms wide. "Let the interrogation begin."

Nico doesn't hesitate. "Are you done being an

asshole to Sofia? I won't let you hurt her again. The woman swooped in and calmed my wife down when she was freaking out about Tobias' fifth birthday. I owe her."

"Char isn't your wife yet, man. You need to have the ceremony and say the vows first," Matthijs points out.

Nico shrugs. "She's as good as. I'm never letting the woman go. I may have been a total fuck up during the beginning of our relationship, but I learned my lesson. Char is mine. I don't deserve her, but hell if I'm going to let her go."

I hear a commotion down the hallway, and I peek around Nico to see Char barreling toward us. She launches herself at him. "I love you, Nicolaas de Ruiter. I can't wait to be married to you."

"Does this mean you'll finally agree to a courthouse wedding?"

"Are you going to tell my family we're eloping and not having a big wedding?"

He grunts. I guess the answer is no, then.

Niels motions to Avery who's trying not very successfully to hide around the corner. "You might as well join us, sweetheart. You'll be able to hear better."

Avery along with Mia and Jenny walk over to join us. The entire group is now standing in the hallway. Except someone's missing.

"Where's Sofia?"

"With me!" A tinny voice answers.

Jenny holds up her phone, and Abby and Sofia wave at me via the screen.

I take in this group of couples, and something occurs to me I hadn't realized before. "You're all Dutch men with American women."

"Once you go Dutch, you'll never want another man's touch," Niels quips.

"Stop being a goofball," Avery tells him.

He waggles his eyebrows at her. "You happen to

love this goofball Dutch guy."

"Yeah, there's obviously something wrong with me."

As much as I'm enjoying their banter, I don't have time for it. "Can we hurry this up? I need to get Sofia food. She hasn't eaten all day."

The men look at each other like they're at a loss to proceed. I turn my attention to the women. "And?"

"Hold on," Abby says through the phone. "I have a list of questions here somewhere."

Sofia snatches her phone away. "No, you don't."

"But—" She pouts.

"No." Sofia glares into the phone. "As much as I appreciate what all of you are trying to do, it's not up to my friends to decide whether a guy is good enough for me. It's up to me."

"And? Have you made a decision yet?" I can't help but ask.

"The jury's still out."

I'm not surprised. Frankly, I'm not sure I am good enough for Sofia. There's much more to her than I thought when I met her. Of course, I thought she was a complete bitch then. Now, I know better. But I have very little of myself to give to her now. I should probably wait until Mieke's better before starting to date, but I can't risk missing my chance with Sofia.

Sofia has captured my attention and drawn me in. Not only is she gorgeous – I dream about kissing those lush lips of hers while burying my hands in her luxuriant hair – but there's more to her than her appearance. She's funny and sweet and a bit cynical. It's a package I'm finding extremely appealing and having a hard time resisting.

"What can I do to hurry up the deliberations?" I waggle my eyebrows.

She giggles. "Keep being yourself and we'll see where we end up."

"Found it!" Abby shouts from behind Sofia.

"What did you find?"

"My list of questions for Rafael, of course."

"But I took your phone away."

Abby snorts. "Like I wouldn't have a spare phone on me."

"You're in the maternity ward of the hospital."

"I am aware. I'm the one whose private parts are—"

Sofia slaps a hand over Abby's mouth. "Nope. No way. Any sentence including the words 'private parts' is hereby prohibited."

"Do you want me to add that to the girl gang rules?" Avery asks.

"No, Uptight, I do not," Abby grumbles. "You guys are no fun."

"I'm fun," Niels declares.

"You're a goofball is what you are," Avery tells him.

I hold up my hands. "I think we're done here. I need to find Sofia food and Char and Nico need to get back to Tobias. And—"

My words are cut off when Matthijs' alarm goes off. Mia glares at him. "Honey," he pleads. She whirls around and stomps off before his groveling can begin in earnest. He scrambles after her.

"I guess we'll give him temporary approval to be reviewed at a later time and date," Niels says.

My response? I walk away in search of the cafeteria.

As much as I'm annoyed with Sofia's friends, I'm relieved she has such good ones. Friends who will protect her and stick up for her. She'll need them because as much as I hate to admit it, I simply can't be there for Sofia all the time. My priority has to be Mieke.

Chapter 25

I'm yawning when I open my apartment door the next Saturday morning. I thought with Abby laid up after giving birth and Mia unable to drink, the Friday evening drinks – aka *borrel* – at the apartment building would be nice and peaceful. As if.

My new friends don't know what the word peaceful means. Avery was pissed about some work thing. Don't ask me what. I have no idea what half the legalese coming out of her mouth means. And Char was upset Tobias didn't get into the elementary school she and Nico chose for him. They took all their frustrations out on a bottle of wine, and I ended up getting home past midnight.

When my eyes blink open from my yawn, my jaw drops practically to the floor at who I see standing before me. "Mama, what are you doing here?"

"Is this any way to greet your Mama, little rabbit?" she asks before kissing my cheeks.

Pai wraps me into a hug and lifts me off the ground. "How are you, baby girl?"

"When did you arrive? Why didn't you tell me you were coming?" I ask instead of answering his question.

"Are you going to invite us in?" Mama asks.

"Of course. Of course." I usher them inside my apartment. "Where's your luggage?"

"At the hotel. We don't want to disturb you and your *lyubov*," Mama says as she surveys the place as if she's expecting to find Rafael hiding behind the sofa.

"We don't live together," I tell her.

She raises an eyebrow. "But he does exist, yes?"

"I didn't lie." Much. "He exists. But he lives in

Amsterdam and takes care of his little sister who's sick."

While I make coffee, I tell my parents all about Mieke and Rafael.

"I think I like this Rafael," Mama declares.

Pai grunts. "I'm not convinced. I need to meet this boy first."

"He's not—" My words are cut off by the doorbell.

Mama claps. "Maybe it's Rafael."

I open the door to find Abby, Mia, Char, and Avery standing there. "What's going on?"

Char groans. "I don't know. I should be in bed recovering from a hangover, but this one," she points to Abby, "called and told me to get to your place pronto. I need to lay down."

Mia grins. "I don't care what's going on. Any excuse to get away from Mr. Overprotective is a-okay in my book."

I cock an eyebrow at Abby and wait for her to explain. She holds my stare for a few seconds before giving in. "I saw your parents are here."

"How? You don't live in this building anymore."

Avery grunts. "I thought Abby living down the street from me would be wonderful. I didn't realize she was going to call me at the butt crack of dawn to come racing over to the apartment building. Do you guys want her back?"

Abby ignores her. "We're here to run interference."

My brow wrinkles. "Run interference? Why?"

"When you tell them about Rafael."

"You're such a liar. You just want to meet my parents."

Abby doesn't deny it. "Of course, I do. Is your mom as beautiful in person as she is in magazines? Inquiring minds want to know."

I throw open the door and invite them in. "Come on in. Let's see, shall we?"

The way Abby pushes her way past everyone and marches down the hallway to the living room makes it hard to believe she gave birth a week ago. Maybe she really is Wonder Woman.

She gasps. "She is as beautiful in person. No wonder all your suitors hit on her."

Mama gives her the dazzling smile and renders Abby speechless.

Mia's head swivels back and forth between the two. "It's a miracle. We finally found a way to keep Abby quiet."

"I'm sorry, Sofia, but your mom is going to have to come live here," Char tells me. "She'll be our secret weapon when we need Abby to slow her roll. Because, lord knows, there are times when the woman needs to slow down. Like now for instance. The woman gave birth to little Olivier a week ago. She should be at home recovering. But no. She's trying to control our lives."

"Your mom can live with me," Avery says. "We converted the attic into a granny flat."

Mama giggles. "I adore your friends, little rabbit. We should have dinner together tonight. Bring your Rafael and his sister."

"I'll make a reservation and send everyone the information," Abby says before she starts tapping away on her phone.

"Our number is—"

Abby holds up her hand to stop Mama. "I got it."

Mama is obviously confused, but I tell her, "I find it's better not to ask."

"Amen," Mia shouts. The doorbell rings and she sighs. "Mr. Overprotective has arrived. Is it wrong for me to call his boss and ask him to assign Matthijs more shifts?" she mumbles as she goes to answer the door.

"Welp. My work here is done," Abby declares as she shoves her phone back in her pocket. "I'll see you tonight."

Avery and Char follow Mia and Abby as they leave nearly as quickly as they came.

"I can't wait for tonight," Mama says.

Pai places his arm around her shoulder. "Come on, my love. You need a nap. Otherwise, you'll have jetlag. And you know how much you hate jetlag."

♥♥♥

"I'm really sorry about you having to miss a night of bartending," I tell Rafael that evening as we walk from the parking garage to the Chinese restaurant Abby booked for our group.

He squeezes my hand. "It's fine."

"And I sprung my parents on you after one date. And we didn't even finish the date."

"What do you mean we didn't finish the date? Eating crappy vending machine food in a hospital waiting room isn't the most romantic date you've ever had?" He clutches his chest. "I'm hurt."

"I for one am glad you called. I wasn't looking forward to another evening of baking with Esmay." Mieke beams up at me. "I can't wait to see your friends again. They're crazy."

Rafael frowns. "Don't overdo it."

She rolls her eyes. "And Mia thinks her husband is overprotective. Please. She has no clue."

The girl gang and their partners are waiting at the entrance to the restaurant. A taxi arrives and stops in front of them. When Mama and *Pai* step out of the taxi, I study Rafael's expression, but he isn't paying any attention to Mama. He's greeting my friends while keeping a protective arm around Mieke.

Mama arrives under a cloud of Chanel No. 9 perfume. I take her hand and lead her to the group. "You ready?" At her nod, I start the introductions. "You met Char this morning. This is her fiancé, Nico, and their son, Tobias. Abby, aka Wonder Woman, and her husband, Jasper. The little girl is Sylvia, and the tiny baby is Olivier.

This is Niels, Avery's partner. The man who's ready to lose his mind if we don't sit down soon is Mia's husband, Matthijs."

Mama dazzles them with her smile. I clear my throat and grasp Rafael's hand.

"And this is Rafael and his sister Mieke."

Rafael steps forward. "Nice to meet you, Mrs. Silva." He takes her hand and kisses it.

Abby coughs. "Suck up."

Like the woman wasn't struck mute when she met Mama for the first time this morning.

Rafael takes Mieke's hand and draws her near. "And this is my sister, Mieke."

"Wow." Mieke's eyes are wide as she stares at Mama. "You're really pretty."

Rafael winks over at me. "But not as pretty as her daughter."

I roll my eyes. "Lying will get you nowhere."

"Who says I'm lying?"

Mama threads her arm through Rafael's and drags him toward the entrance of the restaurant. "My little rabbit does not see her own beauty. I am glad she has a man now who does."

I can't believe it! Rafael didn't need to hit on my mom. She's doing all the work for him. Typical. I huff, but before I can say a word, Rafael's head swivels my way, and he mouths *Help me.*

My shoulders relax. He isn't dazzled by my mom. He's not like the other men I've dated. He might be a model, but only because he needs to make as much money as he can. He's not superficial like the other models I've photographed.

Mieke takes my hand. "Come on. Let's go save my idiot brother. He's been worried the entire day about meeting your parents. He's afraid he's going to screw things up. Like he did when he first met you but didn't realize who you were."

I chuckle. "I don't think he's going to appreciate you telling me his worries."

She snorts. "Then, he shouldn't be trying to win the most overprotective brother of all time award."

"I think brothers are supposed to be overprotective," I tell her.

"I'm sixteen. He acts like I'm six."

I don't respond. This is not an argument I can win. Is it possible to win an argument with a teenager? I cringe to think how quarrelsome I was as a teen.

When we join Mama and Rafael at the table, Rafael stands and pulls out a chair for me. I notice he positions himself on the opposite side of me so he's not sitting next to Mama. He's racking up the good boyfriend points now.

"You have to protect me," he whispers. "Your mother already asked me what size suit I wear and if I'm willing to convert to the Orthodox church. She's going to have us married off before the main course arrives."

I'm surprised when my heart clenches at his words. Does he not want to marry me? It may be way too early to talk about marriage – we haven't even had a real date yet – but he's dismissing the idea outright.

"We can't get married when Mieke is sick. Once she's better, I'm open to negotiations."

"Wait. What?" I realize I shouted the words when the chatter at the table quiets down and ten heads swivel our way. I motion with my hands for them to go back to their own conversations.

Rafael's cheeks darken. "Forget what I said. We'll talk about this later."

I reach over and squeeze his thigh. I could fall for this man. Have I finally found my nice and dependable man? Who knew nice and dependable could come is such a yummy package?

Chapter 26

"I can't believe your parents got to meet Rafael before me," Zara complains as she paces my living room while we wait for Rafael and Mieke to arrive.

"I told you they showed up uninvited. What did you expect me to do? Hide Rafael during their visit to ensure you could meet him first?"

She's been complaining pretty much nonstop since she arrived in The Hague about my parents meeting Rafael first. She needs to get over it because there's nothing I can do about it now. I can't exactly build a time machine. I barely passed physics in college. I don't even know if physics is the discipline you need for time travel.

At the sound of the doorbell, Zara sprints to the door and flings it open. "Who are you?"

I peer over her shoulder to see Char, Abby, Avery, Mia, and Jenny standing in the hallway.

"What are you guys doing here?"

Abby rolls her eyes. "We're here to initiate your friend in the girl gang, of course."

"Shouldn't you be getting everything ready for the party?" I ask Char.

Nico officially adopted Tobias this week and they're throwing a party to celebrate. Her family flew over for the celebration.

"Are you kidding me? I needed a break from my crazy family. The twins, Robbie and Ronnie, are darting around with their pants off and my sister, Robin, is lecturing everyone about penises. I don't know why. She doesn't like the dick. Her words, not mine."

Zara perks up. "How old is Robin? Does she have

a girlfriend?"

I wag my finger at her. "No, no, no. You're not going to have a one-night stand with the sister of my friend."

"Why not? Don't be a hater."

"I'm not a hater. I'm trying to avoid spending months listening to Char complain about how my friend broke her sister's heart."

Char snorts. "Robin doesn't have a heart."

Zara bites her lip. "Interesting."

"Can we get back to the girl gang initiation now?" Abby asks.

"What's your hurry?"

She indicates her breasts. "I'm lactating."

Avery laughs. "And she can't stand not being the center of attention."

Abby doesn't deny it. "I can't help it I'm awesome."

"What is the girl gang initiation?" Zara asks.

"Wait. Don't we need to vote on her entry into the girl gang first?" Mia asks.

"Sofia vouched for her. It's good enough for me."

"I didn't vouch for her."

Zara throws her arm over my shoulder. "But she will. Unless she wants me to tell you all about the time—"

I slap my hand over her mouth. "I vouch for her. I vouch for her."

"Nuh-uh." Abby crosses her arms over her chest. "Now, I want to hear what Zara was going to say."

Zara rubs her hands together. "Ah, where to begin? How about the time she got arrested in Moscow?"

Trust me, it sounds way worse than it was. "It was a mistake. As soon as the police realized I was merely sitting in the car for a photoshoot, they released me. I didn't even get fingerprinted."

"You don't get fingerprinted anymore," Char says.

"It's all digital nowadays. You put your hand on a scanner and that's it. There's no ink or dirty hands. It lacks the charm of when you used to get your finger squished by a pissed off police officer."

My eyes widen. "When were you fingerprinted?"

"It wasn't because I got caught driving in Russia when I wasn't supposed to. I had to get fingerprinted to be an official foster parent to Tobias."

"Sofia has been fingerprinted with ink before."

The bell rings before Zara can tell the story. Phew. No one needs to know about my arrest for slapping a police officer at a Black Lives Matter rally. Anger management courses are no joke.

"This better be Rafael," Zara shouts as she opens the door.

Rafael winks at her. "I am Rafael. And you must be Zara." He takes her hand and kisses it. Always the charmer.

Zara places the back of her hand on her forehead and feigns swooning. "Wow. He's gorgeous. Those cheekbones. Those biceps." She reaches forward and pinches his muscles. "I don't even like men, and I'd consider taking this one for a ride."

"I like her," Mieke says.

Rafael moves around Zara to come to me. He kisses my forehead. My skin tingles at the contact and I want to throw everyone out of the house and see how it feels to have his lips on other parts of my body. Between him caring for his sister and my parents' surprise visit, we've had precious little time alone. The frustration is real.

"How are you, gorgeous?"

"Better now you're here. Someone's been complaining all day about not having met you yet."

"Now can we do the inquisition?" Abby asks.

"Inquisition? What's going on?" Mieke wrinkles her brow in confusion.

"She doesn't mean the actual inquisition, like the

Spanish inquisition. I keep telling her she should stop using the word inquisition as it has a historical aspect, which is not applicable here, but Abby listens to no one but Abby," Mia, our resident history geek, explains.

Mieke stares at her for a moment before admitting, "I'm still confused."

"They want to ask me questions to make sure I'm good enough for their friend, Sofia," Rafael explains.

Mieke places her hands on her hips. "Why wouldn't he be good enough for Sofia? My brother is great. Is he a pain in my ass? Of course, he is. Is he overprotective to the nth degree? Guilty. But he's loving and caring and wouldn't ever harm anyone on purpose."

She glares at my group of friends. "Now, who has a question they want to ask?"

Rafael wraps an arm around his sister's shoulders. "Check out little Mieke becoming a fierce warrior protecting her big brother from the scary women."

She elbows him in the stomach. "I'm not little Mieke. I'm sixteen. When are you going to get it through your thick skull? My kidneys not working doesn't mean I'm a child."

Rafael winces at her words. As do I. I realize being flippant about her illness is a coping mechanism for her, but she needs to take it seriously. She needs a kidney transplant, or she will get sicker and then— Nope. I push those thoughts out of my head. I'm not going to think about what happens after the 'then'.

"Who votes to initiate Mieke in the girl gang?" Abby asks, and her hand shoots in the air.

"Cool." Mieke smiles at my friends. "Do I get a secret name? Do I need to drink blood from a sacred cup and take an oath? Is this when I find out I have magical powers, but can only use them once I'm initiated?"

"Wow. Someone has a bigger imagination than I do." Abby stares at Mieke like she can't believe what she's seeing.

Mieke frowns. "Someone has a lot of time to read."

"I—" My response is cut off by the doorbell.

"That'll be Matthijs." Mia checks her watch. "I'm surprised he let me stay this long. Of course, I didn't tell him I was going anywhere when I snuck out of the house while he thought I was taking a pre-party nap."

"At least you can sneak out of the house. This one...," Mieke tilts her head toward Rafael, "spread a bunch of Legos in front of the door to prevent me from leaving. When I stepped on one and yipped in pain, he scurried out of the bathroom holding up his pants."

Mia points at Rafael. "You are not allowed to talk to my husband."

Someone pounds on the door. "Mia, I know you're in there," Matthijs shouts.

She groans. "He makes me sound like I'm a teenager trying to sneak out after curfew." She rubs her belly. "I'm sorry baby girl, but I don't think you're getting any siblings."

"You want me to schedule an appointment for Matthijs to get the snip?" Abby consults her phone. "Jasper said his doctor was nice and understanding."

Mieke's eyes widen to the size of saucers as she stares at Abby.

"Don't worry, Mieke. Abby's crazy is not contagious. I've been friends with her for a while and I'm perfectly normal," Avery says.

"Normal?" Abby raises her eyebrows. "Uptight is not normal."

Rafael opens the door for Matthijs before Avery can respond.

"What are you doing?" I hiss at him. "You know Mia isn't ready to see him."

"Sorry. I'm not going to keep a worried man from seeing his pregnant wife. It's in the bro code."

Matthijs bumps fists with him. "Thanks, man."

Mia stomps her foot. "I'm pregnant. Not a child."

Mieke drags Rafael away from the two. "I don't need you taking notes on how to be more protective than you already are."

Char's phone rings. She consults the screen and swears. "Shit. Fuck. Damn. Crap. Sorry, I need to get all the swear words out now before my niece, Lucy, shoves the swear jar in my face. Nico is asking where I am and if he can escape with me."

"I guess we need to get to the party," I say and shoo everyone out of the apartment.

Rafael and I lag behind as we walk to Char's apartment.

"You ready to party?" I ask Rafael.

He throws his arm around me and pulls me near before kissing my hair. "To be honest, I'd rather spend the evening on the sofa with you."

My belly warms at his words. "You're a keeper, you know that?"

He winks. "I'm glad you think so."

Chapter 27

Char's apartment is already crowded when we arrive. Tobias runs to the door as we enter. I lift my camera to capture the moment. It warms my heart to see him this happy. The little guy's father died before he was born, and his birth mom didn't want him. He deserves some goodness in his life.

Tobias halts and poses for me by throwing his arms in the air. "I have a mom and dad now," he announces.

Mieke kneels to hug him. "Congratulations. Moms are the best."

"Where's your mom?"

"She's gone."

Tobias wrinkles his little nose in confusion. "Gone? I have a new mom. Do you want to share mine?"

"It's okay. I have a brother instead."

"A brother? I want a brother. Mom!"

Char races to his side. "What's wrong?" She picks him up and cuddles him close, but he wiggles to be let down.

"I want a brother," he tells her. "How can I get one?"

"Do we need to have the birds and the bees talk already?" Abby wades in.

"No!" Char shouts, and Nico comes running.

"What's wrong?" His eyes scan the room for a threat. For a governmental desk worker, he's awful protective. But who can blame him after all he went through with Tobias' mom?

"Abby wants to give Tobias the birds and bees talk."

"He's five. It's a bit early for the *bloemetjes en de bijtjes.*"

"Flowers and bees? Of course, the Dutch would have a name for the sex talk that makes way more sense than the birds and the bees," Abby says. "Now, shall we do this talk here or what?"

Char tries a different tactic. "There's no need for a talk. His brother will be adopted like him."

"You're adopting another child? When were you planning on telling us this, young woman?" A man frowns as he approaches Char.

She sighs. "We're only talking about it, Dad. We haven't made any decisions yet."

I take Rafael's hand and tiptoe past Char and her dad. I can see a guilt trip coming on and I want no part in it. I get enough of them from Mama.

An elderly woman stops us. "Who's this?"

Another woman who could be her twin looks Rafael up and down. "Oh my. They sure do make the men pretty in this country. This one could be a model."

"Actually," Mieke pipes up, "he is a model. He doesn't like it much, but he does it for me."

The first woman's eyes narrow. "He does it for you? Why don't you come with me and tell Aunt Anne all about it."

"This is cool. I've never had an aunt before," Mieke says before traipsing off with her.

I go to follow, but Char stops me. "She's safe. These are my Aunts Alice and Anne. They're perfectly harmless. Unless you have a combover, then she'll get out the scissors." Char mimics cutting with her fingers.

Rafael combs a hand through his light-brown hair. "Um…"

"She did warn Henry if he didn't get rid of the combover, she'd take care of it," Anne explains. "Don't worry. I'll protect you from my sister." She winks.

Rafael's cheeks darken and he takes a step back. An older man growls before taking Anne's hand and leading her away without saying a single word.

Rafael sighs in relief when they're gone. "Holy crap, she scared me. I need you to protect my virtue."

"You said crap! Swear jar!" a girl screams before shoving a jar stuffed full of Euro bills at Rafael. "And what's virtue? Is it the same as virgin?"

"I'm starting to believe Char was right when she told us her family's crazy, which is saying a lot since my mama is a Russian supermodel and my *Pai* is a Brazilian model."

A woman dashes over to us and shoos the girl with the swear jar away. "Sorry, sorry, sorry. I'm Char's sister, Julie, and the little troublemaker is my daughter Lucy. You must be Sofia and Rafael."

"How did you know?"

She points to the camera on my neck. "Photographer." She bites her lip and points to Rafael. "Model."

A man throws his arm around her shoulders. "I thought you promised you wouldn't drool over other men."

She waves at Rafael. "He's not a man. He's a model. He's fair game."

I wag my finger at her. "No, he's not. He's mine."

Rafael's hand spasms in mine. "What? Are you not mine? You put up with a lecture on the Russian Orthodox church from Mama for an hour."

He shrugs. "It was interesting."

I rear back. "It was interesting listening to *Pai* and her debate the merits of the Catholic versus the Orthodox church?"

Julie giggles. "You two are definitely a couple." I cock my eyebrow at her. "He's putting up with your family shit. Totally a couple."

"Everyone puts up with my family. My mama is a supermodel."

"Still not as pretty as you, gorgeous," Rafael insists.

I roll my eyes.

"Beautiful, modest, and a famous photographer." Julie shakes her head. "I don't think we can be friends."

Eek. How do I answer her? I search the room for a distraction and discover Zara cornering another woman on the opposite side of the room.

"I told Zara she couldn't pick anyone up at the party. Did she listen?"

"That's my sister, Robin. Don't tell me my sister isn't good enough for yours because she's a school teacher."

"First of all, Zara is not my sister. Second, I'm trying to protect your sister. Zara is on the prowl for the 'one'."

Julie laughs. "This should be interesting. Ethan, go get us drinks and we can watch the fireworks from here."

Two small boys race past completely naked. A woman chases after them. "Stop this minute!"

"Who are they?"

"My nephews, Robbie and Ronnie, with my sister, Ella, chasing them."

"And they're naked because?"

She shrugs. "Most likely scenario? My pre-teen. Jeremy. dared them to."

I tug on Rafael's shirt. "Is it too early for the 'do you want children' talk? Because I'm thinking my answer is not in this lifetime."

Rafael chuckles as he kisses my hair. "It's not too early, gorgeous. I know you're joking, but I don't think I want children. I raised Mieke. I could use a break."

"I'm with Rafael," Avery announces, and I clutch my chest.

Holy shit. I didn't realize she was standing right behind me. "It's wrong to sneak up on people."

"I didn't sneak up on you. It's not my fault if you were too busy giving Rafael goo-goo eyes to notice me."

"Oh boy, is Ms. Uptight Attorney in the house?" Abby asks as she joins us with Olivier attached to her breast.

"Um, don't you want to nurse him somewhere in private?" I ask her.

"Why? I'm covered. I didn't flash my boob at anyone. It's in my agreement with Jasper. No flashing the boobies. I did it once and the man lost his mind. He gets hysterical over the weirdest things."

Julie looks back and forth between Abby and Avery. "I love Char's friends. I want to move here."

Her husband returns and hands her a glass of wine. "We're not moving overseas. Can you imagine the crap our children would give us if we tried to take them away from their friends and grandparents?"

She frowns before taking a sip of her wine. "I seriously hate it when you're right."

Rafael tugs on my hand and tilts his head toward a quiet corner of the room. I give a slight nod and we slip away as Julie and her husband argue over how much she enjoys it when he's right.

The corner has an alcove positioned behind a bookshelf. Rafael maneuvers us until we're hidden in the alcove out of everyone's view.

He wraps his arms around me and drags me close. "I love your friends, but I need some time with you alone after you said you're mine."

"And what did you have in mind for this alone time," I ask and lick my lips.

He groans and his head descends until his lips meet mine. He teases me with barely there kisses on the corners of my mouth before his tongue peeks out and he licks my bottom lip.

"I love your lips. I can't look at them without wanting to kiss you," he whispers against my mouth.

"You can kiss me now," I breathe out.

He molds his lips to mine in response. I gasp and his tongue demands entry. I open up and his tongue rushes in. I clutch the front of his shirt and hold on as our tongues clash. His hands thread through my hair and he tilts my head to the side to gain better access. *Yes.*

He presses closer to me until I can feel how hard he is against my belly. I'm hitching my leg over his hip to rub myself against his hard length when a little voice interrupts me.

"Whatcha doing?"

I wrench my lips away from Rafael's to discover a small boy staring up at us. An identical boy joins him.

Rafael groans. "Cockblocked by a set of twins."

"At least they're dressed now," I point out.

"I need to take you out on a real date. A romantic date with no friends or family around."

"Promise?"

He winks. "I promise."

"I'm counting on it."

Chapter 28

Rafael

My eyes widen when Sofia opens the door wearing a summer dress that hugs her body in all the right places. Her tall, lean body has the exact right amount of curves for my hands to explore. I long to trail my fingers over her hips and feel her naked breasts in my hands. I haul her into my arms and press my lips against hers.

When she moans, I lift my head. "Hello, gorgeous."

"Hi," she breathes out.

"As much as I'd like to spend the evening feeling your body pressed up against mine, we have plans."

The corners of her lips turn down briefly before she gives in. "Okay."

I force myself to release her. "Grab a sweater. I don't want you to get cold."

It's unseasonably warm for September, but we're spending the evening outside. Once the sun sets, it can get chilly.

"Where are we going?" she asks as we drive out of the parking garage under her building.

I wink over at her. "You'll see."

"Someone's Mr. Mysterious tonight."

I'm trying to be Mr. Romantic. I promised Sofia a real date without friends and family. I want our 'first' date to be a romantic memory for her.

I drive to Scheveningen. This neighborhood of The Hague is a seaside resort and a mere ten minutes from Sofia's apartment. After I park, I scramble around the front of the car to help Sofia out.

Her emerald eyes light up as she glances around. "The beach at sunset? I'm glad I brought my camera."

Sofia always has a camera with her. I nearly asked her to leave it at home. I wanted her to experience the sunset with just the two of us, not from behind the lens of a camera. But having a camera and constantly taking pictures is part of who Sofia is.

I open the trunk and take out the picnic basket and blankets.

"A picnic on the beach at sunset? Someone's trying to be romantic."

"Not trying. Succeeding," I tell her with a wink.

She giggles and all the preparation time and anxiety about making this date perfect disappears. I grab her hand and lead her to the boulevard.

At this time of day, the boulevard is busy. It's lined with restaurants and bars, and it appears as if everyone in the city has decided to take advantage of the unexpected warm weather by having dinner at the beach tonight. We continue past all the restaurants until we reach a quiet spot. We kick off our shoes before traipsing onto the sand.

I lay the blanket out while Sofia takes picture after picture of the sea and the pier. The pier juts into the sea from the boulevard and is two stories high. It's flanked by a Ferris wheel which reaches fifty meters into the sky and offers the perfect backdrop for a picture.

Once I have the food and wine laid out, I take Sofia's hand and force her to sit down.

"Wait. I need to take a picture of this before we dive into the food." She jumps to her feet and takes several pictures before lowering her camera and sitting next to me.

"Let me guess. You have two gazillion social media followers."

She giggles. "I don't think Oprah has two gazillion social media followers. And these pictures are not for social media. I don't post anything private on social media. I learned my lesson when I was young."

I pour her a glass of white wine and hand it to her. "What lesson?"

She takes a sip of wine before answering. "I posted about being with my mother at a certain restaurant. Within thirty minutes the place was packed with people dying to meet Mama."

I study her. Her lips are pinched as she stares out into the sea. "And thus, a cynic was born."

She toys with the stem of her glass. "I'm not such a cynic anymore."

I lift her chin with my finger. "It's okay to be cautious. After all the stories you've told me, I think you've earned it, gorgeous."

I lower my head until my lips meet hers. I nibble on the corners of her lips until she sighs. I take advantage and dive into her mouth. Her hand fists the front of my t-shirt, and she tugs me closer. I love how responsive she is to my touch. How quickly she lights up for me.

When I hear her stomach rumble, I slow the kiss until I can pull away. My heart is pounding in my chest as I stare at her swollen lips. She bites her lip, and my cock swells in anticipation. Not yet, I tell it. I need to feed Sofia first.

"Did you eat today?"

Her nose wrinkles as she thinks about her answer. "No?"

I frown. I don't like how she forgets to eat. "Were you working?"

"I went to the *Schilderswijk* to explore and take some pictures."

The *Schilderswijk* is a lower-income immigrant neighborhood in The Hague. "Why there? I thought you'd be more interested in the architecture of the city."

The Hague has several famous buildings such as the Peace Palace, the Dutch Parliament, and a few royal palaces since it's the residence of the Dutch King and Queen.

She wrinkles her nose. "Taking pictures of buildings is not my thing. But people of different cultures and how they integrate into a new society? That's my jam."

"Do you feel an affinity with them because you were an immigrant in America?"

She gazes out to sea as she answers. "My story is completely different. I'm lucky. *Pai* grew up in a *favela* in Rio. If he hadn't been spotted by a talent scout for a modeling agency, who knows what would have happened to him. But me? I grew up in the lap of luxury traveling the world with my famous mama."

I grab a plate and prepare it for her. I fill it with potato salad, a small sandwich, and some fruit before handing it to her.

"Do you feel guilty because you were lucky and others weren't?"

She bites her lip. "It's stupid, right?"

"Not at all, gorgeous. I feel guilty for being healthy when Mieke's sick."

She grasps my bicep and squeezes. "You can't help it Mieke's sick."

I raise an eyebrow. "And you can't help it you grew up with all your needs catered for while others grew up with nothing."

She narrows her eyes on me. "You're more than just a pretty boy, aren't you?"

I wink before nodding toward her plate. "Now eat before the police show up to investigate what the loud rumbling sound is."

She rolls her eyes, but she does take a bite of her sandwich. "This is good. What is it? Did you make it?"

I chuckle. "It's chicken curry salad and no, I didn't make it. I made the potato salad, though."

She grabs her fork and dips it in the potato salad before taking a bite. Her eyes widen as she chews. "This is good. You can cook?"

"I can hardly order take-out all the time. Even if we could afford it, Mieke has special dietary needs."

She frowns. "That sucks."

"It's my life. Or, I should say, it's my life until Mieke gets a kidney transplant."

I'm done talking about my sister and all my problems. I want a fun night with my girl. Not an in-depth breakdown of how my life sucks at the moment.

"Tell me something about yourself no one else knows."

She taps her chin as she thinks about how to answer. "You can't tell anyone this. Not even Mieke."

Now, I'm intrigued. I motion for her to tell me more.

"When I was sixteen, I snuck out of the house. Zara and I met up with some kids in the park and drank a bunch of wine coolers. I had my camera with me." She lifts up her camera. "I saw a squirrel and decided to take its picture. Suffice it to say, the squirrel did not want its picture taken. We made it home okay and I thought we got away with it. But then I wake up in the morning with my arms full of scratches. It was the middle of the summer and I ended up wearing long sleeves every day for a week to cover up my arms to hide how we snuck out from my parents."

I chuckle. "I guess I now know why you're not a wildlife photographer."

"No thanks." She does an exaggerated shiver. "Your turn."

"Same rules apply. No telling Mieke." She crosses her heart.

"You know how there's a red light district in Amsterdam? Some of my friends dared me to streak through the *Ouderzijds Achterburgwal,* which is like the busiest street in the area. I was nineteen and stupid, so I did it. The thing about the red light district is, it's filled with police. The police chased me, and I ended up hiding in this nasty toilet in a little hole in the wall bar. I fashioned a pair of underwear out of a roll of toilet paper. By the way, toilet paper briefs are fine. The police are used to bachelor parties and kids doing stupid stuff. But naked? Not okay."

Sofia is holding her stomach laughing. "Underwear out of toilet paper? Do you have any pictures?"

I glare at her. "What do you think?"

She calms down and we finish our meal while sitting in silence and gazing out over the water as the sun sets.

"Five stars for romance. Highly recommend," she says once darkness settles.

"Don't forget the scintillating conversation and delicious food."

"Fine. Four and a half stars."

"Four and a half stars?" I wrap my arm around her to haul her near before tickling her ribs.

"Stop! Stop!" she shouts between bouts of laughter.

I pause. "Am I still four and a half stars?"

She smiles up at me and my heart flips in my chest. I could fall in love with this woman. I rub my nose up and down hers before nipping at her jaw. She tilts her head to allow me better access and I run my tongue down her neck until it meets her shoulder. I bite into the joint and she shivers in my arms.

"Wat zijn jullie aan het doen?"

I lift my head to see a policeman glaring down at us. *"Alleen een beetje zoenen. Dat mag toch wel?"*

It's not illegal to have sex in public in Holland, but yet this policeman is glaring down at me like he's ready to throw me into a jail cell.

Sofia climbs off my lap. "What's wrong? We're still fully clothed. I'd think the liberal Dutch wouldn't have a problem with people kissing on the beach."

The policeman's face softens. "Sorry, ma'am. It's not illegal unless other people say they have a problem."

He points to the children's playground behind us. "The parents of the small children complained."

Sofia huffs. "It's after ten. Small children should be in bed and not running around on a playground."

He chuckles. "Maybe, but I'm going to have to ask you to move somewhere more discrete."

Sofia opens her mouth, but I answer before she can speak. "We'll move."

He nods and leaves. I throw our things into the picnic basket while Sofia folds up the blanket. I tag her hand and lead her off the beach to where the car is. She's quiet while I drive back to her apartment building.

"Do you want to come in?" she asks once I park.

My entire body warms at the idea of spending the night with Sofia. I could stay. Esmay is with Mieke all night.

"If I come up, I'm not going to want to leave until morning."

Her cheeks darken. "Good. Because I don't want you to."

Chapter 29

Rafael

I thread my fingers through Sofia's as we walk to her apartment. I want to sprint up the stairs, throw her on her bed, and have my way with her, but I keep my steps steady and even. I don't want our first time together to be a quick affair. No, I plan to show her how much she means to me.

Sofia drops my hand to unlock her door, and I follow her inside.

"Do you want a drink?"

I maneuver her until I've got her pushed up against the wall. I run my nose up and down her neck as I breathe in her spicy scent.

"Is that what you want, gorgeous? To have a drink?" I whisper into her ear.

She shivers. "N-n-no."

"What do you want?" I ask before tracing a circle with my tongue on the spot behind her ear. Goosebumps appear on her skin.

"Y-y-you." She clears her throat and lifts her hands to cradle my face. "You. I want you."

Her words are music to my ears, but I need to make sure. "You're certain?"

Her nod is all I need. I wrap my arms around her stomach and lift her up before throwing her over my shoulder. "Bedroom?"

She points to the room opposite of where we're standing. I stride toward the room while she bounces on my shoulder. I lift her to throw her on her bed but realize the bed is covered with an assortment of clothing.

Sofia groans. "Sorry. I … um … couldn't figure out what to wear tonight."

Her words only endear her more to me. The gorgeous famous photographer was nervous about going on a date with me, a no one.

"Did you call Zara and model clothes for her?" I tease.

"You've been watching too many teenage shows with Mieke."

"I'll take that as a yes."

She pounds on my back. "Let me down, so I can pick up."

I slide her down my body making sure she feels exactly how happy I am to be in this room with her right here, right now.

Her eyes flare when she feels my hardness. "Do you have a rocket in your pocket?"

I burst into laughter. "Your dorkiness rating just shot through the roof."

"I go everywhere with a camera around my neck. You can't get much dorkier than me."

"I disagree. When you take pictures, your self-confidence shines through. It's sexy as hell."

I crowd her until she's forced to take a few steps back. When her legs hit the bed, I stop. "Now, are you going to pick up the clothes? Or do I do a sexy swipe of the bed and clear it?"

Her eyebrows raise. "A sexy swipe. This I gotta see."

I wink before moving around her. I rip off my shirt and throw it on the ground.

"You're cheating."

Damn right, I am. All's fair in love and war after all. I waggle my eyebrows at her before sweeping all the clothes from her bed onto the floor. Once the bed is clear, I prowl to her. Her eyes heat as they focus on my chest.

"Your turn," I say and drop to my knees in front of her.

I help her out of her shoes before placing my hands on her calves and gliding them up her legs under her dress. I gather the garment in my hands as I stand. She raises her arms and I whip it off of her.

I let the dress drop as I stare at the vision in front of me. Sofia is wearing a matching pair of white panties and bra. The white accentuates her glorious mocha colored skin. I nearly drool at the idea of getting my lips on her naked skin. Finally.

Her underwear displays her body in all its glory. The panties are a mere scrap of silk with lace sides. And the bra barely contains her heaving breasts. I take a moment to enjoy the view.

"I want to lick every inch of your skin, but where to start?"

She shivers in response. "I don't care where you start as long as you start."

I trace a finger down her cheek. "Is someone getting impatient?"

"Is someone being a tease?"

I smirk. "Teasing is all part of the pleasure."

I don't make her wait a second longer. I wrap an arm around her waist and throw her on the bed. Before she can settle, I pounce on her. I shackle her wrists and place her hands on the headboard. "Keep those there."

"Maybe I don't want to," she says, but I see the way she rubs her thighs in response to my order.

"Don't make me punish you."

Her chest heaves at my words and I watch as her breasts strain against her bra. I've found the perfect place to begin my torture.

I trace my tongue along the lace edges of her bra. I wait until she's squirming before I add little nibbles. This causes her legs to wrap around my waist. I push the bra cups down, exposing her dark pink nipples. I don't bother teasing her any longer. I use my teeth to gently bite one nipple. Her back shoots off the bed in response.

My hand moves to massage one breast while I concentrate on nibbling and biting her other one until her nipple is a hard peak. I blow on it and she moans. I move onto the other breast and give it the same treatment.

She's now rubbing her center up and down my cock. I lift my head.

"You need to stop doing that if you want this to last."

"What do you expect?" She pants. "You're torturing me."

I reach around and unhook her bra before throwing it across the room. I massage her breasts as my lips trail further down her body. I take a moment to circle her belly button with the tip of my tongue before I reach her panties.

I trace the edge of the silk with my tongue before latching onto the fabric with my teeth. I use my hold to draw the scrap of silk down her thighs.

"Holy cow. Did you remove my panties with your teeth?"

"I'm multi-talented. Wait until you see what I can do with my tongue." I wink.

Her hands release the headboard, and she grasps my head to yank me back up her body. "I already know your tongue is talented. I'm wondering about your cock."

At the word cock falling from her lips, mine twitches. It's more than ready to join the party.

"I want to pleasure you first."

"You have me naked in bed, panting. Mission accomplished. Now, get those pants off and take care of business."

Who am I to deny her? "Yes, ma'am."

Maybe other men would be turned off by a woman ordering him around in bed. Not me. I jump to do her bidding. I grab a condom from my wallet before shedding my jeans.

After I don the condom, I look up to find Sofia licking her lips at me.

"You like what you see?"

She plays it off with a shrug, but I notice her widen her legs. I don't hesitate to take her up on her unspoken invitation. I crawl back on the bed and line myself up with her opening.

Sofia wraps her legs around my waist, and I rub my cock up and down her slit. Once she's writhing in my arms and chanting *please, please, please,* I enter her.

Sofia's fingernails dig into my shoulders. "Hurry up."

I dip my head and kiss her lips. What I don't do is hurry up. I'm taking my time this first time. Maybe next time I'll be in a hurry.

I finally bottom out and pause; buried as deep as I can get. Sofia throws her head back on a long moan. There's a look of happiness on her face. A look I'm determined to change to bliss.

"Look at me."

Her eyes flutter open and she tilts her chin down before smiling at me. Her smile could light up the night sky.

"You good?"

"I'm good, but maybe you could move." I hesitate, but then she squeezes her inner muscles around me, and I have to grit my teeth to stop myself from coming right then.

"You don't fight fair."

"Never said I would," she says and squeezes me again.

"You asked for it."

I slowly withdraw before thrusting into her again. She groans and her legs tighten around my waist. I bury my head in her shoulder as I drive into her again and again. Her hips lift to meet me each time I plunge into her.

"Yes, yes, yes," she chants as her fingernails scrape against my back.

I feel her tighten around me. "Come for me, gorgeous."

"I am. I am. I am," she mutters as she explodes, her back arching and her hips gyrating against me.

I thrust into her two more times before my climax hits me. I continue to thrust into her a few more times, riding out my orgasm, before collapsing on her.

"Is death by orgasm a thing?" Her voice is muffled, and I realize I must be squishing her.

I roll off her before situating her until she's cradled in my arms.

"I don't know, but I'm willing to give it a try."

She chuckles before I hear a quiet snore. She's fallen asleep. I'm not more than a minute behind her.

Chapter 30

My eyes fly open when I feel Rafael kiss my forehead. He's standing next to the bed dressed in the clothes he wore last night. I glance out the window to see it's still dark out. My brow wrinkles in confusion.

"What's going on? Why are you dressed? What time is it?"

"Shh. Go back to sleep. It's the middle of the night."

I sit up making sure to drape the sheet over my naked body. "Why are you leaving in the middle of the night?" The cynic in me rears her ugly head. "Don't tell me you got what you came for and are leaving."

"No," he scowls. "I thought you knew me better."

"And I thought you wouldn't try sneaking out in the middle of the night," I counter.

He sighs. "It's Mieke. Esmay is rushing her to the hospital. Apparently, she's been vomiting nonstop for hours now."

"Why didn't you say so? Give me five minutes," I tell him as I climb out of bed.

He stops me. "You don't have to go with me."

"Don't be an idiot. Mieke's my friend. You're my…" I pause. I don't want to use the word boyfriend. The word is too tame for all the feelings I have for him, "… whatever. I'm coming."

I throw on a pair of jeans and a t-shirt in record time. Although it took me mere minutes to get ready, Rafael is pacing by the front door when I race out. He takes my hand, and we dash down the stairs to his car.

"Should I drive?" I ask him. "You might not be in the best mental state."

"No," he says as he climbs into the driver's seat. "I need something to concentrate on to keep my mind from spinning out of control." Fair enough.

The drive to Amsterdam usually takes forty-five minutes to an hour. We make it to the hospital in less than thirty minutes.

"I'm surprised we didn't get pulled over by the police," I say as we park.

"There are speed cameras everywhere. I probably got five tickets."

Damn. It's not like he has money to throw away and it's all my fault he wasn't home. But if I offer to pay the tickets, he'll lose his mind. I'll talk to Matthijs. Maybe the cop can help me figure out what to do.

Rafael doesn't bother stopping to ask for directions. He marches through the lobby to the emergency room entrance.

"Mieke Driessen," he grunts at the receptionist. "She was brought in an hour ago."

A woman hurries over to us before the receptionist can answer. "I'm sorry. I should have brought her in earlier. But Mieke said she was fine." She wrings her hands.

Rafael kisses her cheek. "It's okay, Esmay. It's not your fault."

I bite my lip. It's my fault. He should have been home with Mieke and not with me. He squeezes my hand.

"And whatever you're thinking is bullshit, too, gorgeous. But right now, I need to deal with my sister. We'll deal with the crap in your head later."

The receptionist speaks up. "You can go back and see her now."

I step back, but Rafael's hold on my hand tightens.

"I'll wait here," Esmay says as we leave. I wave back at her, and she gives me a thumbs-up.

Rafael seems to know his way around the emergency room. How bad have the last years been? How sick is Mieke? I know she needs a new kidney, but I guess I assumed she could live for several more years while she waits for an organ to become available. Now, I'm not sure.

We arrive in a room to find Mieke lying in a hospital bed. Her skin is so pale it's nearly transparent. Despite the multitude of machines making a bunch of noise, her eyes are closed. She opens them when she hears us enter. She smiles but the brackets around her mouth indicate how unwell she's feeling.

"I'm sorry. I didn't want to interrupt your date." Her voice is barely louder than a whisper.

Rafael drops my hand and hurries to her side. I stand on the opposite side of the bed and take her hand.

"You didn't interrupt us," he tells her.

She studies me. "Are you sure? Someone has sex hair."

Rafael groans but I wink at her. "Trust me. You didn't interrupt any of the good stuff."

"Good," she says as her eyes close. "Big brother may be annoying, but he deserves to have some good in his life, too."

My eyes itch at her words. This girl. She's laying sick in the hospital, and she's worried about her brother having a good time. Biggest. Heart. Ever.

"I do have good. I have my sister. She's a total brat, but I love her anyway."

Mieke laughs but it turns into a cough. Rafael finds her glass of water and helps lift her head to help her take a sip.

A doctor sweeps into the room. He opens Mieke's medical file, and I loosen my grip on her hand. Time to go.

"No," Mieke pleads. "Don't go."

I lean down until I can whisper to her. "This is personal. I can wait outside. I don't mind."

"I want you here," she insists. "And before you ask,

I'm sure."

The doctor clears his throat and I roll my eyes causing Mieke to smile before I stand up and give the doctor my attention.

"The good news is she is not at end-stage renal disease – yet."

End-stage? I want to ask what he means, but now is not the time for me to ask questions.

"The bad news is she needs a new kidney sooner rather than later."

Rafael gulps. "How much time are we talking?"

"I hate to give specifics because every person is different but suffice it to say months."

"And in the meantime?"

The doctor briefly glances up from the file to answer. "Keep doing what you're doing. Eat healthy, take your medicine, and continue with dialysis." He shuts the clipboard and hangs it up on the end of the bed. "She'll need to stay here until her fluids are replenished and her levels are back to normal."

He doesn't bother asking if there are any further questions before sweeping out of the room.

"I rate him a seven," Mieke says once the door closes.

"I'm going with an eight."

"What are we rating?" I ask.

"His god complex. All doctors have one," Mieke explains.

"Ten being the worst?"

"Yep. How do you rate him?"

I frown as I consider her question. Honestly, I haven't met enough doctors to rate one's god complex. "I say seven, too."

Rafael huffs. "The guy was a complete dick. A seven is too mild."

"He let me stay and he spoke English to allow me

to understand. He gets points for those aspects. Besides, aren't all doctors dicks?"

Mieke yawns in response.

"Do you want me to stay?" Rafael asks her.

She rolls her eyes. "Do I want you to stay and watch me sleeping all night? Gee, let me think about it."

He bops her on the nose. "No need to be a smart ass."

"I did learn from the best."

"We'll go then," Rafael says, but he doesn't make any move to leave.

"And no hanging out in the waiting room until the morning either."

Rafael frowns. "I only want to make certain you're okay."

She sighs. "I'm pretty sure that's the job of the doctors and nurses."

Speaking of which, a nurse bustles in and startles when she sees us.

"They were leaving," Mieke says before Rafael has a chance to speak. "They're on a date."

The nurse looks between the two of us and smiles. "I guess we'll let them get back to their date then, won't we?"

Never mind it's now five o'clock in the morning. I lean over Mieke and kiss her forehead. "You behave," I tell her.

"I'll behave as long as you promise you won't." She winks at me.

"You do realize you're talking about your brother having sex."

She plugs her ears with her fingers. "Na na na. I can't hear you."

I ruffle her hair before walking away. I stand in the hallway and wait for Rafael to say goodbye to his sister. He smiles when he joins me, but it's clearly forced.

"Do you want to stay anyway?" I ask him as we head toward the waiting room.

"Nah, she'll have the nurses check if I'm waiting. If they find me here, she'll throw a fit."

"What about a hotel nearby? It's a good compromise. You're not in the hospital, but you're closer than being at home."

The hospital is on the southwest outskirts of Amsterdam while I know they live in the northeast. There are apparently hospitals closer to their home, but this is a university hospital and is better prepared for the care Mieke needs.

I check the hotel app I use when traveling. "According to my app, there's a hotel three blocks away."

He checks his watch. "It's nearly morning. It doesn't make sense to check in now." I can tell he wants to, though. Decision made. I click on book now.

"You do what you want. I already booked a room for myself, so I can see Mieke in the morning."

He grunts. "You're as bad as Mieke."

I flutter my eyelashes. "I have no idea what you're talking about."

He takes my hand. "Come on. Let's try to get a few hours rest before we come back. Mieke will give me hell if I appear tired."

"Mieke's awesome."

I'm not blowing smoke up his ass. His sister is awesome. Now to find a way to ensure she stays awesome for years to come. Months to live? Not if I can help it.

Chapter 31

I clap my hands to get everyone's attention. "Quiet, please. Quiet, please. Time to get down to business."

Abby's hand shoots into the air. "What business are we getting down to? And where's Rafael? You didn't dump him, did you?"

"I hope not. We like Rafael," Mama says from the computer screen where she and *Pai* have joined us on a video call.

Pai grunts. "Speak for yourself."

"Maybe she wants to plan a surprise for him." Mia sighs as she rubs her ever-growing belly.

"If you do surprise him, remember to keep your clothes on," Char says. "There's nothing like being in the throes of passion and someone," she eyes Abby, "walking in on you. I'm surprised I haven't ended up with some sort of sexual PTSD from the entire incident. The bedroom door now has to be closed and locked before any clothing comes off. Couch nookie is a thing of the past."

"Sucks to be you," Abby sings as if she isn't the entire reason Char is afraid to have sex without the door locked.

Avery clears her throat. "Maybe we can let Sofia speak and tell us why we're here."

"Yes, Uptight."

Everyone's attention centers on me, and I explain. "Mieke is nearing end-stage renal disease. She ended up in the hospital on Saturday night."

Abby's hand shoots into the air again. I sigh.

"This isn't a classroom. You don't have to raise

your hand."

"Sorry, I blame Mia."

Mia glances up from her telephone. "Wait. What? Why am I to blame?"

"Enough!" I shout. "As much as I love everyone's usual banter, today is not the day."

"What did I miss?" Zara interrupts to ask. She's on the same video conference with Mama and *Pai*.

"I do not know. Something about Rafael and Mieke." Mama does a great job of not explaining.

Avery stands and joins me at the front of my living room. She takes my hand and squeezes. "If everyone could please give Sofia their attention without interrupting for a few minutes," she says in what I imagine is her courtroom voice.

I clear my throat. "As I was saying, Mieke was in the hospital on Saturday night where I learned she's near end-stage renal disease." Abby raises her hand again, but I ignore her. "The doctor said she has months to live unless she gets a kidney transplant."

I feel my bottom lip tremble as I admit, "I got tested, but I'm not a match."

The second I realized Mieke needed a kidney as bad as she does I ran to my doctor to find out if I'm match. She didn't bother to do any tests. Once she found out Mieke has blood type O positive and I have A positive, she sat me down and explained I couldn't donate a kidney to Mieke.

Avery wraps her arm around my shoulders and pulls me close. "I'm sorry, Sofia. The news must have been devastating."

I take a deep breath and step out of her arms before I have a complete breakdown. "I don't suppose anyone has O blood type and an extra kidney?"

My shoulders drop as everyone shakes their heads. I figured as much, but I had to ask.

I clear my throat. "I guess we should move on to

the main reason I gathered you here today then."

"What do you want us to do?" Mama asks.

I smile at her image on my computer. "Thanks, Mama. I'm thinking of doing a campaign to raise awareness for living kidney donation."

Abby waves her hand in the air. "What about Mieke's family? Can't one of them donate a kidney?"

"Rafael isn't a match, her mother has passed, and her father's whereabouts are unknown."

She's already taking out her phone and typing away. "What's Mieke's last name? It can't be Van Dijk like Rafael's."

Do I dare ask? "How do you know?"

She shows me her screen. "Because there's no one registered living in Amsterdam with Mieke's birth year with her first name and Van Dijk as a last name."

Avery plants her hands on her hips. "Did you seriously hack into Amsterdam city records with your phone?"

Abby rolls her eyes. "This information is public record. No hacking needed." She sounds disappointed. I'm glad she's on my side.

"Mieke's last name is Driessen," I say before Avery and Abby can get into the merits of hacking.

"Got it. Her father is Arnoud Driessen." She swipes and clicks away. "Darn." She stands. "I need my computer. I'll be right back."

"I don't think Mieke's dad is going to give her a kidney," I shout after her, but she's already gone. "He took off after she got sick and hasn't been in touch since," I explain to everyone else.

"*Zalupoglazaya mondavushka. Unbju*!" Mama curses in Russian.

"What did she say?" Mia asks.

"She called him a slut with pee hole eyes and said she's going to kill him." Despite having a Russian mother, my Russian isn't great. But Russian swear words? Those I have down.

Mia nods to my mother as a sign of respect. "I'll join you. Anyone who can abandon their child doesn't deserve to breathe air."

Char growls. "I second! And I'm in. I don't know how to hide a body but Mia the history nut can help us, and Abby can research anything on the dark web, so we don't leave any internet trails behind us."

Pai sighs. "And I will make the coffee for those lovely Homeland Security men when they come to question you."

Char's eyes pop. "Oops! I guess I shouldn't have mentioned hiding bodies while on a video conference call."

Avery makes a note on her phone. "I'll have Niels contact his criminal law buddies and line up good defense lawyers for everyone."

"We were speaking hypothetically. No need to go all lawyer on us," Mia insists.

I stare at the ceiling for guidance. I asked everyone here today to help me and now they're plotting murder? This is not how the conversation was supposed to go.

"To sum up," Avery says, and I return my attention to the room, "you want to do some sort of awareness campaign for living kidney donation. Do you want to use Mieke as the poster child?"

I bite my lip. "What do you think? Will it make her pathetic?"

I don't want Mieke to think I pity her, because I don't. She's the strongest, sweetest, nicest person I know.

"You can always ask her."

Abby charges into the room. "I found him!" She lifts up her computer to show us the screen. "Arnoud Driessen, forty-year-old male, currently living in Antwerp. The Belgian thing is what threw me. I could have found him much quicker if he lived in Holland."

"What's the plan?" Mia asks.

"I guess I'll approach Arnoud Driessen to ask him about donating a kidney. In the meantime, we need to think about how we want to do this campaign. Encouraging people to donate a kidney to a stranger is not going to be easy. Mama, I need your contacts."

"Of course, my little rabbit. Whatever you need for that darling girl."

"I'll take care of the finances," Char says. "They'll be printing costs, advertising costs, photographer costs. Oh, wait. I guess we have the last one covered."

"I'll donate some seed money," Mia volunteers. "And I have an idea. Why don't we have Mieke come to school to give a talk about living with kidney disease? Obviously, the children can't donate a kidney, but the American school is private and obnoxiously expensive. The parents are wealthy, influential people."

Abby snorts. "As if you're not a wealthy, influential person."

Mia cringes. "I can try to use my American connections, but I've been kicked out of the elitist club in Atlanta."

"And I'll help with any legalities, of course," Avery says.

My eyes itch as I survey the room and my friends. "What did I do to deserve this?"

Abby rolls her eyes. "Love you, girl. But we're not doing this for you. We're doing it for Mieke."

"Speaking of Mieke, why isn't Rafael here spearheading this campaign?" Avery asks.

I wring my hands. "Because it's my fault Mieke ended up in the hospital on Saturday night. If I hadn't been selfish and wanted to spend time alone with him, she never would have gotten sick."

Mama sighs. "Stop acting like a martyr. This is not the Great Patriotic War." If Mama would deign to roll her eyes, they'd be rolling right now.

"Sofia does tend to blame herself when no one is at fault," Zara says with a raised eyebrow as if daring me to contradict her.

Avery squeezes my hand. "It's not your fault. You didn't give Mieke kidney disease. She's been sick for a long time."

"According to my research on kidney disease," Abby chimes in, "Avery is correct. The current situation is a cumulation of years of illness due to low functioning kidneys."

I don't bother asking when Abby had time to research kidney disease. The woman is remarkable. Two children, a busy job, and a husband don't slow her down any.

Char stands. "Good. We have a plan. Who wants wine?"

"This is where we say goodbye." Mama throws me an air kiss before disconnecting. Zara mimes call me before ending her call, too.

Mia groans. "I wish I could have wine. I'm lucky Matthijs hasn't barged in yet to drag me home for a nap like I'm a toddler."

We all pause to listen for the doorbell.

"I got you covered, girl. Matthijs is at my house learning how to change a diaper. Considering Olivier's stomach problems last night, he'll be a while." The smirk on Abby's face is downright devious.

Char hands me a glass of wine before throwing her arm around my shoulders. Together we watch as Abby and Mia discuss babies while Avery makes calls, probably already throwing herself into her role as legal advisor.

"These girls can be crazy, but you can't deny they are the best."

I agree. The best. I can only hope our efforts result in a new kidney for Mieke because a world without her is not a world I want to live in.

Chapter 32

"Thank you for doing this, gorgeous." Rafael kisses my forehead.

"Stop thanking me. I'm not doing this for you. I'm here because I want to spend time with my girl, Mieke."

Rafael called this morning and asked me to spend the day with Mieke. Usually, Sunday is their day together, but the bar where he works called and begged him to take the lunch shift. I didn't hesitate to agree to spend the day with his sister. I know he needs the extra income and doesn't like leaving Mieke alone.

"Then, thank you for being awesome."

"I can't help it. The awesomeness happens all on its own."

He shakes his head. "And modest, too."

I push him out the door. "Get out of here. It's girl time."

He nabs my hand and tugs me into the hallway with him. "I need to taste those luscious lips before I leave you."

You won't hear me complain. I stand on my tiptoes to reach his mouth. As soon as my lips touch his, he takes over. He wraps his arms around me and crushes my body to his. I can feel every inch of his hard muscles. Hard muscles my hands itch to explore every inch of again and again.

His taste explodes in my mouth; a natural musky flavor combined with coffee. I moan and his arms around me tighten for a second before he slows the kiss until he's nibbling at my lips.

"I think I'm addicted to your mouth," he mumbles

between nibbles.

"Right back at ya."

The door behind us opens and Mieke steps out with her hand over her eyes. "Rafael, you're going to be late for work if you don't stop dry humping your girlfriend in the hallway."

"Be nice or I'll make you watch the documentary about font types."

"Hey! I saw that documentary. It was really interesting. It discussed the influence of font on typography, advertising, and design."

Rafael smirks. "My gorgeous photographer is a secret nerd."

"De-sign. Do I need to spell it out for you?"

Mieke taps her wrist. "Tick tock."

Rafael glances at his watch and curses. "I'll see you two in a few hours. Behave."

"I will," Mieke shouts at his back. She removes her hands from behind her back and shows me her crossed fingers. I ruffle her hair as we walk back into their apartment together.

I lift my bag. "I am prepared for the most awesome of girl days. I have Disney movies and cookie dough. I also have supplies to give ourselves facials. Plus, I have make-up to do a make-over should you wish. And, last but not least, I have enough nail polish to paint all the fingernails and toenails of every single person in Amsterdam."

"Disney movies." Mieke feigns gagging. "No thanks."

"I'm confused. Rafael said you make him watch Disney marathons."

She smirks. "I do."

"You're bad." I take the movies out of my bag and set them apart.

"Are those DVDs? What are we? In the twentieth century? There's this new thing now. It's called streaming.

Maybe you've heard of it."

I stick my tongue out at her. "You're a troublemaker."

She beams up at me. "And proud of it."

"Okay, if you don't want to watch a Disney movie, what do you want to watch?"

"*To All The Boys I've Loved Before.*"

I should have known. "Alrighty then. Shall we put the cookies in the oven and get our facial masks on first?"

At Mieke's agreement, I remove several different bottles and jars from my bag. "I have a clay mask, mud mask, hydration mask, single sheet mask, and a gel mask with chamomile which is supposed to be calming."

"You're either a beauty freak or you went overboard in the 'entertain Mieke' event."

I may have gone overboard, but I'll never admit it. "How about my mother is a supermodel who takes skincare very, very seriously?"

"I didn't think vampires had to worry about skincare."

I sigh. "I'm never going to hear the end of that, am I?"

"Nope," she says making sure to pop the P.

She bites her lip as she studies the array of choices before picking up the single sheet mask.

"Let's get this cookie dough into the oven first." I shake a plastic bowl at her. "Don't worry. It fits within your diet. It's vegan, paleo, and gluten-free."

She makes a face. "And probably gross tasting."

"I don't know. Abby made it for us. She did some research on diets for kidney patients and started cooking up a storm."

Her eyes widen. "Abby can cook?"

I understand the confusion. Abby's style doesn't exactly scream domesticated with her purple-striped hair, ripped jeans, and shitkicker boots. "She's disgustingly good at it. The woman is good at everything she does. It's annoying as hell."

Oops. I shouldn't be swearing. "Don't tell your brother I said hell."

"Why the hell not?"

Oh boy. The troublemaker is strong in this one.

Together we form the dough into balls and place them in the oven. While the cookies are baking, we wash our faces and put on the masks. I snap a picture of Mieke with hers on and send it to Rafael.

Rafael: I hope this means she's behaving.

Me: Stop being a Debbie Downer.

"You're right about your brother. He takes overprotective to the next level."

The timer dings to indicate the cookies are ready.

"Huh." Mieke stares at the tray of cookies. "They actually look yummy."

I hip check her. "Told you. Abby is disgustingly good at everything."

She piles a plate high with cookies. "Mine." She darts to the couch with her booty. I let her. I know she doesn't eat nearly enough, and the cookies are fairly healthy considering they're cookies.

I sit down next to her on the sofa with my plate of two cookies. Mieke shakes her head at my measly plate. I'd roll my eyes, but my mud mask currently has my face immobilized.

"Start the movie," I tell her.

I nibble on a cookie as I watch the opening credits.

"Wow. These are good."

I glance over at Mieke to see her chowing down. Her face mask slips a bit and I warn her, "Watch out before—"

Too late. The face mask rolls into her mouth, and she chews on it before she realizes what's happening. Her action causes the mask to slip further until it flips over and lands smack dab on top of her pile of treats. I burst out laughing and she glares at me.

I raise my hands in surrender. "Who's laughing at my tiny plate now?"

The gel from the face masks drips down her face and I can't help myself. I pick up my camera and snap a picture.

"You didn't!" She lunges at me. I jump to my feet and run away from her.

I head to the kitchen and pick up one of the remaining cookies. I cock my arm back as if to throw it at her.

"You wouldn't!"

I feign throwing the cookie and she tackles me to the floor. I hold the cookie up high as she wrestles me. Her breathing sounds heavy. Shit. We shouldn't be horsing around. I don't say anything of the sort, of course. I'm not an idiot. She won't appreciate me pointing out her weakness.

Instead, I fall back and lift my hands in surrender. "I give up. You won, brat." She snatches the cookie from my hand and shoves it into her mouth.

I notice my top is now covered with gel from Mieke's mask. "I think I need to get cleaned up." I point to her face. "And you need to wash up."

After we've washed our faces, Mieke finds me a t-shirt of Rafael's to wear since my shirt is in the dryer. I lift the fabric to my nose and inhale. It smells like the man himself. I put it on and now I feel engulfed by his scent. He's not getting this t-shirt back.

I grab my bag and set my make-up out on the kitchen table.

"Who wants a make-over?" I ask when Mieke returns with a fresh face and wearing a clean top.

She hesitates. "Rafael doesn't like me wearing make-up."

"One, Rafael isn't here. Two, you're sixteen, not

six." I point to a chair. "Sit down. I make you beautiful," I say with a thick Russian accent.

I spend the next twenty minutes applying the skills Mama insisted I learn the day after I got my first period. When I finish, she resembles a healthy teenager and not the tired one who opened the door when I arrived today.

I place a mirror in her hand. "What do you think?"

"Wow. I kind of look pretty."

I slap her shoulder. "No kind of about it. You look pretty because you are pretty."

She blushes. "Thank you. Can you show me how to do this myself?"

"Of course." I spend half an hour showing her how to apply make-up before packaging all of it up to give to her.

"I can't take this from you."

"Um, Mieke, have you seen the color of my skin? I can't use any of these products. I bought them for you."

Her eyes widen. "You did?"

I roll my eyes. "Yes, silly girl. I did. Now, put your stuff away, and let's finish watching these movies I'm way too old for."

"You are kind of old," she says and hurries off before I can reply.

By the time Rafael returns in the early evening, we've finished watching *To All The Boys I've Loved Before* and are watching *To All the Boys: P.S. I Still Love You.* There's a third movie in the series lined up next.

"I brought Chinese take-out," he announces as he strolls into the apartment.

"Let me guess, stir-fried vegetables with no sauce for me." Mieke feigns gagging.

He smiles before heading toward the kitchen with the food. He stops halfway there. "What's going on? Why do you look like you're a thirty-year-old and not my sixteen-year-old sister?"

Mieke frowns. "You don't like it?"

"Honestly—"

My growl cuts him off. "Tread very carefully with your next words."

His head swivels back and forth between the two of us before he groans. "Shit. Now I have two women running my life."

"Aren't you the lucky guy?" I wink at him.

"I sure am. I sure am."

I hope he feels as lucky as I do because I think my heart has found the one it's been searching for.

Chapter 33

Rafael

I stomp up the stairs to Sofia's apartment. I cannot believe her. I can't believe she did this. I thought she was different. I thought she was the one. I thought I was falling in love with her. But now this? Sofia is not the woman I thought she was.

I pound on the door to her apartment. When the door flies open and she smiles up at me, my heart – the traitor – misses a beat before quickening and my blood thickens at the memory of those lips on mine and other parts of my body.

I ignore my body's response to her. My head knows better. This woman is not to be trusted.

When I merely stare at her without speaking, the smile falls from her face. "What's wrong? Oh no, is Mieke okay?"

She moves to wrap her arms around me, but I step away. Hurt flashes in her eyes and her hand grips the door as if she needs the help to stay upright. I ignore her reaction. I'm the injured party here. Not her.

"Do you want to come in?"

I grunt and she opens the door wide. She doesn't make it to the living room before my patience expires. "How could you?"

She spins around. "How could I what? Don't tell me you're still mad about the make-up. Mieke is sixteen. She's not too young to wear make-up."

My nostrils flare as I take deep breaths to stop myself from shouting at her. "I don't give the first fuck about the make-up."

She throws her arms in the air. "Then, what are you talking about?"

"I'm talking about Mieke being your charity case."

Her brow wrinkles. "I don't understand."

I take a step closer until I'm right up in her space and glare down at her. "Guess who I had a call from today?" Her mouth opens but I speak before she has the chance. "Arnoud Driessen."

"And? What did he say?" The excited look confirms what I already know. Sofia was the one to contact him.

"You're not going to ask me who he is?"

Her cheeks pinken. "Um, no. I know he's Mieke's father."

"And you know he's Mieke's father because you stuck your nose in my business."

She winces as if I slapped her. "Your business?" she whispers.

I point to myself. "My business."

She drops her gaze to the ground and her hands fiddle with the hem of her t-shirt. "I thought you and Mieke were my business, too."

"Is that your excuse for contacting a man who has had nothing to do with his daughter?"

Her head lifts and her emerald eyes sparkle with anger. "I thought if he knew how sick Mieke is, he'd consider donating a kidney to save her life. The doctor said—"

"I know what the doctor said," I explode. "I know what every single doctor has said for the past six years because I'm the one who has been there for her every day for all those years, not her father."

Her brow wrinkles in confusion. "No one is saying you haven't been there for her. You said yourself. Your kidney isn't a match."

"And somehow me not being able to donate my

kidney became an excuse for you to contact her father?"

She puffs out a breath of air. "I apologize if I stepped over the line. I only want to help Mieke. I love that girl."

I run a hand through my hair and step back from her. Am I overreacting? Am I being a total douchebag? How do I explain? "It's been me and Mieke against the world for years now. I'm not used to other people caring."

She grabs my t-shirt and drags me close. "Then, get used to someone caring, because I care. I care a lot."

"Okay." I swallow and force my anger under control. "But please tell me in advance next time. Getting blindsided by Arnoud is not fun. The guy is a total dick."

She bites her lip and her nose wrinkles as she looks up at me. Her eyes are filled with trepidation.

"What?"

"I may have done this other thing."

I take a step back, forcing her hands to drop their hold on me. "What did you do?" The question whips out of me.

"Please don't be mad."

Never a good way to begin a conversation.

She takes a deep breath before plowing forth. "I'm working on a campaign to raise awareness for live kidney donation. I thought we could use Mieke as an example to show the world the necessity for live donations. People donate bone marrow for someone they don't know but kidneys are a different matter. I—"

I hold up a hand to stop her there. "Are you out of your mind?" I shout.

Her eyes widen. "I don't understand. Why are you angry?"

"Why am I angry? You want to exploit Mieke for your own goals and you're asking why I'm angry?"

"No. No. No." She reaches for me, but I step back. "I'm not exploiting Mieke. I'm trying to help her. You know yourself, she needs a kidney."

"Which is why she's on the transplant list."

She grasps my hand and squeezes. "What if an organ doesn't become available soon enough to save her?"

I shake her hold off of me. "It will." Because it has to. I am not going to live in a world without Mieke.

"Don't you see? This living donor campaign might reveal someone who's willing to give her a kidney now. Then, she doesn't have to wait for someone to die to donate their kidney."

I flinch. I hate how someone has to die in order for my sister to live, but I've made my peace with it. I've had to. My sister comes first. She will always come first.

Sofia uses my obvious discomfort with the situation to dive right in. "This campaign is going to be wonderful. My parents are rallying their friends and connections. Abby and Mia have already donated funds. Avery is taking care of all the legalities. And Char is in charge of finances."

"And what about you?"

"I'm in charge of photographing, of course. I'm going to ask Mieke to do another photo session with me. She'll be our poster child."

At the words poster child, my anger returns. "Mieke is no one's poster child."

"Shit. I didn't mean it like it sounded."

"Like what? Like Mieke is a charity case for you to rally around?"

"Charity case? You make Mieke sound pathetic."

"Isn't that how you see her?"

She rears back. "No. Of course not."

"And yet you want to use her," I scoff. "I'm done with this conversation. And I'm done with you."

She gasps. "Are you serious? I'm only trying to help. You want to end us because I care about your sister?"

I get up in her face. "You don't care about Mieke. You care about using Mieke to further your career."

"You think I'm using Mieke for my career?" Her eyes widen and I can see tears form in them. I know better than to be swayed by her act, though.

I sneer at her. "I don't think it. I know it."

Her shoulders hunch. "After everything we've shared together, you think I'd exploit a child for my career? I guess you're right. This is over."

Her eyes close for a second before she lifts her hand and points to the door. "You can see yourself out."

I don't let the obvious hurt on her face affect me. "You are no longer welcome in our lives," I tell her before stomping to the door and yanking it open.

As I sit in my car in Sofia's parking spot under her apartment, my heart screams at me that I'm making the biggest mistake of my life. My head disagrees. Sofia is a user, and I won't let her use Mieke to further her career.

I switch on the car and drive out of the parking lot. I don't look back.

Chapter 34

I wait until I hear the sound of the door snick closed before I fall to the ground. I wrap my arms around my knees and drop my head. The tears I managed to hold off during the conversation with Rafael come now.

"Someone help me. I can't lift her."

I raise my head to find Abby standing next to me. Mia and Char are behind her.

"How did you get in here?"

"It's better not to ask questions," Mia says.

Char pushes Mia and Abby out of the way. "I got this."

She squats like she's going to help me up. I raise my hand. I can stand on my own. "I'm half a foot taller than you. I don't think you can lift me."

She indicates her body with a sweep of her hand. "I'm not exactly some dainty woman."

I stand and stare at everyone in my hallway. "Dare I ask what you're doing here?"

Abby rolls her eyes. "We're here to cheer you up after your break-up with Rafael, of course."

"How do you know I broke up with Rafael? Are you spying on me?"

"Like I said, it's better not to ask questions. Come on, let's move this to the living room where I can sit down." Mia shoos us out of the hallway. "Don't tell Matthijs but my back is killing me, and my feet are beyond tired. I think I have cankles."

Avery dashes into the room. "Sorry. Sorry. Sorry. I got here as quick as I could. If someone would have given me a ride, I could have gotten here faster." She glares at Abby who shrugs in response.

"Is it my fault you weren't ready when I messaged you?"

"Believe it or not, I don't spend all my time sitting around waiting for you to contact me."

"I don't know why not." Abby appears genuinely confused about the matter.

Char takes my hand and leads me to the living room where Mia is already sitting with her shoes off and her feet up on my coffee table. I wince when I see how swollen her feet are.

"What happened?" Char asks.

I collapse on the sofa and cover my eyes with my arm. I should probably go wash my face. I can feel how puffy my eyes are from crying, and I don't even want to think about the state of my make-up. Mama would be appalled I let anyone see me when I'm not showing my best. As if I have a choice with Abby the tornado.

"He found out about the campaign to raise awareness for live kidney donors."

When no one responds, I drop my arm. "What?"

Abby motions for me to continue. "And?"

"And he lost his mind. He thinks I'm using Mieke and her disease to further my career goals."

Abby snorts. "Does he not realize you're one of the most sought after fashion photographers in the world?"

Char grimaces. "Again. I'd like to—"

"If you apologize about asking me to photograph Tobias' party one more time, I'm going to tell Tobias it's okay to run around naked in public."

She gasps. "You wouldn't."

I cock my eyebrow. "Try me."

Avery sits down on the chair opposite the sofa. "I'm confused. How can he possibly be mad about you wanting to do this for his sister?"

"He thinks I think he's a charity case. Plus, he's pissed we contacted Mieke's dad. Apparently, the asshole called Rafael and gave him an earful."

"Some people are not fit to be parents," Abby mumbles. She would know. Her adopted parents actually gave her back to the orphanage.

"Does this mean we're stopping the campaign?" Mia asks as she rubs her belly.

"No. This campaign is too important to give up because some guy got his pride hurt." And I'm not giving up on Mieke. Her brother may be a total asshole I never want to see again, but she's my friend. I won't let her down. But I will give Rafael some time to cool off before I contact her.

Char rubs her hands together. "I say we give Rafael a good old-fashioned pranking."

"Like what? You can't exactly glitter bomb his apartment. Mieke lives there, too."

She taps her cheek as she considers the possibilities. "We could put grape Kool-Aid in his showerhead."

"Am I talking to myself? I told you Mieke lives with him."

Her eyes widen. "I know. We'll get him a subscription to a filthy magazine. It will embarrass the hell out of him." Yeah, because the Dutch are such prudes. Not.

I don't bother responding to her idiotic idea. "Can we talk about something else besides pranking my ex-boyfriend?"

My heart squeezes at the word ex-boyfriend. I'm such an idiot. I thought Rafael was the 'one'. Once again, I've been fooled into thinking a man is someone he's not. Why I thought I could date and find someone to love is beyond me.

I don't need love. I need nice and dependable. Not someone who makes my heart race whenever I see him, and goosebumps break out on my skin whenever we touch. My body no longer gets a vote in who I date.

"Where's your 'cheer up a girlfriend'-kit?" Avery asks Abby.

Abby's eyes nearly pop out of her head. "I forgot it."

Avery removes her phone from her pocket. "I need to write this down. Abby aka Wonder Woman being forgetful. You don't see this happen every day."

Abby slaps Avery's phone out of her hand. "I'm allowed to be forgetful once a year. I have a newborn, a toddler, and a busy job. I have a lot of balls in the air."

Mia moans as she rubs her belly. I scoot away from her. "You're not in labor, are you? Do you want me to call Matthijs?"

"No!" she shouts. "Do not dare call my husband or I will have Char glitter bomb your apartment."

"She's not due for another five weeks," Abby says.

"I'm fine. My girl is quite the kicker. I'm afraid Matthijs will have to accept she's going to play football."

"Speaking of forgetting things, I think Abby forgot to tell everyone her news," Avery prods.

"I didn't forget. I didn't think it was appropriate to share good news while cheering up a girlfriend. I read it somewhere. I actually added it to my girlfriend rules."

I lean close to Char to whisper, "Does she seriously have these rules written down?"

"Like Mia says, it's better not to ask questions."

"Before Abby shares her news, I want to hear what Sofia's going to do," Avery says.

I wrinkle my brow. What is she talking about? "Do about what?"

"Rafael, of course."

I shrug. "What is there to do? We're done."

"That's it?"

"Yep. I should have stuck with the plan. Find a

nice, dependable man."

Abby sighs. "Not this again. You don't want a boring man."

"I certainly don't want an asshole model either." My head nods in agreement, but my body disagrees. It thinks I should rush to Amsterdam and apologize to Rafael again. Explain and make him understand I'm trying to help.

Char takes my hand and squeezes. "Sometimes men do stupid stuff when it comes to family. It's not because they're assholes."

I cock an eyebrow. Char told me the story of how Nico ghosted her after she moved to Holland to be with him. I don't think I could have forgiven him. I can see how much he loves her now, but he also caused her a ton of heartache. I'm self-aware enough to know my cynical heart wouldn't deal with those ups and downs with the grace she did.

"Really, they're not all assholes," she pushes.

Whatever. I'm done with this conversation. I'm not going to sit here and listen to her try to convince me to give Rafael another chance. It's not like the guy wants another chance anyway.

"What's this news?" I ask Abby.

Avery nudges her. "It's okay to share your news. The heartbroken girl asked. I think her asking is an exemption to your 'no good news when trying to cheer up a girlfriend'-rule."

"Okay." She throws her arms out to the sides. "Before you stands the new Chief Technology Officer of Petroix Oil."

I jump to my feet and grab her hands to haul her off the chair and engulf her in my arms. "Congratulations."

"Group hug!" Avery shouts and the other women pile onto us.

Everyone is laughing and shouting in happiness for Abby, and I realize I may not have found romantic love, but I did find the love of good friends.

Screw Rafael and his hurt pride. These women are worth a thousand Rafaels.

Chapter 35

Rafael

I slam the beer tap back into place with a grunt.

"Whoa! Who pissed in your Cheerios this morning?" My boss, Mats, asks.

I grunt again before bringing the beers over to the waitress who serves them to the customers. She stares at the beers for a second before looking past me to Mats.

I move to block off her view of him. "Is there something wrong with the beer?" I sneer.

She grimaces before answering, "There's a lot of head on these."

I glare down at the beers as if it's their fault I'm grumpy. I snatch them back and return to the tap to top them off. I don't bother to skim the top to get rid of the excess foam. I bring the glasses back to her with the foam pouring down the sides.

"You're on break," Mats says when I return to stand behind the tap.

I survey the bar. It's lunchtime on a Saturday in the center of Amsterdam. He needs me out here.

"Go take your break and try to come back less of an asshole. That's an order."

"Whatever," I grumble before throwing my towel on the bar and marching off.

I make my way past the toilets and the kitchen and open the door leading to the alley in the back. I pace the alley as I try to get my raging emotions under control. I shouldn't be this upset by Sofia's betrayal.

It's not like we dated for very long. We hardly know

each other. My heart calls me a liar. It claims it knows all it needs to know about Sofia. She's kind, generous, and funny. It doesn't need to know more. Except she pities me enough to start some fucking campaign for Mieke. Guess my heart doesn't know everything after all.

The rest of the afternoon drags by until Mats sends me home early. He also tells me to get my head on straight before my next shift. I manage not to flip him off as I leave.

When I enter my apartment an hour later, things don't improve. The first thing I notice is Mieke sitting on the sofa wearing make-up.

"What the hell are you wearing make-up for?"

"It makes me feel pretty."

"There's no reason to feel pretty when you're sitting at home on the sofa watching a movie."

"Why are you being such a jerk? Are you sexually frustrated? Do I need to call Sofia?" Her face falls.

"What is it?"

"Sofia hasn't been answering my messages."

Fuck. This is all my fault.

I sit on the coffee table in front of Mieke. "I'm sorry."

Her eyes narrow. "Why are you sorry?" My chin drops to my chest to avoid her gaze. "What did you do?"

I stand. "Sofia and I are over."

She gasps. "Why? What happened? Did you cheat on her?"

"No, I didn't cheat on her. Why would you think that?"

"Why else would Sofia dump you? It's plain to see how much she loves you. Her eyes practically get those cartoon hearts in them whenever she gazes at you."

"She didn't dump me."

Her eyes widen and she stands to confront me. "You broke up with Sofia? You are the biggest idiot in the world."

"Hey! You don't know what she did."

She fists her hands at her hips. "Fine. Bring it on. What did Sofia do that was horrible enough for you to break up with her?"

"She found your dad and then called him and asked him to donate a kidney to you."

She flinches. "I bet dear old dad loved getting called out by a stranger."

"He was pissed. He called me to complain."

She freezes. "You have contact with my dad?"

I frown. "Not really. I haven't spoken to him for several years. I talked to him about four years ago when we found out you'd eventually need a new kidney. He told me not to call him again. And I haven't."

Her shoulders relax. "Okay." Her brow wrinkles. "I'm confused. You dumped Sofia because of this? Thanks for confirming you're the world's biggest idiot for me."

"There's more."

When I pause, she motions for me to get on with it.

"You may want to sit down for this."

I wait until she's comfortable on the couch before I tell her the words I know are going to rip her world apart. Shit. I should have lied and said I cheated on Sofia. I clear my throat.

"Sofia pities you."

She barks out a laugh. "Did you stop at the coffee shop on your way home? Been smoking too much reefer? Sofia doesn't pity me."

"You don't know. You don't know what she did."

"I do know. I've been able to recognize the pity look since I was twelve. But come on, tell me what Sofia did that shows how much she pities me."

"She's putting together a campaign to help raise awareness for live kidney donorship."

Her eyes widen, her jaw drops, and she slaps her

palms on her cheeks. "Holy cow! You have got to be kidding me. What a complete bitch. She's using her own time and energy to raise awareness for a cause near and dear to my heart. I can't believe this. No wonder you kicked her to the curb."

"Stop being a smartass. She wants to use you as the poster child."

Mieke waits for me to explain further, but when I don't say more, she demands, "And?"

"And she's obviously using this campaign to further her own goals."

Her forehead wrinkles. "Her own goals to fight kidney disease?"

I slash a hand through the air. "No. Her photography career."

She tips her head back to stare at the ceiling for a few moments before returning her gaze to mine. Her eyes are spitting daggers at me.

"You're telling me you think Sofia Silva, the artist who currently has an exhibition at the Photography Museum, and who also happens to be Fifi Silva, famous fashion photographer, set up a campaign to raise awareness of kidney disease because it will further her own photography career?"

It sounds stupid when she puts it this way. "She wants to make you the poster child for the campaign," I remind her.

She opens her arms wide. "Do I look like I care?"

"You should. It shows she pities you."

"Again with the pity. I'm starting to think the person we should pity is you, because you, my dear brother, are a fool."

"If she isn't doing the campaign to further her career or because she pities you, why didn't she involve me? Or at least tell me what she was doing?"

"Let me count the ways." She holds up one finger. "One, this is about me, big brother, and not you." Another finger. "Two, she doesn't need to run every single thing in her life by you first. That's not how relationships work." Another finger. "And, finally, maybe she was being considerate because she knows how thin you're spread. You work three jobs in case you forgot."

"Maybe two after today."

She sighs. "Don't tell me Mats is going to fire you for being a grump."

I cringe. "I might have been a jerk to some of the waitstaff and customers."

She points to the door. "Go! Go apologize to Mats and your colleagues right now."

When I don't move, she wiggles her finger. "And afterwards, you can drive to The Hague and grovel at Sofia's feet."

I growl. "Sofia and I are done."

"Sofia loves you. Blind people can see how much she loves you. Not only did she befriend your sister—"

"Hey! Don't sell yourself short."

"I know. I know. I'm perfect in my own right. But most women in their early thirties would not be willing to deal with a boyfriend who's raising his little sister, let alone a little sister who's sick. And what does Sofia do? She pulls out all the stops to launch a campaign which may lead to me getting a functioning kidney."

She takes a deep breath and blows it out. "How you can stand to be in the same room with her is beyond me. She's obviously a horrible person."

I grab my hair with both hands and yank. "Fuck. I screwed up."

She crosses her arms over her chest and purses her lips in my direction like she's the adult and I'm the kid. "Yes, yes, you did. The question is how are you going to fix it?"

"Maybe I should let it go."

She snorts. "In case I forgot to mention it, it's also obvious to blind people how much you love Sofia."

My heart stalls before stuttering to life again. I clutch my chest. Love? Do I love Sofia? My heart rolls its eyes at me. Duh. Of course, you love her. Damnit. What have I done? I love Sofia, and I broke up with her. I need to fix this. But how?

Chapter 36

I trudge up the stairs to Abby's house and knock on the door. I don't want to be here. I don't feel like celebrating Abby's perfect promotion and her perfect life with her perfect family today.

Abby throws the door open with a huge smile on her face. "Thanks for doing this, Sofia."

"You do realize I'm entirely too expensive for this. You could easily find another photographer to take your headshots for half the price."

"And miss the opportunity to have my picture taken by the great Sofia Silva?" She winks.

"I use the name Fifi Silva for fashion photography."

"I know. I want my picture taken by the artist."

Damn. She scored some points with her comment. Judging by the grin of satisfaction on her face, she knows it, too.

"Come in. I'll give you a tour and then you can decide where you think the best place to take pictures is."

My mouth drops open as I follow her into the living room. The ceilings are at least twelve feet high and decorated with ceiling cornices. On the floor, the parquet flooring is laid out in a herringbone pattern. The street side of the room has a large bay window, above which is a stained glass window. The light shines through the stained glass causing prisms to appear randomly throughout the room.

"This room is too busy for a picture, I think," Abby says and continues to the dining room, which is connected to the living room with pocket doors. The pocket doors have cut-outs with stained glass, which match the front windows.

"This might work," she says as she points to the wall of bookshelves behind the oak dining room table.

I have her pose while I take a few snaps. I lower my camera and study the pictures. "I don't think I've ever seen you wear a shirt that wasn't a t-shirt before."

"Stupid board and their stupid 'make sure you appear professional in your headshot'-comments," Abby mutters.

Jasper saunters in holding little Olivier. Abby raises her hands and steps back. "Don't you dare. He already spit up on me twice this morning."

She looks at me. "Welcome to the glamorous life of a mother with a two-month-old."

Sylvia runs into the room. Her hands are covered in a white substance. She lifts her arms to be picked up by Abby.

Abby glares at her husband. "You planned this, didn't you? You know this is the one day in my entire life I need to appear professional and stay clean."

Jasper chuckles. "I planned your daughter to be experimenting with flour in the kitchen? I must be awfully clever."

Abby's face softens. "You sure are. You married me, didn't you?"

"Knocking you up was the best mistake of my life."

"What's knocked up?" Sylvia asks.

Abby squats down. "It's like—"

"No," Jasper shouts before grasping Sylvia's hand and dragging her toward the door. "You are not giving our two-and-a-half-year-old the sex talk."

"What's sex?" I hear the little girl ask as they leave.

Abby wipes her hands on her pants. "And that, Sofia, is how you get rid of your husband and children."

"You're evil," I tell her.

"An evil genius." She winks. "Come on. The kitchen might be a good place for a picture. It shows I'm more than the Chief Technology Officer."

The kitchen is open to the living room. Abby skirts the enormous marble island and comes to a screeching halt. "Um, I think we'll skip the kitchen."

I peer over her shoulder to see the floor is covered in flour.

"The caterers are going to love me," she mumbles.

Abby is throwing a party this afternoon to celebrate her promotion. Because it's October in Holland – meaning rain is a near certainty – she's set up a tent in their backyard where I can see people bustling around preparing for the party.

We continue through the hallway and up the stairs. I stop her. "These stairs are gorgeous. Let me get a few pictures of you here."

The staircase is traditionally styled with oak treads, a woven patterned runner, and Edwardian spindles. Oak wainscotting decorates the wall behind the stairs. It's the perfect background for a professional headshot.

"I didn't figure you for a traditional girl," I comment as I snap away. Her penthouse at the apartment building was ultra-modern and sleek.

"It's my first home," she answers with a shrug.

I lower my camera and review the pictures I've already taken. "I think I have something useable if you need to get ready for the party."

"I'm pretty much ready. Besides, I want some pictures of me in my office."

I follow her up two flights of stairs to the attic. When I enter the area, I don't think I'm still in the same house. This room is filled to the brim with computer monitors and sleek office furniture.

"I know. I know. A completely different vibe up here, isn't it?"

Abby looks right at home here. "Sit at your desk.

Let me work my magic."

I spend the next half an hour taking pictures of Abby in various poses – behind the desk, next to the desk, glasses on, glasses off – the usual variety until Jasper arrives with a screaming baby.

"You can't brush me off this time, *mijn schat.* Someone's hungry."

Abby immediately reaches for the buttons of her blouse. I back away. "I'll see you downstairs," I say before fleeing the room.

Don't get me wrong. I have no problem with nursing mothers, but I prefer not to see my friends topless.

There are already a few guests in the tent when I arrive. Avery waves me over to where she's standing with Niels.

"How did it go?" she whispers.

"Great. I think I have several photographs she'll be able to use."

Her face falls. "Oh."

I giggle. "What did you expect?"

"You never know with Abby. Speak of the devil."

Abby strolls into the tent. She's changed into a t-shirt and ripped jeans. Her t-shirt says *just a girl boss building her empire.* It's not wrong. The rest of the girl gang and their entourage follow behind her.

Abby grabs a tray of champagne and orange juice from a waiter before joining us. She hands out the drinks before lifting a glass of orange juice. "To me!"

Avery clutches her arm to stop her from drinking. "I don't think you're supposed to toast yourself."

"Actually," Mia says, "I don't think there's any taboo or bad luck associated with toasting to yourself. Toasting with water, on the other hand, is definitely bad luck. The Ancient Greeks would drink from the River Lethe in the Underworld in order to forget their past, corporeal lives. Thus, toasting with water is akin to wishing bad luck or death upon the person toasted."

Matthijs kisses her forehead. "My little history geek."

Char raises her glass. "I think we can all agree the modest train doesn't stop at Abby's house. Now, let's toast before Tobias decides to take a dive into the chocolate fountain buck naked."

I lift my glass and sip my champagne. When I see who's entering the tent, I nearly spit it out. I slam my glass down on a table and snatch Abby's hand to drag her away.

"What's going on?" Avery asks as her gaze darts around the tent.

"Rafael's here," Mia whispers.

"Told you. Once you go Dutch, you won't want another man's touch," Niels sings, and I give him the finger behind my back.

As soon as we've reached a quiet corner of the tent, I hiss at Abby, "If your nose were as big as you are nosy, you wouldn't be able to fit through doors."

She wags her finger at me. "For your information, I didn't invite him."

I cross my arms over my chest. I don't believe her for one second.

"He's the one who called me."

My stomach clenches at her words. Rafael called her? And not me?

"Geez. Get the puppy dog look off your face. He called me to arrange a meet with you since he thought you wouldn't answer a call from him." She steps closer. "Would you have answered if he rang you?"

Huh. I think about it. I don't know. I've checked my phone about a million times in the two weeks since Rafael cast me aside like yesterday's trash. But would I have actually picked up the phone if he called? No idea.

"Yeah. Exactly what I thought."

Enough of this. "You couldn't have arranged for us to meet somewhere less public?"

She opens her arms wide to indicate her backyard. "This isn't a public setting."

"You know what I mean." I indicate all of the people milling around, most of whom are not bothering to hide their curiosity at our conversation.

She smirks. "And miss the explosion? You have met me, right?"

She puts her hands on my shoulders and whirls me around. "Now, go get 'em tiger." She shoves me toward the corner where Rafael is waiting for me.

"What the hell are you doing here?" I shout when I'm halfway there.

The chatter dies down, and I feel the gaze of everyone in the tent on me. Ugh. I couldn't keep my mouth shut until I reached him? Whatever.

I shackle his wrist and tug him toward the exit.

"The guest bedroom has clean sheets," Abby shouts after us.

I give her a one-finger salute.

Chapter 37

Rafael

Sofia is trembling with anger as she drags me out of the tent and into Abby's house. She glances around as if searching for a good place to give me a piece of her mind. But then she notices everyone outside is gathered at the entrance to watch us. She glares at them before grabbing my hand once again and drawing me further into the house.

"No, this isn't going to work," she says as she stands at the bottom of the stairs. "I can't trust Abby hasn't put listening equipment in the house. After all, she knew you were going to show up today."

"I didn't put listening equipment in the spare bedroom," Abby shouts.

I chuckle. "Your friends are seriously crazy."

Sofia doesn't respond to Abby's statement and instead asks, "Do you have your car?"

We pile into my car and head to her apartment building. While we drive, Sofia drums her fingers on her thigh. She's nervous. She's not alone.

Once we're in her apartment, she sets her camera and the accompanying equipment in her spare bedroom before marching to the kitchen and opening the refrigerator. She removes a bottle of wine for herself and a bottle of beer for me.

"Sit. Spill," she orders, but before I can respond she lets me have it. "I can't believe you crashed Abby's party. What were you thinking? You broke my heart and then show up at a party like it's no big deal."

Damn. I really hurt her. "I broke your heart?" I

whisper.

She ignores me. "This is not okay, you know. This violates the break-up etiquette."

She takes a gulp of her wine while I wait for her to run out of steam. "Aren't you going to say anything?"

"I was waiting for my turn."

"Don't be a smartass. It's not attractive."

I sigh. "Sorry."

"Is that all you have to say for yourself? Sorry?"

"I—" Sofia cuts me off again. I should have known she wasn't done yet.

"First, you tell me I pity you and you don't need my charity and then you accuse me of using your sister for my own gain. How I could possibly gain from finding a kidney for your sister is beyond me. Are you mental?"

Her chest heaves as she glares at me. My pants tighten at the sight of her perky breasts moving up and down. I tell my cock to calm the eff down. Now is not the time to try and get into Sofia's pants. She certainly wouldn't welcome an advance right now.

"Can I explain?"

She flicks her wrist at me.

"I'm an idiot." She snorts. "The world's biggest idiot. I panicked when you told me about the campaign." I gulp before admitting, "In all honesty, I feel guilty for not doing something similar before. Maybe if I had, Mieke would have the kidney she needs already and she wouldn't have spent the past years in and out of the hospital."

The guilt is what caused me to become a raging lunatic. It took me a while to realize it and admit it to myself, but guilt is what pushed me over the top and made me do the stupidest thing I've ever done in my life – walk away from the woman I love.

"You're a bigger idiot than I thought. And I already thought you were pretty much the biggest idiot in the world."

I grunt. She's not wrong.

She takes my hands in hers. "You have worked yourself to the bone making sure Mieke has everything she needs. No one – least of all Mieke – expects you to do more than you already do."

I frown. "Mieke said the same thing when I complained you didn't involve me in the campaign planning."

Her brow raises. "You're mad I didn't involve you? I thought you would be too busy."

I groan. "Mieke said that, too. I'm going to be hearing I told you so from her for the rest of my life."

"Does this mean you realize I'm not taking advantage of Mieke to further my career?"

I place my forehead against hers. Relief fills me when she doesn't move away. "As Mieke also pointed out, I'm an idiot for thinking a campaign about live kidney donation would help your career in any way."

"Your sister obviously got all the smart genes in the family."

I chuckle. "She also pointed another thing out to me."

"What?"

"She said it's obvious I love you." I wasn't planning on confessing my love to Sofia, but it feels right.

Her breath hitches and her eyes widen. "You do?"

I thread my hands through her hair. "How can I not love you, gorgeous? You're everything to me. You're fun, interesting, a little bit of a cynic, and are taking the world by storm with your art. You also love my sister. Not because she's my sister but because Mieke is her own person. And you're doing everything in your power to help her. Plus, you're sexy as hell and one look at you has me hard."

I lower my head until my lips meet hers. "I want to kiss these lips every day for the rest of my life."

I bite her bottom lip and then sweep my tongue

across it. She climbs onto my lap and cradles my face with her hands.

"I love you, too, you big idiot," she whispers against my lips.

I lean back to gaze into her eyes. "You do? After all the idiotic things I've done?"

She giggles. "Apparently, I'm a sucker for an idiot."

I close my eyes and drop my forehead against her chest. "Thank you. Thank you for forgiving me. And thank you for giving me your love."

She palms my neck and squeezes until I lift my head. "Don't thank me for loving you. Show me how you feel."

I growl and my cock twitches at the idea. I don't waste any time ripping her shirt off of her. She's wearing another lacy white bra. I'm almost tempted to leave it on. The sight of her breasts straining against the lace material drives me wild. But I want to put my hands on her soft skin.

I reach around and unsnap her bra before dragging the straps down her arms. I moan when her rosy nipples are exposed.

"I love these," I say as I toy with her nipples.

"You don't think my breasts are too small?"

I grin up at her. "Not at all. They're perky and perfectly shaped for my hands." I wink. "Or my mouth."

With her on my lap, her breasts are at the perfect height for my mouth to devour them. I suck on her nipple until it forms a hard peak. Sofia uses her hold on my head to keep my mouth right where she wants it.

"More," she groans.

I'm happy to oblige. I move to her other breast and nibble on her nipple. She undulates herself on my hard length and I punch my hips up. She grunts and throws her head back pushing her chest further into my face.

I grasp her hips and use my hold to help her roll herself against my cock.

"Oh god, Rafael. I could come like this."

"Then come, gorgeous."

She stills and her head tilts to stare down at me. "I want to come with you inside of me."

I smirk. "I can arrange that."

I help her to stand. She reaches to unbutton her pants, but I stop her. "That's my job."

I kneel before her and slide her pants down her legs. I take my time, enjoying watching the goosebumps my hands on her skin create. She steps out of her pants, and I stare up at this beauty clothed in a mere scrap of lace panties.

"If I were the photographer in the family, I'd take a picture of you like this, gorgeous. You look like a goddess staring down at the mere mortals below her."

She grasps my shoulders and attempts to force me to stand. "I'm not a goddess. I'm impatient is what I am."

"You're also not naked yet."

I slip my hands under the lace at the side of her panties before ever so slowly drawing them down her legs. She shivers and I lower my chin to keep my grin hidden from her. I slide my hands up her legs as I stand.

"My turn."

I worry she'll torture me like I've done to her, but it seems I've got her too worked up for her to want to slow down. She tears my t-shirt off of me. She licks her lips as she stares at my chest. I can't help but puff it out to show it off to her.

She sighs before reaching for my jeans and popping the first button off before lowering the zipper. It's slow going with my hard cock making my jeans tighter than normal. She licks her lips when my pants are open, and the head of my cock is revealed poking its head out of my boxers.

She shoves my boxers down before fisting my cock and pumping up and down twice before releasing me to push my jeans and boxers the rest of the way down my legs. Once my clothes are around my ankles, she shoves me until I fall onto the sofa.

"Don't you want to go to the bedroom?" I ask despite not wanting to move from where I am.

She climbs onto my lap and rubs her core against me. I groan and squeeze her hips to stop her movement.

"Condom. Wallet. Back pocket." She's reduced me to talking in sound bites.

"I'm on birth control."

I kiss her nose. "Thank you for giving me your trust, but I won't abuse it. I'll get tested before I enter you bare."

She hesitates a second before reaching down to get my wallet and retrieving the condom. "May I?"

I may come before she gets the damn thing on me, but I nod. Whatever she wants, she can have. The idiot has left the building. Hopefully, for good.

She tugs on my cock a few times before rolling the condom on me. Then, she situates herself above me. She doesn't hesitate to lower herself on me until I'm fully seated in her wet warmth.

My head falls back, and I let out a long groan. She lifts up but I grasp her hips to stop her. "If you don't slow down, I'm going to finish before you."

The crazy woman leans forward and nips my ear before whispering, "Race you."

She uses her hold on my shoulders to lift and lower herself on me while contracting her inner muscles to squeeze my cock. Is she trying to ensure I win this race? Two can play at this game. I sneak one hand between us to find the hard nub of her clit. I rub against it while my mouth descends to play with her nipple.

"Yes, like that," she moans as I bite her nipple.

"I'm going to… I'm nearly …"

"Come, gorgeous. Come all over my cock."

"Rafael," she shouts as her movements become jerky and her inner muscles squeeze my cock harder than ever.

I wait until her orgasm wanes before I start thrusting up into her. I use my hold on her hips to keep her where I want her as the telltale tingle in my spine tells me I'm nearly there.

"I love you," I shout when my release hits me. My thrusts become shallow as I come down from my high.

She collapses on my chest. "Love you, too, idiot."

Chapter 38

I wake when I feel Rafael lift his arm off of me and roll out of bed. I groan. Not this again.

"You aren't trying to sneak off, are you?" I ask without bothering to open my eyes.

He chuckles and I open my eyes to find him standing at the side of the bed deliciously naked and smiling down at me.

"No, gorgeous. I was going to surprise you with breakfast in bed."

"Joke's on you. Unless you're planning to make a breakfast of protein bars and wine, you're out of luck."

He kneels on the bed to lean down and kiss my forehead. "I guess I'll have to take you out to brunch instead."

"Don't you need to get back to Mieke?"

"Nope. Mieke kicked me out of the house with instructions to 'fix my screw up'. I'm not supposed to come back until tonight."

I sit up in bed. "But Sunday is your day to do stuff together. I can tag along. I don't want her to be alone."

"She's not alone. Laura from the apartment building is with her."

"Which means we have the entire day to spend together." I waggle my eyebrows. "I have some ideas."

I grab his hand and he topples on the bed onto me.

"I can get on board with this plan," he says before he sinks his fingers in my hair and his lips find mine.

An hour later, Rafael tries to sneak out of bed

again.

"This is becoming a pattern."

He yanks the sheets off of me. "Get up. Get showered and dressed. I'm worried the neighbors are going to call the police about a monster in your apartment if we don't feed your stomach soon."

I pose on the bed like those models I photographed for the sexy magazine that shall remain unnamed. "Don't you want to stay in bed all day? We can order take-out. I'll let you eat in my bed."

He smirks. "I've already eaten in your bed."

I throw a pillow at him. "Dork."

"Come on. I've got an entire day planned."

Okay. Now, I'm curious.

Thirty minutes later, we're sitting at the café down the street from the apartment building where I first met Abby, Mia, and Avery.

"Let's hear this itinerary then." I lift my camera. "I brought my camera as instructed." Like I ever leave the house without it.

"If you hadn't ordered a second coffee, we'd be on our way already."

I mock outrage as I draw my coffee cup near. "Do not get in between me and my caffeine fix."

"You could have gotten it to go."

"And have Abby lecture me about single use plastic again? No thanks."

He looks around the café. "Abby's not here."

He doesn't understand. "Trust me. Abby always finds out." I gulp the rest of my coffee and stand. "I'm ready."

He stares at me. "Did you burn your throat?"

"As if." I scoff. "Try drinking tea in Russia some time. The country may be cold, but they drink their tea hot as Hades."

An hour later, Rafael parks next to a large visitor's

center.

"Where are we?" I ask because despite my needling him, he hasn't divulged any information about his plans for the day.

He steps out of the car and walks around to open my door for me. He wraps an arm around my shoulder before spinning me around. "This is why we're here."

I gasp when I see the view of the windmills along the dyke.

"This is the *Kinderdijk*."

I've heard of the *Kinderdijk*. It's a world heritage site containing nineteen monumental windmills. I've wanted to come here for ages but it's hard to reach without a car. And me not having a car is the only reason Abby didn't string me up by my entrails the time she found me with a to-go cup of coffee. The woman takes saving the planet to extremes.

I squeal. "This is awesome. Thank you."

I don't hear his reply as I'm already snapping pictures.

He taps me on the shoulder. "The view from the roof above the visitor's center is supposed to be amazing."

We spend the next hour strolling around the area while I take tons of pictures. I'm surprised by how clean everything is. Despite the number of tourists traipsing around, I don't see a scrap of trash on the ground, because of course, I'm looking. Photographing trash is my thing after all.

"You ready for our next stop?" Rafael asks when I finally lower my camera.

"There's more?"

He chuckles. "There's more," he says as he takes my hand and leads me back to the car.

We drive in the direction of The Hague, but Rafael takes an exit for the center of Rotterdam. "I know you don't photograph buildings, but I thought you might make an exception for this," he says as he parks.

"And what is 'this' exactly?"

He doesn't bother to respond to my question. He takes my hand, and we exit the carpark into the sunshine before turning left. "What are those?" I ask when I see a row of yellow cubes tilted on their sides and resting on hexagon-shaped pylons.

"Our next destination – the cube houses. There are thirty-eight small cubes and two larger ones. They're all attached to each other. Each house contains three floors and is about 1,000 square feet but around a quarter of the space is unusable because of the angle of the walls and ceilings."

"You sound like a tour guide."

His cheeks darken. "I may have done a bit of research before today. We can visit one if you like."

"No need. I'd like to take some pictures, though."

"That's what we're here for."

I snap several pictures as we head toward the houses. Once we arrive, I realize the best angle is from the ground. My fingers tingle in excitement when I lay on the ground at the center of the houses and discover this isn't the best angle, it's the perfect angle.

"Remind me to carry a blanket in the car for when you decide to lay on the filthy ground," Rafael grumbles as he helps me get to my feet.

I brush the dirt off my jeans. "I'm used to it. Do you not remember the first time you saw me photographing I was standing in a field covered in cow shit?"

He grasps my chin. "I don't care if you're used to it. I don't want you to get dirty if you don't have to."

"What? You don't like me dirty?" I give him a saucy wink before pushing up on my toes to peck his mouth. Rafael threads his fingers through my hair and holds me close to nibble at my lips.

I tug him near causing my camera to dig into my ribs. "Ow."

Rafael jumps back. "What's wrong? Did you hurt

yourself on the ground?"

"Enough with the laying on the ground thing. I forgot about my camera is all."

He waggles his eyebrows. "You were blinded by passion."

I tilt my head back and burst into laughter. After two weeks of thinking I lost this man, I am bursting with joy at having him here with me making corny jokes. He smiles as he watches me and happiness beams from his eyes.

"There's one more place I want to show you and then it's time for lunch," he says as he takes my hand.

"Lead the way."

We walk a block to a small harbor.

"This is the *Oude Haven* or the old harbor. The first jetty was built here around 1350, making it the oldest port in Rotterdam." He points to a white building across the water. "This is the *Witte Huis,* aka the White House, the first skyscraper in Europe."

"Is it art nouveau?" I mumble my question as I study the harbor and White House through my viewfinder.

"Yes, it is. It was constructed in 1889."

I take a few pictures of the old barges in the harbor and the White House. The area is unique looking with its historical buildings, but like I said, I'm not much for taking pictures of buildings. It doesn't take long for me to finish.

"Now, I'll feed you," Rafael announces.

We return to where the car is parked, but instead of going down into the carpark, we enter a horseshoe structure.

"This is the *markthal.* Look up."

I'm already looking up. The doom of the building is adorned with artwork showing enlarged fruits, vegetables, seeds, fish, flowers, and insects in bright colors. I take a few pictures but without my specialized equipment, I won't be able to capture the essence of the artwork.

"What do you want to eat? Fish, Greek, pizza,

Lebanese, tapas, ramen, Middle-Eastern, Chinese, Japanese..."

I hold up my hand. "Whoa. Did you memorize all the restaurants in this place?"

He points to a legend. "Sorry to disappoint."

"I vote for Basque. I could go for some *pinchos*." I love the tapas from Northern Spain.

We find the place and settle at a table right inside the restaurant where we can watch the people moseying around the market. When our glasses of Tempranillo arrive, I raise mine and indicate for Rafael to do the same.

"Thank you for making today a special day."

We clink glasses.

"Of course, gorgeous. I want to make every day special. I love you."

His words and lack of hesitation to say them cause my heart to tumble in my chest. Nice and dependable can take a hike, because I love this man. This gorgeous, sometimes infuriating man who has the biggest heart in the world.

Chapter 39

Rafael sighs as he opens a box of campaign posters. "Mieke is going to think she's a star with 10,000 posters of her face hanging up everywhere in the country."

I slap his shoulder. "Mieke is a star."

"And she won't let me forget it," he grumbles.

"Can we talk about how using posters like this is going to ruin the environment?" Abby asks.

Char frowns at her. "We're trying to save Mieke's life. Can't you give it a rest for a minute?"

"Uh oh. Someone woke the crusader," I whisper to Rafael.

"Do you know how many people have been killed due to climate change? The forest fires, the cyclones, the hurricanes—"

"Abby," I cut her off before she can give us a ninety-minute lecture on saving the planet. She has a PowerPoint presentation and everything. "I contracted the green printer you recommended. The soy and vegetable-based inks they use are non-toxic and recyclable. And the paper is one-hundred percent biodegradable."

"Oh." Her shoulders drop and her lips purse. "I guess it's okay then."

"I'm more concerned with the legality of putting posters up everywhere in the city," Avery says.

Niels wraps his arm around her shoulder and kisses her hair. "There's my little uptight attorney I fell in love with."

"Can you be serious for one second?"

He rolls his eyes. "Fine. How's this for serious? In

the city, there are designated billboard areas where anyone can post a sign. Additionally, you can put a sign in the window of a store as long as you have permission from the owner of the store. Satisfied?"

"Give me a box." Mia motions to the stack of boxes in the corner of my apartment. "I'm going to put them up at school. I've also talked to teachers at the International School and the British School. They'll put up posters, too."

Before anyone can hand Mia a box, Matthijs is there taking one. "You are due to have our baby girl any minute. You will not be carrying a box. It's bad enough you're still working."

Mia plants her fists on her hips and glares at him. There's practically steam coming out of her nostrils and ears. "I am not an invalid. I'm pregnant. Women have been having babies since the beginning of the species. You know in China women had babies in the fields and then went back to working."

"Yeah, yeah, we all read *The Good Earth* in high school. I thought Pearl S. Buck was a man for the longest time. She's actually this really interesting woman who grew up in China the daughter of missionaries. Her life is quite fascinating. Come to think of it, it would make a good movie."

Nico chuckles at Char's long-winded reply to Mia. "Your motormouth is sexy."

"What else do you find sexy about her?" Abby asks, and I groan.

I hold up my hands. "No! We aren't talking about sexy stuff. We're here to get these posters divided up and talk about the next steps in the campaign."

Abby frowns. "But Jasper is babysitting the kids and isn't here to stop me. This is my only chance to hear the details from the horse's mouth."

I ignore her to address Avery, "Do you foresee any issues with me being a guest on a talk show?"

When I mentioned the campaign to the curator at the photography museum, she got me in touch with an

English-language radio station. I have an interview scheduled there next week. I'm also a guest on a late-night talk show on a Dutch television program. I can thank Mama for arranging it. The woman has admirers everywhere. It's about time I take advantage of them instead of the other way around.

Rafael's phone rings and he exits the room to answer it in private.

"Do you have the receipts for the printing?" Char asks when he's left the room.

"They were a bit more than we budgeted due to the eco-friendly materials and printing, which our investor insisted on." I tilt my head toward Abby.

Rafael dashes into the room. "*Ik moet gaan.*"

I look to Niels to translate. "He needs to leave."

I grab Rafael's hand before he can run off. "What's wrong? What's going on?"

"Mieke. Hospital," is all he manages to say.

I survey the room. I need to go with Rafael, but I can't leave all this work for my friends to finish. Abby takes charge and, for once, I'm not going to bitch about it. She places her hands on my shoulders and pushes me to the door.

"Go. We'll take care of this."

"Thank you," I shout as I rush out of the door after Rafael.

"What's happening?" I ask once we're in the car flying down the highway.

"Mieke collapsed and Esmay couldn't wake her. She called an ambulance. They're on their way to the hospital now."

Damnit. This is bad. Very bad. Mieke has been getting weaker and weaker over the past month. Every time I try and bring the subject up with Rafael, he shuts me down. I get it. Talking about the end of life choices for a loved one can't be easy. But decisions will have to be made.

Now is not the time, however. I reach across the console and squeeze his thigh. He grabs hold of my hand and doesn't let go until we arrive in Amsterdam.

"Fuck!" Rafael swears when we arrive at the hospital and the parking lot is full.

"Pull up to the ER. I'll park the car and find you later."

He doesn't hesitate to do as I suggest. He screeches to a halt and jumps out of the car without another word spoken.

Between finding a spot in the parking garage and walking back to the hospital, a good thirty minutes have passed by the time I return to the emergency room. When I arrive, Rafael is pacing the room.

"Where's Mieke? What do you know?"

He shoves his hands into his hair and yanks at the strands. "Nothing. I don't know anything yet."

I spot Esmay sitting on a plastic chair in the corner. "What happened?" I ask after a quick hug.

"We were talking, and she said she didn't feel too good. I asked what I can do, but she collapsed on the floor before she could answer." She clutches my hands. "I couldn't wake her up."

Pressure builds behind my eyes, but I won't succumb to tears now. I need to be strong for Rafael. "Has anyone come out to tell you how she's doing?"

She shakes her head. "We're still waiting."

The minutes crawl by as we wait for news on Mieke. I try to get Rafael to eat a sandwich or at least drink a cup of soup, but he's not interested.

Nearly an hour later, a woman enters the waiting room and announces, "Rafael van Dijk?"

I jump to my feet to stand next to Rafael. He clutches my hand in his. "How is she? How is my sister?"

She frowns. "Why don't you come with me to my office where we can talk in private?"

I step back when Rafael moves to follow her. I don't want to interfere. But Rafael refuses to release my hand. He tows me behind him until we reach a small office. I force him to sit in a chair before taking the seat next to him.

"I'm afraid it isn't good news," the doctor begins. "Mieke needs a new kidney sooner rather than later."

Rafael's hand spasms in mine. The pressure behind my eyes is nearly blinding now, but I will remain strong for Rafael.

"What about dialysis?" I ask when Rafael remains quiet.

"Unfortunately, at some point, dialysis is no longer a viable option. We've reached that point with Mieke."

"How long?" Rafael grits out.

"Weeks if we're lucky."

He swallows before standing. "Can we see her now?"

"Of course."

The doctor leads us through the corridor until we reach a curtained off area. "They'll be here soon to move her to a hospital bed," she says as she parts the curtain.

I stumble when I see Mieke laying on the bed. She's practically hidden by the amount of machines she's hooked up to. Rafael drops my hand to rush to her side.

"Mieke," he says as he takes her hand. "Talk to me."

I stand on the other side of Mieke's bed. She groans. "I'm sleepy."

Rafael's sigh of relief fills the room. "You're lazy is what you are," he teases.

"Hey girl," I greet.

The corners of her lips tip up the smallest amount. "Sofia. You're here."

"Of course, I'm here. You're my girl. Where else would I be?"

The curtain slides open behind us, and I glance over my shoulder to see an orderly and nurse step inside the area.

"I'm sorry, but we need to move the patient now," one of them says.

"Mieke," Rafael insists. "Her name is Mieke."

"Sorry. Yes. Of course. We need to move Mieke. You can visit her upstairs once she's settled."

I kiss Mieke's cheek. "See you upstairs."

Rafael clutches Mieke's hand. I move to him and place my hands on his shoulders. "We need to let the staff do their job," I tell him.

He takes a deep breath before leaning over and kissing his sister's forehead. "Behave."

"Never."

I wrap my arm around Rafael's waist and direct him out of the room. Once we're in the hallway, I survey the area before I notice a family bathroom. I push Rafael inside and lock the door behind us.

"We're alone," I tell him. "Mieke can't hear you in here."

He wraps his arms around me, and his body shakes with sobs. My legs give out from under me, and we fall to the floor. I lean against the door as he cries against my chest. I soothe my hand down his back as he lets out all the fear and frustration he's feeling.

When his cries wane, I tell him, "This isn't the end, you know. We're going to find a kidney for Mieke. There are more than seven billion people on this planet. Someone, somewhere is a match and willing to donate. We will find them."

He takes a deep breath before sitting up. I hand him some toilet paper and he wipes his face. "I'm sorry. I bet sitting in a family bathroom with your boyfriend blubbering all over you is the last place you want to be today."

I palm his neck and bring his face close to mine.

"There's nowhere I'd rather be." And I'm not lying.

Chapter 40

I'm reviewing some photographs on my laptop when I hear Mieke stir.

"What are you doing?" she asks. Her breaths are shallow, but I know better than to remark on it after several weeks of her being in the hospital. She does not appreciate or need my concern. Her words.

"Editing some of my work." I close the laptop. "Am I allowed to ask how you're feeling or are you going to take my head off?"

She sticks her tongue out at me. "I'm fine."

Fine is her standard answer. I'm about done with her being 'fine'. I'm ready for her to be a normal teenager who shouts at me when I ask how she's doing and then stomps off before slamming her bedroom door in my face.

"Where's Rafael?"

"At the bar."

It took a lot of persuading and some yelling, but I finally convinced Rafael he needed to get back to work. He didn't want to leave Mieke alone, no matter how much she begged him to leave already. The argument was finally settled when I reminded him I'd be here with Mieke whenever he's gone anyway.

"Good. We need to finish watching *To All the Boys: Always and Forever.*"

I groan to cover up my relief at her question. Mieke hasn't been feeling up to doing much, not even watch movies, for the past week. If she wants to watch a film, we're watching a film. At this point, I'd let her watch pretty much whatever she wants. Even those horror films that scare the hell out of me.

"Do we have to?"

Mieke giggles and it's the sweetest sound in the world. A sound I will do anything to continue to hear for decades to come.

"I know you love the movies."

"I do not!" I feign being indignant.

She raises an eyebrow. "Then why did I find the books on your kindle when you lent it to me."

Because I bought the books for her. I don't tell her the truth, though. I look away and pretend to be embarrassed, which causes Mieke to giggle again.

I get the film queued and we settle in to watch it. My phone rings fifteen minutes later and I pause the movie to answer it.

"Hi Mia! Are you okay?"

"It's not Mia. It's Abby."

"What are you doing with Mia's phone?"

"She gave it to me to call everyone because someone's having her baby!"

I rest the phone against my chest to tell Mieke, "Mia's having her baby." Her eyes widen and she gives me two thumbs-up.

I return to my conversation with Abby. "Yeah! How is she doing?"

"She's fine." She snorts. "Matthijs not so much."

"We knew he'd freak out when she went into labor."

"Get this. Mia is insisting on having her baby at the VU."

I wrinkle my brow. "The *Vrije Universiteit*? In Amsterdam? Where we are? But why?"

"She wants Mieke to be able to meet the baby."

My eyes itch and I turn away from Mieke so she can't see my reaction. Mia wants to have her baby here because she thinks Mieke won't be around to see her baby otherwise. Fucking hell.

"Stop it," Abby growls into my ear. "Mieke is going to make it. This is merely a precaution."

"How do you know what I'm thinking?"

"Maybe because I'm sitting in a car with two other women who have the same stupid concerns." She scoffs. "We will find Mieke a kidney before it's too late."

I can't talk about whether we'll find Mieke a kidney. Last month when we launched the campaign, I had such high hopes. After I was on a popular talk show, the calls came rushing in. But there were precious few people who actually went to their doctor to discuss live kidney transplants. And none of those were a match.

"You're all on your way to the hospital?" I ask.

"Of course, we are. We're not going to miss Matthijs losing his mind when Mia's labor pains hit."

"And we want to see the baby girl when she's born," Avery shouts.

"Gotta go. We're here," Abby says and hangs up without further ado.

I stare at my phone. "The girl gang has arrived."

Mieke's smile stretches from ear to ear. At the sight, I want to kiss Mia for making this happen.

Abby is the first one to arrive fifteen minutes later. "I come bearing gifts," she announces and hands Mieke a paper bag.

Mieke opens the bag and screeches in delight at what she sees.

"You better have not brought her smutty magazines. I won't hold Rafael back when he decides to murder you for corrupting his little sister."

Abby rolls her eyes. "Welcome to the twenty-first century, Sofia. No one needs smutty magazines anymore. There's this thing called the Internet. It's pretty cool. You should check it out."

I stick my tongue out at her before asking Mieke, "What did she bring you?"

Mieke bites her lip. "Promise you won't be mad."

"I promise if I'm mad, I'll be mad at Abby, not you." It's the best I can do.

She opens the bag and shows me the contents. My eyes widen when I see it's filled to the brim with Dutch black licorice. Licorice she's not allowed to eat because some unpronounceable ingredient in it increases blood pressure.

I take a deep breath to stop myself from lecturing her. No one wins if I go into lecture mode. "Here's the deal. I won't tell Rafael as long as you let me control the bag." Mieke opens her mouth to reply but I hold up a hand to stop her. "I'll let you have three pieces a day." She glares at me. "It's the only deal I'm offering. Take it or leave it."

She stuffs a piece of licorice in her mouth before handing me the bag with her eyes narrowed.

"Sorry. Life sucks sometimes." And in her case, a lot more than sometimes.

Avery is next to arrive. She's also carrying a gift bag. I groan. "If you give Mieke licorice too, I'm going to lose my mind."

Her brow wrinkles. "You made us read those information pamphlets on what she's allowed to eat. Of course, I didn't bring her licorice." She smiles at Mieke. "I brought you some of those graphic novels we talked about. I know you can read them online, but it's not the same."

Mieke rips the packaging open, and her eyes widen. "These are the latest ones I haven't had a chance to read yet. Thank you."

Avery inclines her head. "You're welcome."

"What did I miss?" Char asks as she enters the room. "Nothing's happening yet with Mia's baby." She hands Mieke a piece of paper. "This is from Tobias. He drew it for you. Don't ask me what it is. Rembrandt, he is not."

Mieke props the drawing on a flower vase on her

side table. "Tell Tobias I said thank you."

Abby's phone pings and she reads the message. "Time to get a move on. Jasper says Mia is screaming at Matthijs to get the hell out of her room." She rubs her hands. "Let the fun begin." She blows us air kisses before leaving.

"I can't miss this," Char says and follows us.

Avery sighs. "It's like the two of them think giving birth is a television show. I blame reality programs. If I ever get pregnant, I'm not telling anyone when I go into labor." She waves before leaving, too.

She's barely out of the room before a nurse arrives with a wheelchair. "Here we go."

"What's going on?"

"We're going to see the baby," Mieke says with a roll of her eyes.

I bite the inside of my cheek to stop myself from screaming no. Although Mieke has left her hospital bed a few times, I don't like it when she's not hooked up to all the machines that are prolonging her life.

"It could take hours before the baby arrives," I say instead.

She shrugs. "And when I get tired, I'll let you know, and you can bring me back up here."

"Promise me you'll tell me if you're tired or not feeling well," I order.

"Yes, ma'am." She salutes.

We get her situated in the wheelchair, which is no small task, before heading off in search of the maternity ward.

"It's the second floor," Mieke says when we enter the elevator.

"How do you know?"

She shrugs. "I like to look at the babies when I can't sleep."

"Who doesn't?" I say as I push the button for the

second floor.

We don't need to ask which way when the elevator doors open. "Matthijs de Vries if you don't stop being overbearing this minute, I will have you removed from this room!"

"Shoot," Abby mutters when we enter the waiting room. "I figured she'd be swearing by now." She slaps a five euro bill into Char's hand.

The waiting room is packed to the gills. In addition to the girl gang, their partners are here as are several people I don't know.

Jasper, Niels, and Nico notice Mieke. They come over one by one to kiss her cheeks and check on how she's doing. Every single one of them has stopped by the hospital at least once a week since Mieke was admitted. I can't ever repay their kindness.

"Who are they?" I ask Avery as Niels jokes with Mieke.

"This is Matthijs' family. I didn't realize you hadn't met them." She takes my hand. "Come on, I'll introduce you."

Before I have the chance to move, Rafael rushes in. "What are you doing out of your room?" he shouts at Mieke who glares at him in response.

"I'm not a prisoner. I'm allowed to leave my room once in a while."

Before Rafael can answer, a tall bald guy approaches us. "Are you Mieke?" At her nod, he smiles. "I'm Wessel. Matthijs is my brother."

She waves at him. "Nice to meet you. This is my brother, Rafael. He's in the finale to compete with Matthijs as to who is the most overprotective."

Wessel chuckles as he shakes Rafael's hand. "I think I know who's going to win." He winks at Mieke as Rafael squeezes his hand.

"I'd like to talk to you," he says and Rafael growls. I pinch his side.

"Sure." Mieke grins up at him. "Do you want my autograph?"

Rafael wasn't wrong when he worried Mieke would become a star due to the campaign posters with her picture on them. She's become quite the social media icon.

"Um, no. I think I have something you want."

The chatter in the room dies down and my friends circle us.

Mieke appears confused. "You do? What's that?"

"I saw Sofia on the television program, and I got myself tested."

My heart clenches in my chest, and I cling to Rafael's hand.

"Turns out, I'm a match. I'd like to offer you my kidney."

My hands tremble, and tears form in my eyes. Mieke, on the other hand, is completely calm and controlled.

"I would be honored." Wessel smiles but she's not done. "As long as you assure me, the loss of one kidney won't affect your health or your work."

He drops to his knees in front of her wheelchair. "I promise you it won't. I have two healthy kidneys and I already talked to my employer about the donation. No worries there."

Mieke inclines her head. "Then, I accept your gracious offer."

Rafael stumbles and I throw my arms around him before he can crumble to the ground. I let the tears fall from my eyes. There's no way I can stop them now. A baby's cry echoes throughout the room, and I lift my head toward Mia's room.

"Two miracles in one day," I whisper. Best. Day. Ever.

Chapter 41

Rafael

My knee bounces up and down as I sit waiting for news on how Mieke's operation is progressing. Sitting is for the birds. I spring to my feet and pace the room. The kidney transplant operation should take three hours and it's already been two and a half. Why haven't we heard anything yet?

Sofia blocks my progress. "Do you want a coffee? Scratch that. How about an herbal tea?"

I shake my head. My stomach is in knots. The idea of food or drink is not appealing.

"How about some soup?"

I cup her cheeks and kiss her forehead. "I promise I'm fine, gorgeous."

She studies me for a moment before stepping back. "Feel free to return to your pacing then."

Before I can take another step, Joris, Matthijs and Wessel's father, claps me on the shoulder. "Let's take a walk."

"I—"

His hand tightens on my shoulder. "We won't get any news for at least another thirty minutes." He uses his hold on my shoulder to push me out of the room. We march down the corridor to the elevator and find ourselves outside in the interior courtyard of the hospital a few minutes later.

"Mr. De Vries," I start, but he lifts a hand to stop me from speaking.

"When Wessel came to us to tell us he was donating a kidney, I'm ashamed to say I tried to forbid it. I was afraid and it made me mad. But then he sat me down and forced me to watch Sofia's interview. To be honest, I got a little choked up when I heard Mieke's story. She was already dealt a shitty hand when her mom died and her dad abandoned her, but on top of that, she's sick."

I don't know why he's telling me this. I know this. I lived this.

"And then I realized there's another story here. A story about the brother who sacrificed to make certain his sister had everything she needed. Who didn't get to have a fun and carefree time in his twenties because he was basically a father to a sick teenager."

I glance away. "I didn't do anything more than anyone else would have done."

"Look at me, son." I face him. "What you did, what you're doing, for your sister is being a parent. I know you don't have a father anymore and I thought it was about time someone said this to you. I'm proud of you. I'm proud to know you. And I'm damn proud my son is donating a kidney to the girl you raised as your own."

I take a deep breath and blow out a puff of air before I break down and blubber like a child in front of this near stranger.

"Thank you, sir," I finally manage to say.

He slaps me on the shoulder. "It needed to be said. You ready to get back in there?"

I nod and we head toward the entrance together. Before we make it there, Matthijs opens the door and steps out. He glares at his dad. "If you made him feel bad about Wessel donating his kidney, I am going to be extremely disappointed in you."

Joris claps his son on the back. "As would I, son. As would I." He saunters off without a backward glance.

"You okay? My dad didn't give you too hard of a time, did he? He's worried about Wessel. I hope he didn't take it out on you."

"It's all good, man."

"What a relief. I had to hold Mia and Sofia back from coming after you two. One at a time, I can handle them. But when they gang up on me? I haven't got a chance. Especially when I can hear Abby and Avery plotting with Char." He shivers. "When Abby starts plotting, I start running."

The door flies open, and Jasper, Nico, and Niels rush outside.

"What's going on? Is there news about Wessel?" I gulp. "Or Mieke?"

"Wessel's out and in recovery. Mieke is still in surgery," Jasper says, and I feel some of the tension leave me.

"What's going on?"

"We're checking on you," Nico explains.

"Yeah, but we had to evade our women first. Those women are fast." Niels shivers.

Jasper glares at him. "You didn't need to throw Olivier at them."

"Hey! I was out of options."

Matthijs growls. "No one had better be throwing my daughter, Elin, around."

Niels raises his hands, palms out. "Dude. She's strapped to Mia's chest. She's as safe as she can be."

"There was no need for you guys to evade the women to check on me. I'm fine," I lie. I feel like I could crawl out of my skin at any moment.

Jasper cocks his eyebrow. "Fine? Hardly."

"I thought you were going to deck Matthijs' dad when he shoved you out of the waiting room," Nico adds.

"I wasn't going to deck him."

Niels shakes his head in disbelief. "Dude, your face was bright red and your hands fisted."

"As a police officer, I can attest those are definite signs of suppressed anger," Matthijs adds.

"Suppressed anger? I'm a lover, not a fighter."

Matthijs snorts. "Not a fighter? Maybe not physically but I dare anyone to stand in between you and your sister."

At his words, my hands fist.

Niels points to them and shouts. "Told ya!"

"Where's Sofia? How is she?" I ask because I'm not talking about whatever suppressed aggression they're accusing me of.

"She's fine. The girls have her. And we've got you."

Jasper's words surprise me. It's not like I've become close friends with the group of them. Frankly, I haven't had the time. Between working several jobs and Mieke in the hospital, I haven't had much time to spend alone with Sofia – except to fall asleep in bed the minute we get home – let alone time to spend with friends.

To be honest, most of my friends disappeared once I no longer had time to hang around with them. I don't blame them, but it does suck.

A hand slams against the window and I glance over my shoulder to see Sofia standing there.

"Now there's some not suppressed aggression right there," Matthijs mutters as he opens the door for her.

Sofia steps outside and places her hands on her hips as she stares down the men. "If you guys are giving Rafael a hard time, I promise I will make your lives miserable. And, trust me, I won't need Char's amateur prank kit. I have connections you can only dream of."

I approach her with my hands up. "It's okay. They're checking on me."

She does another sweep of the group with her eyes spitting arrows. "They better be."

Jasper shivers. "And I thought Abby was scary."

Matthijs herds the group of men back into the building. As soon as they're gone, Sofia wraps her arms around me. "Are you okay? They really didn't say anything to upset you?"

I kiss her nose. "Nothing bad happened, gorgeous."

She beams up at me. "Good. Because Mieke is out of surgery and the doctor wants to talk to you."

I grab her hand as I rush back inside. "Why didn't you say so right away?"

"Because as much as I love Mieke and want the surgery to be successful, you're just as important and I needed to check you were okay, too."

I stop in the hallway and yank on her hand to haul her near. "What did I do to deserve you?"

She scoffs. "Are you kidding? Do you want me to count all the ways you deserve happiness and goodness in your life? Because we'll be here for a while."

I touch her lips in the briefest of kisses. "I love you, gorgeous."

"And I love you. Now, can we go talk to the doctor and see your sister?"

"Smart ass."

The doctor is waiting for us when we arrive in the waiting room. "The surgery went well, and your sister is in recovery. I have full confidence the operation was a success." The waiting room erupts in cheers. "A nurse will take you back to see your sister as soon as she's out of recovery."

"Thank you," I whisper, and he nods before leaving.

Sofia wraps her arms around me. I can feel her body shaking with her sobs. I cradle her face and tug until I can look her in the eyes. Her gorgeous green eyes are filled with tears, but a smile reaches from ear to ear on her face.

"And thank you, gorgeous. Without you ...." I swallow. I can't say the words.

"Without me, you would have found another way," she whispers before lifting up on her toes to touch her lips to mine.

Our kiss is brief as we have an entire waiting room of people ready to congratulate us. I can hardly believe what I'm seeing as I survey the room. A year ago, Mieke and I were alone fighting to keep her healthy. And now there's a room full of people who care about Mieke nearly as much as I do.

Sofia has brought unbelievable amounts of love into my life. I don't know how I can ever thank her enough. I do know one thing, though. I am never letting her go. I am tying her to me as soon as she'll let me.

Chapter 42

"**B**e careful!" I shout when I see Mieke stand.

She blows a raspberry my way. "You're as bad as an overprotective brother." She indicates Rafael with her thumb. "I'm only going to the toilet."

"Do you need help?"

She rolls her eyes. "No, Mom. I've been potty trained for a while now."

The chatter in the room quiets as everyone watches Mieke gingerly make her way to the hallway. Wessel doesn't watch. He approaches and wraps an arm around her waist. "How ya doing, squirt?"

She reaches up and rubs his bald head. "For luck," she tells him.

"And it feels silky smooth." He winks at her, and she giggles in response.

Rafael growls and I grab hold of his arm to stop him from going after Wessel. "He's not making a move on her. He's helping."

He frowns at them, but the tension in his body subsides. "I can't help it. I keep seeing her in the hospital room before the surgery."

I wrap my arm around his waist. "Me too, babe. Me too."

Mama sighs as she surveys the room. "The Dutch are such pretty men. Too bad you are coming home now. There is much opportunity for shooting pretty boys, yes?"

Rafael's brow wrinkles before he asks. "Coming home now?"

"Yes," Mama answers for me. "She said she would

stay in Holland for six months. It has been seven months. Time to come home."

Rafael grasps my shoulder and whirls me around. "When were you going to tell me you're leaving?"

"I—" He cuts me off before I can answer.

"This is unbelievable. You're exactly like Mieke's father," he spits out. "Leaving when things get difficult."

"Hey now! I've been here through all the difficult moments for the past several months."

"And Mieke's recovery? Where will you be then?"

"I—"

Abby pushes her way in between us. She points at Rafael. "You might want to stop running your mouth because you're going to regret it when you hear what Sofia has to say."

"And you!" she shouts at me. "Why haven't you told him already?"

She knows my secret. Of course, she does. You can't keep a secret from Abby. "How do you know?"

She huffs. "I wish everyone would stop doubting me. Like the t-shirt says, assume I know everything at all times."

Jasper takes her hand and tugs her away. "I'd say sorry but there really is no excuse for her."

"And yet you love me."

He sighs. "With all of my heart, *mijn schat*."

"What is going on? What is your crazy friend saying?" Mama demands.

I raise an eyebrow at *Pai*, but he shakes his head. I know the expression. It means *you got yourself into this mess, you can get yourself out*. Dang it. I didn't want to do this in front of everyone I know in Holland, but here I am.

"We're supposed to be celebrating Mieke's return home from the hospital. Maybe we should concentrate on her."

Mieke grunts. "Please, no. All of you have

concentrated on me ad nauseam for the past month. Give a girl a break."

Wessel ruffles her hair. "Not going to happen for a while, squirt."

Mia raises her hand. "I'm with Mieke. I want to hear Sofia's secret."

"Secrets are never good," Char points out. I can't argue with her. Nico's secret nearly ended their relationship. "Rip the bandage off. Whatever it is, however bad it is, we'll deal. You've got the girl gang at your back."

I survey the room and notice everyone is staring at us. Some, like Abby and Mieke, with excitement. Others, like Mama and *Pai* and Rafael, with trepidation. Ugh. Fine. I give in. But I'm not making some big announcement in front of everyone.

"Can I talk to you alone?" I ask Rafael. He nods and I take his hand.

Mama steps in our way before we can escape. "No, my little rabbit. I want to hear."

Pai soothes a hand down her back. "Now, now, Sasha, let the children have some time alone." He mouths *go now* at me and I drag Rafael off to his bedroom.

I shut and lock the door behind me. It won't stop the girl gang from eavesdropping, but I have to try.

"What's going on?" Rafael grits out when we're alone behind a closed door.

I wring my hands. I hope I made the right decision. I know I should have talked to him before I decided but everything happened while Mieke was sick. I didn't want to distract him. A little voice in my head calls me a chicken. Stupid little voice.

"You know the grant I got to come to Holland for six months?" He nods. "They offered me another grant, this time for a year, and I took it. I know we should have talked about it before I accepted it as this affects both of us and we're in a relationship, but Mieke was in the hospital at the time and—"

He places a finger over my mouth to stop my babbling. I finally take my eyes off my hands and glance up at him. His smile spreads from ear to ear.

"You're staying?"

I bob my head and he hauls me into his arms. His lips meet mine and fire immediately rushes through my body. It's been entirely too long since we've spent any sexy times together. With Mieke in the hospital, we've barely had the chance to be alone in the same room together when we weren't sleeping let alone had time to explore each other's bodies.

I wrap my arms around him and sink into the kiss. Rafael's taste of musk and pure man hits my tongue and I moan as my fingers dig into his shoulders. I wind my leg around his and he lifts me up until my center is rubbing against his hard length. *Yes*.

I hear shuffling in the hallway before someone knocks on the door. "You better come out now," Matthijs shouts. "We can't keep the girls back any longer."

Rafael grunts before lowering me to the ground. "Your friends have the worst timing."

"Our friends," I correct him. "We'll be right out!"

"Can you get me another t-shirt?" Rafael asks before whipping his shirt off. I bite my lip as my eyes rove over his muscles. He chuckles before pushing me toward his dresser. "Top drawer."

I open the drawer but instead of finding a stack of t-shirts, it's empty except for one thing – a jewelry box. My hand trembles as I reach into the drawer to remove the box. "W-w-what?"

Rafael places his hands on each side of me on the dresser, trapping me with his body. "Open it," he whispers in my ear, causing goosebumps to erupt and travel down my neck.

I gasp when the box springs open, and I see triple rolling rings nestled in it. The three interlocking bands of rose, white, and yellow gold symbolize the past, present, and future of a couple.

"Google wasn't real clear on whether the so-called Russian wedding ring is actually part of the Russian culture or merely named Russian for unknown reasons. But Mieke and I saw this one and thought it was perfect for you."

"Mieke knows about this?"

Someone knocks on the door before shouting, "Mieke wants to know if you say yes!"

"He hasn't asked me yet," I shout back.

"Smartasses, the two of you," Rafael mumbles before clearing his throat. "Sofia Silva, I want you by my side forever. Will you surrender your title of world's greatest cynic and become my wife?"

I toy with the rings I've already placed on my left ring finger. "Do you promise to never prank me again?"

"I guess."

"And to burn the rubber snake?"

He sighs. "If you insist."

"Okay. Let's make this official."

The door flies open and Mieke rushes in. She tackles me and I nearly stumble to the ground. "How did you get in here?"

"As if I haven't been able to pick big brother's lock since I was twelve."

Wessel plucks her out of my arms and carries her off. "No overdoing it, squirt."

"Giving me a kidney doesn't mean you can go all overprotective on me!"

"Of course, it does."

"Welp." Abby places her hands on her hips. "I guess it's time to retire my 'cheer up a girlfriend'-kit. The girl gang is full. We are no longer taking applications."

"I told you. Once you go Dutch, you'll never want another man's touch." Niels winks.

Avery elbows him in the ribs. "It was funny the first time but not the three gazillionth."

"You do know gazillionth isn't a word, don't you?"

She sticks her nose in the air and ignores him.

Once all my friends and their partners have tried to hug me to death, we return to the living room where Mama and *Pai* are waiting for me.

"Mama, *Pai*." I hold Rafael's hand and stand in front of them. "I'd like you to meet my fiancé."

"Finally!" Mama shouts before snatching Rafael from me and hugging him while *Pai* slaps him on the back.

Rafael's eyes widen, and he mouths *help* at me.

Not a chance. I laugh. "Welcome to the family."

Chapter 43

Several years later

Abby

I watch as Sylvia walks into the garden carrying a tray of oranges. Our back garden is full of all of our friends and family. It can barely contain the lot of them. For someone who grew up without any family whatsoever, it can be overwhelming how much family I now have. But I wouldn't give them up for the world.

Tobias, as he has done since the first day he met Sylvia, follows behind my daughter. Olivier is the last member of their little group. He's carrying a pen and paper while trying to push his glasses up his nose. He's the spitting image of Jasper. I pray he remains oblivious to girls as much as his daddy. Otherwise, the teenage years are going to be brutal.

Avery grins as Sylvia offers her an orange slice. I bite my tongue to stop myself from laughing out loud. Avery will never learn. You never, ever accept anything from my daughter without asking her what it is first. She won't lie to you, but if you don't ask, you're almost always in for a surprise.

Avery bites into the orange and her eyes widen before she searches around for a napkin to spit it out.

Niels breaks into laughter and she slaps him. "Don't encourage her," she mutters at him before asking my daughter, "What did you put on the orange?"

"Baking soda. It's an experiment."

Everything is an experiment with my daughter. She's smart like me, but instead of being interested in gadgets and how they work, she's fascinated with chemistry and blowing things up. I couldn't be prouder of her.

"How much did you use on the slice?" Olivier asks as he takes notes for his big sister.

"Maybe you should warn people before you offer them an orange," Avery suggests.

Tobias steps in front of Sylvia and crosses his arms. He's growing like crazy, but he's still a foot shorter than Avery. He doesn't appear to care.

"Watch how you talk to my Sylvia."

His Sylvia? I have no doubt Tobias considers Sylvia his girlfriend. Sylvia, on the other hand, strolls off to her next victim without a backward glance.

Jasper places his arm around my shoulders and pulls me near before kissing my ear. "Your daughter is going to break that boy's heart some day."

"My daughter?" I huff. "Why is she only my daughter?"

"I remember someone complaining when she was pregnant about me saying *we* are pregnant."

I roll my eyes. Will he never stop bringing up what I said when I was pregnant or giving birth? Everyone knows you can't be held responsible for your words when the hormones are raging in your body.

"Olivier is going to be a heartbreaker, too," I point out. "He looks exactly like his daddy."

"If he's like his daddy, he'll wait for the right woman to come around."

"And then get her pregnant to tie her to him?"

He shrugs. "Whatever works."

We fall into silence as we watch the people in our backyard laugh and joke with each other.

"You happy?"

I smile up at him. "I couldn't be happier. Thank you for giving me this life."

He chuckles. "I didn't give you a damn thing.

You're the one who cobbled these people together and made them into a family."

He's not wrong. "Thank you for putting up with me then."

"Of course, *mijn schat.* Until my dying breath."

Avery

My phone rings and I remove it from my purse, but before I can bring it to my ear, Niels snatches it from my hand.

"No."

"But I'm the Chief Operating Officer of Petroix Oil. It might be an emergency."

He places my phone in his pocket. "And, if it is an emergency, they'll call back."

"But—"

Our son, Tijn, crashes into my legs. The boy doesn't know the word for slow down, let alone stop. He's exactly like his dad. He sees what he wants, and he goes all out to get it, consequences be damned.

I pick him up and whirl him around before hugging him close. He's four now and the chances to cuddle him are becoming less and less. I'm not ready for him to start school and become an independent being, but it doesn't matter what I want. Time stops for no man, or woman in this case.

Niels ruffles Tijn's hair. "Having fun, kid?"

How could he not be having fun? Abby always goes all out for her parties. There's a bouncy castle, a swing set, and a treehouse. The kids are having a ball, although Abby's own kids aren't interested in any of the 'kiddy activities'.

Tijn looks up at me and widens his eyes before asking, "Can I play on treehouse?"

Ugh. I hate it when he begs me with those blue eyes. They're the exact same shade as Niels' and I can never say no. I created a mini-Norse god and I have never been in this much trouble in my life.

"Of course, you can, kid," Niels tells him, and Tijn wiggles to be let down.

I watch as he runs to the treehouse. "I don't know about this. He's too small for the treehouse. What if he falls out?"

"He'll be fine," Niels says in a breezy voice. He never worries about Tijn. No, I have to worry for the two of us.

"Why don't we sneak off for a few minutes?" Niels whispers into my ear before biting my earlobe.

"But we're in the middle of a party."

"Good. Built in babysitters for Tijn."

"But…" My voice cuts off when he licks the skin behind my ear. I tilt my head to give him better access.

"Our house is two doors down. We can nip over there for a little afternoon delight and be back before anyone is the wiser."

I raise an eyebrow. "What you're saying is you want a quickie."

He waggles his eyebrows. "I'm saying I want to get down and dirty with the boss."

Niels now has my former job as Head Legal Counsel. Between my director position and his job, we work a lot of hours and don't see each other as much as I'd like. We hired a live-in nanny to take care of Tijn's every need but hiring her hasn't assuaged the guilt I feel for spending time alone with Niels when I can be with Tijn.

Niels cradles my face with his hands. "You're a wonderful mom." I open my mouth, but he doesn't let me get a word in edgewise. "Do you work a lot? Yes, you do. But you've also been there for every single milestone in our child's life. You, sweetheart, are kicking ass as a working mom."

He tells me this all the time, but I'm always surprised to see the sincerity in his face and hear it in his voice. "Thank you."

He tugs on my hand. "Now, it's time to see to your husband." He gives me the same puppy dog eyes Tijn did. "I have needs."

I giggle before following him out of the yard and back to our place.

Mia

I pick up a tray of buns to carry to the barbeque, but before I can take a single step, Matthijs arrives to yank the tray out of my hands.

"What are you doing? You shouldn't be carrying anything."

I growl at him. "It's a tray of buns. It weighs less than a pound. I'm not some fragile woman despite what you may think."

"I don't think you're fragile."

I roll my eyes. "You don't? Then explain why I'm not allowed to carry a tray of stupid hamburger buns."

His gaze roves the party, obviously searching for an ally, but all of the men turn away. I guess my friends have husbands who are smarter than mine.

"You're pregnant. I don't want you to overdo it."

"I'm aware I'm pregnant." I point to my belly that looks like I'm about to go into labor any moment despite having another month to go. "I'm the one with cankles here, not you."

He reaches for me, but I step back. His hand drops and he frowns. "This is why I'm trying to help."

"Then, you admit I have cankles," I shriek at him.

"Dude," Rafael shouts from across the yard. "Admit you fucked up and apologize."

Matthijs wraps his arm around me and leads me away from the crowd. He kisses my hair before speaking. "I'm sorry. I know I go into overprotective mode, but I can't seem to stop myself."

"You're going to have to learn. We have two girls and you're going to push them away if you continue to try and control their lives."

"The universe is testing me, giving me all girls. I hope the next one will be a boy. I need another man in the house to help me."

Unlike the previous two children, we agreed not to learn the sex of this child before birth. Except at my last doctor appointment, the doctor let the cat out of the bag. Fortunately, Matthijs wasn't there to hear the verdict. I've been keeping the knowledge secret ever since.

"I think I need to tell you something." This secret is burning a hole in my stomach.

"Family meeting?" he asks, and I nod.

Since my birth family abandoned me, I've ensured my real family – my girls and my husband – are involved in all big decisions and discussions that affect our family. I want Elin and Nova to understand we are a unit, and we will always make decisions as one.

Matthijs gathers our girls, and we find a table away from the crowd. Nova climbs into my lap while Elin sits next to Matthijs. Elin is daddy's little girl while Nova is the spitting image of me.

"We have news," I begin.

"Is it time for the baby?" Nova asks. She can't wait to meet her sibling. She's tired of being the baby of the family.

"No, but it is about the baby."

Elin, serious like her father, asks, "Is the baby all right?"

I rub my belly. "She's fine."

The girls don't pick up on what I said but Matthijs sucks in a breath. "She?"

"I know you want a boy—"

He holds up a hand. "Stop. I don't care if the baby is a girl or a boy as long as she's healthy."

Elin and Nova look back and forth between us. "What's going on?" Elin asks.

"The baby is a girl. You're getting another sister."

Nova cheers. "Yes! A baby sister." She scrambles off my lap. "I need to tell all the cousins," she says before rushing off.

Elin sighs before standing to follow her. "I'll make sure she's safe."

Matthijs moves to sit next to me. "Thank you, honey. Thank you for giving me a beautiful life."

He kisses my hair and I melt into him. "Thank you for giving me a family."

Char

I watch as Tobias follows Sylvia as she cons everyone into taking part in her orange slice experiment. "If Abby doesn't take over the world, her daughter will."

Nico chuckles. "Maybe she'll save the world."

"She's definitely going to break Tobias' heart at some point." I bite my lip as I watch them. Sylvia doesn't seem to notice Tobias and his devotion to her. He's on a one-way trip to heartache and I don't know how to protect him.

Nico squeezes my hand. "You can't shield him from all the evil in the world."

"Why not? I'm his mom. I should be able to keep him safe."

"You can't protect his heart. Just like you can't protect Jens from the hurt caused by bullies."

I deflate. Jens, our son we adopted two years ago, is now eight years old. He's had problems with bullies at school the past year. He's small and quiet and the other kids think his traits make him weak. They don't.

Jenny walks over to the table we're sitting at. "Hey, Jenny. How are you?"

She hesitates before answering, "Bram said I

should keep my mouth shut, but I can't."

I sit up straight. "What is it?" My eyes scan Abby's backyard but nothing appears amiss. "Is Tobias hurt?" She shakes her head. "Jens?" Another shake. I deflate. "Shit. What is Tom doing now?"

Tom is our foster child. He's thirteen years old and has bounced from home to home until joining ours last year. Both of his parents were addicts and died soon after his birth. He was born prematurely and fought to stay alive, and he's been fighting ever since.

Jenny points to the side garden. I take Nico's hand and stand. When we round the corner, we find Tom leaning against the house smoking.

I drop Nico's hand and fist my hands on my hips. "What do you think you're doing, young man?" Geez, I sound exactly like my mom.

"What does it matter? You're going to send me back anyway."

"Where did you get such an idea from?" Nico asks as he comes to stand behind me and present a united front.

"I heard you whispering about me the other day."

"You need to learn to eavesdrop better. Maybe take some classes from Abby." What am I saying? No one should be able to eavesdrop as well as she can.

"Then, you aren't kicking me out?"

"No. We're planning to ask you if you're interested in joining our family permanently. As in adoption."

His hands tremble causing the cigarette in his hand to fall to the ground. "Y-y-ou're serious?"

"The lawyers already drew up the paperwork." We're kind of experts with how the whole adoption thing works now.

"What about Tobias and Jens?"

At his question, I know we made the right decision. He's concerned what our other children think? Totally the right decision.

Jens peeks around Nico's legs. "I vote we adopt Tom."

Jens has a bit of hero worship going on with regard to Tom. Tom arrived to pick him up from school one day and witnessed the other boys bullying him. He didn't hesitate to wade in and protect his little brother. It's one of the reasons I want to adopt him despite knowing it's going to be an uphill battle to get him settled in our family.

"Let me get Tobias. I know he'll vote yes, too," Jens says before rushing off.

In less than a minute, he's back with Tobias in tow.

"What's going on?" Tobias asks.

"We're discussing adding Tom to our family."

Tobias' nose wrinkles in confusion. "He's already our family." Enough said.

"And?" I address Tom. "What do you think? Are you up for being a permanent member of this family?"

He hesitates for a moment before launching himself at me. I lift my head and find Nico. He winks at me, and I mouth *thank you.* He doesn't need to ask what I'm thanking him for. He knows.

"Love you, Lotje."

Sofia

I smile as I look around Abby's backyard. "It's good to be home."

Rafael's arm squeezes my middle. "It sure is."

After Mieke recovered from her surgery, I began traveling for work again. Rafael insisted on tagging along. He quit his bartending gig, gave up on modeling, and concentrated on his web design business – work he can do from anywhere in the world.

Whenever we're gone for more than a month, we fly Mieke out to visit us. The Hague has replaced New York City as home base now. Mama still complains about it whenever she has the chance, but Zara loves it. I swear she's in The Hague more than we are.

Less than a month after Rafael proposed, we married in a small ceremony at city hall. I never dreamed of a big wedding with a fluffy dress and Rafael wasn't waiting. Mama sighed so much during the ceremony, I was worried she was going to cause herself to hyperventilate.

Once we were married, Rafael gave up his place in Amsterdam and we found a house near Abby and Avery in The Hague. Mieke lives there. It works since we travel too much to get on her nerves. Her words.

Rafael growls and I search the area to see what has him bent out of shape. Uh oh. Mieke brought her boyfriend. Mieke's twenty-one now, but my husband can't stop thinking of her as a little girl. He can't get the picture of her sick and dying in the hospital out of his head.

"What is he doing here?"

Not this again. "Boris is Mieke's boyfriend. Of course, she brought him."

"I don't approve."

"I think the whole world knows you don't approve by now."

"And what kind of name is Boris anyway?"

Now he's grasping for straws. I don't bother replying. It will encourage him to whine and complain more.

Abby claps her hands to gain everyone's attention. "I have a few announcements to make."

Avery, Mia, Char, and Jenny gather around me while Rafael moves to stand with the men.

"What's she up to now?" I ask.

Avery shrugs, but Mia and Char won't meet my eyes. Interesting. I cock an eyebrow at Jenny who shrugs, too.

"The first news of the day is Mia is having another girl!"

I squeeze Mia's hand to congratulate her. I know

better than to hug her when she's this far along. Matthijs would lose his ever-loving mind.

Once the hubbub quiets down, Abby speaks again, "And Char and Nico have a new addition to their family, too. Tom is now a permanent member of their family."

I jump Char before anyone else has a chance. "Yeah! I'm happy for you."

This time when everyone quiets down, Mama and *Pai* exit the house to stand next to Abby. My eyes widen and I glance over at Rafael. He shakes his head. He has no idea what's going on either.

I motion to him, and he returns to me. I clutch his hand. "I'm afraid."

He snorts. "You stared down a bear in Siberia."

"This is worse. Way worse," I tell him.

Mama clears her throat. "I am retiring."

I clap with everyone else. It's about time she retires. She has enough money to live very comfortably for the rest of her life. She should enjoy it.

"And we are moving to The Hague."

All eyes swivel to find mine. "We bought a house down the street."

I should have known Mama wouldn't accept me living in another country. I bury my face in Rafael's shoulder. "I'm sorry."

I feel his body move with his laughter. He doesn't find Mama nearly as irritating as I do. "You promised me an adventure when we got married. And you definitely delivered."

I lift my head to look him in the eye. "I love you."

"Always and forever, gorgeous. Always and forever."

About the Author

D.E. Haggerty is an American who has spent the majority of her adult life abroad. She has lived in Istanbul, various places throughout Germany, and currently finds herself in The Hague. She has been a military policewoman, a lawyer, a B&B owner/operator and now a writer.

Made in the USA
Middletown, DE
10 November 2021